THE HIDDEN PHOENIX

GEORGINA MAKALANI

Also by Georgina Makalani

The Magics of Rei-Een:
The Hidden Princess
Hidden Promises
The Hidden Phoenix

The Raven Crown Series:
Raven's Dawn
The Caged Raven
Raven's Edge

Other Stories:
The Mark of Oldra

The Legend of Iski Flare (Novella series):
The Legend Begins
Red Wolves
The Riddle of Daralis
The Last Child
The Tree Maiden
Reflections
The Beast

Short Stories:
Stuffed Frogs and Spinning Teacups
Searcher
The Silence (in Glimpses)

For all the hidden princesses

1

Lis blinked into the dim early-morning light. The walls and bare room were familiar, and yet it took her a moment to recognise the room she had previously stayed in at the Hidden school. She stretched beneath the covers, but then curled again as the aches in her body protested. Every part of her ached. The silence of the room was somewhat overwhelming, and she closed her eyes to the world again.

Remi flashed behind her eyes, burning brightly. All she wanted was to save him. Hot tears rolled down towards her ears as she refocused on the ceiling above her. It had been the first time she really wanted to help him. Not just because he was to be her husband, but because of the man he was. He was lost, and she should have been the one to stand up for him rather than against him. But the magics hadn't helped either of them. They were only using the prince to get what they wanted. They weren't trying to put him on the throne—they were planning a revolution.

She wasn't sure how she had survived the explosion that had followed her trying to end the fight peacefully. She had wanted to pull him inside her barrier and keep him close. But instead, the action had pushed them apart. Even breathing hurt now, and she could only hope he had survived her failed attempt to save him.

She looked around then, a little more panicked. Who else might she have lost that day? Her father came to mind. She had already lost her family when she'd been chosen, and yet her father had managed to find her again and again. Lis wasn't sure he would fight on the right side, but then she wasn't really sure which side was right. The Empire was not as it had been, and the comments of her sister Ting's new husband had worried her more.

She shivered at the thought of him. She had planned to marry him herself before she had been chosen for the new crown prince and sequestered into a life she had never imagined. She doubted now that a life with Peng would have been what she had hoped.

Lis was relieved she'd had Ting removed from the Palace Isle. She would be safer elsewhere, away from the fighting and Peng. Wei-Song had allowed herself to be talked into taking Ting to the little island, and now Lis wasn't sure if Wei-Song was safe. She closed her eyes again, trying to remember the chaos of the square, the movement of people and soldiers. But more than she wished came to mind, including the smell of blood and the crackle of the magical storm threatening to strike them down. She couldn't picture where Wei-Song had been standing. Remi returned in sharp focus, his face pale, his hair loose and his body being pushed away from her. She had tried to maintain a distance, but she couldn't.

'How do you feel?' Healer Yang asked, sliding open the door to the small room.

'Well enough.' She tried to sit, but she quickly gave up. 'Sore,' she murmured.

'You took quite a beating,' he said softly, sitting gently on the edge of the bed, and she tried not to moan at the pain the movement caused.

'How long did I sleep?'

'Days,' he said, resting a shaky hand on hers. 'I wasn't sure I was going to be able to bring you back.' He looked down at her hand, and she put her other one over the top of his. 'He nearly knocked the life right out of you. But I think it is now time to get you moving. You will be stiff, but if you don't move now you may never.'

'You have always done too much for me.' Lis struggled into a sitting position and reached for her old friend. He felt frail and uncomfortable in her arms. 'What have you done?' she asked, hearing the fear for his welfare in her voice.

'What I had to. What I would always do for you.'

'You have given too much,' she said, holding him tighter although it hurt her to do it.

'I would do all I could for you,' he said. Then he pulled back from her and stood, and Lis noticed he was a little shaky.

'You need to rest,' she said.

He nodded slowly and left her room. Despite her pain, she moved carefully from the bed and stood, holding on to the bed post and hoping she wouldn't crumple to the ground.

She sucked in a breath and steadied herself. She looked towards the door, but she knew she could not make the distance. She hadn't asked after the crown prince, she realised. She hadn't asked if Remi had survived. For a moment she wondered if they would tell her the truth. Yang was still protecting her, giving all he had to keep her alive. Did others know she was alive? How had they gotten her out of the square and off the Palace Isle?

She squeezed her eyes closed, but all she could see was Remi burning. She remembered being exhausted and having no energy to hide. She couldn't remember getting to the school, and she wasn't sure if her being there might have put them all in more danger. She stumbled towards the door. What if someone had followed?

She slid the door open and looked out into the silent hallway. What if this was the dream? That had happened before, where things weren't quite what she'd hoped. The hidden princess compound came to mind, and she wondered if the prince might have hidden there. Or had his mother taken him in and somehow kept him safe from his father?

She shook her head, trying to clear the idea of him and what might have happened to him. Despite their fight, she hoped she wasn't the one responsible. She stumbled along the hallway towards the sound of hushed voices. She tried to keep her feet moving, but it felt as though they were dragging across the floorboards.

She paused by a door and leaned against the wall.

'She has found her reason,' a child's voice said, and Lis wondered who she was and who she was speaking of.

'Truly?' Wei-Song asked. Lis could hear the relief in her voice. 'It is the only way they will end this.'

'It will not be so easy,' the child continued. 'The hidden princess has found her love for the crown prince. But there is still a barrier between them.'

Lis thought of her own barrier and wondered what might have happened if she had allowed the prince inside it. She shivered. She was sure they would have burned together. Then she realised what she was listening to. This was the child with visions, the child who could see what they would become.

'Tell us,' an older man said.

'I cannot see it all,' the child said. 'Only what the gods have granted me.'

Lis wondered then who else might have visions and whether they would see anything different. There had been stories before, and the magics who had tried to kill her had spoken of visions and prophecies. Did this child prophesy their end or their salvation?

Lis tried to rest over the next few days, but her mind wouldn't let her. All she could think about was Remi, whether he had survived or not, and what he was doing if he had. Yang checked on her regularly, but he wouldn't stay with her, partly because he was so clearly drained himself. She heard from Wei-Song that he kept to himself. Not that Wei-Song was willing to talk much about what might have happened or what the child thought was to come.

Lis looked out over the little rocky beach below the school and across the water at the horizon. It looked like it went on forever, yet it still felt so close. It had taken more effort than she wanted to admit to reach the little space. She needed the air, despite the discomfort it took to reach it. Wei-Song was going to let her talk with the child today, and she hadn't given any indication that she had heard some of what the child had seen.

She sucked in a deep breath, then closed her eyes and blew it out softly. It wasn't going to change what had to be done. The emperor and his men would not accept the Hidden or any other magics after the very public demonstration that the crown prince was a magic himself. She was sure the rest of the Empire was in uproar, mostly out of fear. Rumour would have reached the little island school, Lis thought. But if it had, they weren't sharing any of it with her.

Lis was sure the people would want to know how the emperor had protected a magic of his own blood while killing so many others. He was determined to remain in power, yet Lis wondered how it could be done.

'They have closed the gates,' a soft voice said behind her, and she blew out another long breath before turning.

Master Yangshing smiled kindly. Lis had grown to care for the man over her time here, in the same way she cared for her father, although they were very different men. The master was always very level, and Lis had learnt much from him in remaining calm even when her insides were tied into knots.

'Is that to keep them in or to keep others out?'

'A good question, and one I cannot answer. In some ways, I wish you were there to ensure things would be as they should.'

'They may never be as they should,' Lis said. 'They haven't been for some time, and I may not be the one to fix it, despite what the child might say. Who is to say that what she sees will happen?'

'Who is to say it won't?'

'It was so hard to fight him,' she whispered. 'I don't think I can do that again. And we nearly killed each other. I might have killed him,' she added, wondering if it was indeed possible for her to kill him, or he her. 'I suppose he nearly killed me before,' she mused aloud.

'I don't think he could,' the older man said, looking beyond her out across the water. 'There is something there, whether you want to admit it or not. The crown prince did far more for you than he had done for anyone in the past.'

'He looked after Mu-Phi,' Lis added, looking back at the view.

'Do you think he does so now? She might be quicker to kill him than you.'

Lis shook her head slowly. 'I saw her die in the square,' she said softly, closing her eyes as the memory of her swift death played out again in her mind.

'I don't think she knew who to fight,' he said.

'Are we really safe here?' Lis asked, shaking the vision of the girl's death.

He nodded. 'All those years of fighting, and we have continued on without any notice from the Empire.'

'What if I were found here, or Wei-Song?'

'Many know who she is, yet she was able to grow in peace here.'

'Her father doesn't know.'

He sighed. 'It is difficult with the emperor to be sure of what he knows.'

'I saw his face when he first laid eyes on her. He didn't know.'

'It is time for you to meet the little one,' the master said kindly, indicating the buildings, and she followed him back towards the little school. The greying wood looked as though the building had stood for long in the weather. The lacquer around the eves was cracked and peeling. The tile roof was faded. And yet it looked lived in, as though many students had used it. And they had. Lis just wished she'd had the chance to study here, to learn all she could of herself before she had been thrown into her strange new life on the Palace Isle. But then if she had been at the school, she might have had a very different life.

'Do any of your students go on to be priestesses?' she asked as they entered the building.

'A different kind of calling,' he said, walking ahead of her.

But a life of seclusion, she thought.

The child sat on the floor, her legs crossed, her hands in her lap and her eyes closed. Wei-Song put her finger to her lips, and Lis continued quietly into the room. Wei-Song stood beside the child as the master followed Lis in. The girl opened her eyes, smiled up at Lis and tapped the floor before her.

Lis lowered herself quickly to the cool ground. The girl reached out and took Lis's hands quickly in her own, then sucked in a sharp breath.

'Close your eyes,' the child directed.

Lis nodded at her very young face and then did just that.

'Breathe,' she continued.

Lis struggled to maintain her quietness in the darkness behind her lids. She wasn't sure what she had expected or even what she had hoped for, but this wasn't it. After several moments, she concentrated on the small warm hands in her own and slowed her breathing.

'Good,' the child said.

Lis wondered if Wei-Song and the master remained in the room or if they had left them alone. As her mind began to wander, the child squeezed her hands. Lis wondered who she was, what her name was and who she had been before the visions and the school had taken her in.

'I am not the focus of this session,' the child said, her voice deeper and more commanding now.

Lis nodded again and tried to focus only on her breathing.

A flash of colour penetrated the darkness behind her lids, and she leaned back, only to be pulled forward again by the girl. Another flash followed, and she was sure she saw flames, like those she had seen in the prince's eyes.

The girl sighed loudly. Lis wondered if she saw the same

images or something very different. Perhaps Lis only saw part of what she did.

The flames changed and flickered, growing smaller and then taller again before turning into a rose, like the one she had created with the prince. And then it changed into another creature—she wasn't quite sure what as the flames licked around its form, changing the shape and obscuring the beast beneath. She thought she saw a wing. Could it be a bird of fire?

'What did you see?' the girl asked, shaking her. Lis opened her eyes to the bright room. She shook her head and realised they were alone. 'You must tell me.'

'What did you see?' Lis countered.

'Death and destruction,' the girl whispered, leaning towards Lis, her hands still holding her tight. 'But I don't know if you work together or against each other. What you saw might give us that answer.'

'It wasn't clear,' Lis said.

'But you recognised what it was,' the child continued confidently.

Lis shook her head and pulled her hands from the child's tight hold. 'Do you not see anything clearly?'

'I know you must work together, but it is a challenge for you both to trust each other. I saw blood, but I don't know who sheds it.'

'Could it be another war that goes on until there is no one left?'

'The Empire continues. Two will rule.'

'And if we don't work together and I am killed, will he take another?'

'Who would know such a thing?' the child asked, confusion knitting her brow.

'You would,' Lis said, standing suddenly, although she still felt somewhat shaky on her legs. 'Who sits on the throne?' she asked too loudly.

'I can't see that either.'

'How do you know two will rule?'

The girl shrugged. 'I just do.'

The door slid open and Master Yangshing entered. He looked serious. The child turned to him, her face pleading, and Lis was reminded of when she was a child and hoped her father would give in to what she wanted.

'Tell her she *must* tell me what she saw,' the child demanded.

The tutor looked at Lis and then back to the child. 'Why won't she tell you herself?'

'I don't know,' she said.

'I thought you knew all,' Lis said.

The girl turned back to her, and Lis realised just how young she was. 'I only know what I am shown. I can't choose what that is. And when it comes to you, I see blood and darkness, fire and...' She stopped, shaking her head.

'You don't know,' Lis whispered.

The girl shook her head again.

'I think there was a bird in the flames, but I'm not sure,' Lis said.

'The phoenix,' the master whispered.

'When was the last one seen?' the child asked.

'It is just myth,' he murmured. 'There are stories of dreams and images, but no certainty that they ever existed.'

'They do,' the child said.

'Do you think it means we will work together?'

'You have great skill,' the master said.

'That doesn't answer the question.'

'I only know you must work together,' the girl said.

Lis shook her head slowly. 'Only I have no choice about whether or not we do. It must be his decision. He is the one who chose to turn away—only he can turn back.'

The child suddenly smiled at her. 'You are getting closer,' she said, 'but you have more choices than you realise.'

2

Remi sat on the edge of the bed and looked over the cobwebs surrounding him. He had wanted so desperately to push them away, but he feared they lent themselves to the magic that kept them all hidden. He didn't know where the magics had hidden themselves before, other than the little houses he had visited, but they had managed to keep themselves from the hunters.

Now they filled the hidden princess compound he had discovered with Lis. The one he had dreamed of, that they both had. He felt the loss of her. The entire world was in chaos. It was what he had thought he wanted. But he had never really imagined her gone.

She had wanted to save him, and that hurt more than her death. She had faced him, not because she had felt she was an option for the Empire, or that it was the only thing she could do to stop him. She had been there because she had thought she could save him. And in trying to do that, she had died.

Some of the magics had suggested she had hidden or been hidden away. But she wouldn't have had the energy left to do that. He'd barely had the energy himself, yet the flames had swirled around him.

There had been something about her before she'd disappeared in the flames, maybe a sadness that it had come to this, like she too had lost him. He pressed his hand into his chest. All the anger, all the hatred, all the confusion seemed insignificant now that she was gone.

It was a physical pain he felt at her loss. He gulped as it threatened to tear him apart. The fire was hot beneath his skin. He appeared to have maintained his power, but he had even less control. It should have scared him, what he had become, what he could be, but he only wanted it to consume him and end his suffering.

He lay back and closed his eyes. His body ached from the fight, but the sharp pain in his chest was worse. Lis had tried to talk with him, tried to tell him what it would do to him, and the magic had pushed her away. Again, he had raised his sword to her, and he understood now why she had been so scared of him. He had never given her the opportunity to understand how much he had wanted to protect her. And then he had lost her. In the one moment as they'd faced each other across the square, the moment he'd realised she was trying to save him, the moment before she'd died.

A memory of Mu-Phi flashed before him. Her anger had made his flames swirl higher, and her sword had been sharp. He rubbed his hand over the still-healing wound on his arm. It was only luck that she had just managed to graze him before one of the magics had taken her down. Just like that, she was gone.

His brother would have been very disappointed if he'd been alive and that had cut him, but not as much as Remi was at the idea that Lis might be gone forever. And they were in hiding, not taking the Empire for themselves as the magics had predicted. The knowledge of where the visions had come from was still a secret. He didn't know who had told them of what he was and what he could become. Chonglin wouldn't speak of it. And no matter what Remi tried, he wouldn't even hint or confirm that Remi could meet the person in question.

There was nowhere he could go and no one he could talk to.

He wondered what his mother thought, although he knew Lis had told her long ago of what he was. And she had been accepting of his sister, even if his father hadn't been. There was no way his father would forgive him for this. Not only did Remi have magic, he had started a fight in the middle of the Palace Isle—which told the people that his father had lied, or at least that he was wrong and magic was not gone from the Empire.

If only Remi could have the chance to talk to his father about what he really believed. There had never been a chance for them to talk other than Remi receiving directions. There were some stories of his father's reign during the magic war, but even those were vague. Although his father was a strong man, Remi was sure it was men like General Long and the hunters who had done all the work and saved the Empire. They might have been covered in the blood of the magics, but it had stained his father.

The emperor ordered things to be done but did little himself. Remi wondered for a moment if his father might have delegated other duties, perhaps he wasn't really his father, and yet it was the line that was most important.

He threw the covers off, trying to throw his frustrations and sadness with them. The dust swirled up around him, and he wondered why no one had cleaned up in all the days they had stayed in the hidden princess dormitory. But perhaps he was right and cobwebs were part of the magic of the place that kept them hidden from the rest of the Empire.

He slowly moved his legs around and onto the floor. Sharp pain rippled through his feet as he tried to stand, and then the high priestess was there, hooking her arm around him and helping him to his feet.

'It will take some time,' she said softly, 'but movement is good for you.'

He nodded and leaned heavily into her small frame. He wondered if he would have survived without this woman. The magics needed him, he thought, and yet when they had dragged him here after the fight, they'd left him alone in the dark corner of the room. They had huddled and talked at the other end, and then the priestess had appeared.

She had fed him soup, wiped his brow, massaged his limbs. She had brought him back to the world, although he certainly hadn't wanted to come back and they didn't appear to need him. When she led him out into the sunshine, he wondered when the storm had cleared.

'Have you heard anything?' he asked, his voice raspy from underuse.

'No, I have not,' she said without looking at him as she carefully walked him towards the dark water of the pond.

'Have you seen anything?' he asked. He tried to pull her to a stop, but he only managed to nearly fall.

She glared at him as though he was a child. 'Nothing that makes any sense,' she murmured. 'And no, I have not seen her.'

A part of him, a large part of him, hoped there had been some mistake and Lis lived, but the priestess had not heard anything about her, nor seen anything, no matter how many times he asked. Other than a certainty that Lis was dead.

'Why are you not with the others?' he asked, leaning into the railing around the gazebo as she rested him against it and stepped back.

'I am needed here,' she said simply. 'You need me.'

'And what if others need you? Do they know where you are?'

She shook her head and leaned beside him on the railing. 'I will return to the temple now that you are up. It is decided that the priestesses are to return to the Sacred Isle.'

Remi took a step forward. 'You are the visionaries,' he said, the idea coming to him quickly. It was the only explanation.

She nodded once. 'I have always known that we needed to keep our abilities secret. That to be able to do what we do, we need to do it in isolation. If the world knew what we could see, they would be forever asking us what the future holds, which in itself would change that future.' She sighed and looked down at her hands. 'Many of the magics know what we are, and I can't discover how they were told, who told them, or for what reason. But I can guess that it was done after the start of the magic war, to enable us to do what we can for the Empire.'

'Such as destroying the princess?'

'She would have destroyed the Empire if we had not stopped her.'

'Would she have?' he asked. The question was serious, but the woman before him smiled, a knowing smile. 'Surely someone would have seen what was to come,' Remi said.

'But I cannot see what occurred. I wonder if the person, or priestess, had some skill in hiding that and knew what telling them would do to change the future. Maybe it was the way to defeat the princess. I couldn't see how that could be done, only what it would mean. What it would do to the future. You were unseen until your magic developed.'

Remi nodded slowly. He was an anomaly the magics had been quick to try and influence—and he had been influenced so easily, he realised now. He thought it was due to the lies Lis had told, the way she had hidden her true self from him, as well as his sister. And learning that the magics had in some way tried to save his brother had helped lead him to their cause. Yet he knew that wasn't what he wanted. He hadn't wanted to fight his own men, or Lis, and he certainly didn't want her dead.

If he could go back, he would have worked with her. He would have found a way to accept what he was. The priestess jumped back, and he realised the flames were flashing over his skin. Any control he'd had was gone. And as his frustration at his predicament increased, so did the reason for it.

'You are where you are meant to be,' she said softly, but he shook his head. 'You are a magic, just like these men. A man trying to live in an Empire where the world wants you dead.'

Her words moved over his skin with the flames, fuelling his

frustrations and anger. But she was wrong. 'What did you see?' he asked, and she looked away again, over the water. 'Why were you so sure we could win?'

'You didn't lose,' she said quickly.

'But we are not in control. We haven't won. There will be more fighting.'

'And you will win that fight too. The hidden princess is gone. It is only men you face, only men with swords, whom you can demolish before they come close enough to scratch you.'

Remi thought about the magics he had killed in his time as a hunter, many of them in close range, pushing his sword through them. They'd had so many chances to kill him, and yet... Maybe they weren't as strong as he thought. Maybe they couldn't win this as easily as the priestess claimed.

Remi shook himself off. He was starting to think of all sorts of craziness rather than focus on what they had to do next. But then, he wasn't sure he wanted to know what to do next. And he wasn't the one making the decisions. Lis had cried out something like that, that he needed to remember who he was. It was all too foggy now, the memory of what had happened, and he stopped and looked around. The compound contained men of all ages and magical abilities.

'I have seen what you must do. I have seen what you will become. If you had sided with her, the world would be a very different place.'

He nodded once. 'Is different worse?'

'It could be.' She stepped forward and placed a hand on his shoulder. The movement surprised him, but he didn't pull away. She closed her eyes, stepped closer and leaned her forehead on his chest. For a strange moment, he wanted to close his arms around her, to hold her closer, but he remained as he was.

'There is something very special deep inside of you. The people have waited generations for an emperor such as you.'

'I'm not Emperor.'

'You will be. You will be great,' she whispered, looking up at him. Then she pushed herself against his chest and raised herself up to press her lips to his. He froze. And yet, as he closed his eyes, he saw himself on the throne, wearing the royal garb that marked him as Emperor.

He closed his arms around her and pulled her closer to him. She ran her hand around his neck and through his hair as she kissed him more passionately. He felt a surge of wanting he hadn't felt before, and then she was pulling away from him.

She licked her lips and smiled. 'I would have the greatest of visions with you,' she said, then cleared her throat. 'But it would be my last.'

The lust that had surged through him disappeared as suddenly as it had appeared.

'There is a great future for us,' she whispered, adjusting her white cloak. Then she turned and walked away from him. He didn't feel the same wanting as he watched her walk away, and he wondered where it had come from in such force to disappear so completely. He shook his head.

He moved along the path from the gazebo towards the little rooms on the other side of the compound. No one had come to stay in these rooms. He wondered how long it would take and what they might do if they were to see the image of the lookalike Lis on the wall. He moved into that room first and sat back to look at her.

In some ways, it reminded him of the way she had looked when they'd fought each other. The dress flowing around her, the serious look upon her face… but there was something else there, a kindness or gentleness beneath. She was a very beautiful woman. He knew he had chosen her for more than just her looks, but of all the girls that had lined up that day, he could only remember her.

He stood quickly and moved to the next room. The faces that had been so overwhelming on his first visit and then disappeared had returned, and he didn't know what had happened to make that occur or whether Lis herself had been involved. She had seemed so disappointed that day they had found them gone. Just the smooth white stone.

He walked slowly around the room, studying each face. He hadn't taken the time to do that before. One of them looked almost like Wei-Song, and he stopped to study it in more detail. In many ways, the white masks all appeared the same, but it could be her.

The tiles covered the entire room, from the ceiling to the floor. Remi dropped to his knees to look over those on the lower levels. He paused at a chubby face smiling at him. She didn't look familiar in any way, yet he felt something as he looked at her. He blinked back the odd feeling and continued. There was nothing of Lis here, and as he got to his feet, he realised he'd been looking for her here as well.

He closed his eyes. He had been so determined to kill her. He needed to kill her to be what he was meant to be. But he missed her. And she had looked so amazing that day. It was a strange thought to have. He headed back out into the morning light, where others were starting to move about, and he followed their path towards the black gate and the training ground beyond.

It had refused to provide him with any more information. The silver symbols remained locked away and he couldn't pull a message forth no matter what he tried. One of the fire bearers had offered to burn through the black paint for him, but Remi knew it could only come from him. If he truly wanted, he could have done such a thing himself.

The training ground was just as it had been when he had first visited it with Lis, and despite her skills he could still see a faint outline where her circular garden had been.

'It is time to forget what you had,' the priestess said, standing beside him and looking over the dried grasses and weeds that sat amongst the cracked stones. 'You must focus on your future.'

He nodded and looked over the group filling the yard. The woman beside him ran her hand along his arm, and he shivered. There was much for him to do.

3

'Explain to me again how this has happened?' the emperor asked. Sitting back on his throne, he looked across the room rather than at the empress as she stood before him.

She tried to maintain her composure and keep the frustration from her voice. 'This isn't my fault. It was bound to happen sooner or later given the amount of magic around.'

'Where have you heard such things?' he demanded, glaring at her.

'I have seen it with my own eyes. What do you think I do with my days? Were you not aware that your eldest son was murdered by magic?' Her anger bubbled to the surface, and she was scared she would say too much. Although he knew it all by now.

'The girl,' he said simply.

'Is your child, the one you ordered me to kill when she was an infant.'

'But you didn't.'

'She was my child.'

'And that is why you hid the boy.'

'You mean the crown prince, the future emperor of our Empire and the last of your line. He had no magic skill other than that of a hunter. Not until the hidden princess and their connection.'

'Did you know what she was when you chose her from the

line?'

'Again, no I did not. And it was your son who selected her, as well as yourself.'

He grumbled something, and she chewed on her lip.

'What else have you hidden from me?' he asked finally, not for the first time in the last few days.

She knew why he kept asking, but she had hoped he would have some trust in her and what she had done to support him over the years. She sighed. 'No matter what you want to believe, he is your son and she is your daughter.'

'You were directed…'

'I saw your face when she stood before you all those months ago,' she said quickly. 'And despite your concerns for magic, you are pleased I didn't carry out such an order.'

'But you won't tell me who else you involved in your plan, and Remi has been destroying the Empire I have built.'

'He is finding his way. If he were to find Lis, I am sure they could help each other.'

'What skills does she have? Could she burn us to the ground?'

The empress shook her head.

'How did they hide so well from the hunters?'

'We have discussed this,' she said shortly, losing her patience. 'And it does nothing to fix the problems we are now faced with. We need help to determine what magic we can work with and what we must fight against.'

'Work with?' he asked, leaping from the throne. 'Have you lost all your senses?'

'There are some who want to work with us, some who want to destroy us. There is a prophecy that Lis and our son may be the answer to this, to bring the people and magic back together.'

'A prophecy,' he scoffed.

'Like the one that foretold you would be the strongest emperor the world has ever seen.'

He sat back down slowly.

The empress looked at her husband, the strong, distant man who was in control of so much. Not only his feelings, but the entire Empire. In some ways he was covered in more blood than their son, yet he had never lifted a hand. He had always directed others to do his bidding.

Now he sat slumped on the wide throne, which made him look small and lost. She stepped forward and sat beside him, putting her arm around his shoulder and pulling him closer. He didn't resist her in any way. It had been many years since he had rested his head on her shoulder, and she had never once sat with him on the throne.

'I have proved myself,' she said quietly, stroking his hair gently back from his face. 'The Empire needs unity. It needs your strength, and it needs our son and his bride to work together.'

'She has magic. They can never wed now.'

'He has magic. Half the world has magic. You can't stop it, and thinking you can only shows foolishness. The Empire does not want a foolish emperor.'

'You push my limits,' he said, his voice carrying some of the strength she was trying to pull from him. 'Bring me a priestess,' he murmured, leaning closer to her.

'I don't...' the empress started.

'Yes sire,' a quiet voice murmured from the other side of the screen. She heard the soft footfalls of a retreating servant.

'We are never alone,' she said, pushing him away. 'After all I have done, there is still no trust.'

'We are alone now, and what you are about to learn is known by no one but myself. Even they do not know that I know.'

She glared at him. 'I don't trust the high priestess,' she said. 'Her predecessor tried to kill me.'

'As they have tried at times to kill me and probably will again.'

'How?' she asked.

'Not well enough,' he said, standing slowly and straightening himself. He ran his hand over his hair to smooth out where she had touched him.

He held out a hand and she took it, surprised by the strength in his grip as he pulled her to her feet. He looked her over and then ran the back of a finger down her cheek. The motion surprised her, and the feel of his skin on hers shocked her.

'A united front,' he whispered as the door opened.

'The high priestess,' the man announced as she appeared. Then he disappeared, and the woman moved forward in a smooth gait. She smiled and gave a shallow nod of her head. A priestess never bowed low to the emperor. They worshipped a higher power even than his, the empress had once heard claimed, but she had rarely seen them bow down to the gods of the temple either.

'You wish to see me, Your Eminence,' she said, her voice calm as she smiled, again, at the emperor. She hadn't even glanced at the empress.

'I have called you here because of the troubles currently plaguing our Empire.'

'The magics?' she interrupted.

He nodded once.

'I know nothing of the magics,' she said, 'other than what I have seen in the streets. How does Your Eminence bear such a burden?'

'More easily than you would like, I am sure. But it is your knowledge that I have called you here for.'

'I have just…'

He held up a hand and cut her off. 'You will tell me what you have seen.'

'In the streets?'

'In the temple. In your visions.'

She took a step back, then dropped to her knees and bowed before the emperor. 'I have no visions.'

'I know where the prophecies come from. I know that the priestesses have a long history of visions. Some have seen more than others; some claim to see it all. You are now the high priestess. Young as you are, your power must be great. And despite your gods, I am your emperor, and you will tell me what you have seen.'

She sat back slowly and looked at him carefully. 'Where have you learnt such stories?' she asked, and the empress knew he was right.

It seemed everyone had a power of some kind. She wondered what the priestesses might do with it. Or what they were trying to do with it now.

'When I was a boy, and my hidden princess was hidden away learning to be my bride, I met a girl.' The empress looked at him. He had never told her such things before. He turned with a friendly smile and indicated that she sit on the throne. Which she gladly did. He held out his hand, and she took it. 'She was my friend.'

The empress nodded once, her hand still held tight in his, and he turned back to the priestess.

'She was a sweet girl, a maid, in the laundry, I think. And one day when I was hiding from my father and his anger at my lack of skill with a bow, I found her hiding in my usual place. She was crying and unable to stop. Her cheeks were red and swollen where she had been wiping over them with her sleeve, attempting to stem the tears.' He took a deep breath. 'She was so pretty,' he mused, 'and I took her hands and asked her to close her eyes and breathe slowly. I had seen my father do the same with my mother when she became excited. Her tears stopped and she smiled, but then she gripped my hands tight and chewed her lip. I wondered if she was scared we would be discovered, because she looked so frightened.'

'When she opened her eyes,' he said, turning to the empress, 'she told me she'd had a vision of me, as a man, strong and ruling a peaceful kingdom. I thought she was trying to be nice, but there was still an uncertainty there. After we talked for a little while, she told me she had dreamt of me, and of the danger and blood we would see. That was why she'd been crying. She feared what was to come. But she didn't want to tell the laundry mistress what she had dreamed in case they thought she was planning to harm the royal family.'

He sat down beside his wife. The priestess drew in a breath.

He smiled. 'You have seen the two sharing the throne. But no one has been clear as to who they are. I think what you have seen is yet to come.' He pulled his wife's hand into his lap, and she wondered at the contact, for he had never been so close before other than to produce children. Was this other girl the reason? Did he care for someone else?

'She had more visions, both waking and sleeping, that showed her various moments of my life to come. She foretold my son's death by magic, and it was why I was so keen to go to war once we realised the true threat that they were.'

'What happened to her?' the empress asked.

'Our hiding place was not discovered,' he said with a smile, 'but her skills were, and she disappeared. It was a long time before I saw her again, and when I did she was a priestess, visiting the Palace Isle before she returned to the Sacred Isle to teach others. I didn't have the chance to talk with her. But I visited the temple hoping she was still there. I asked some questions of the priestesses, thinking I was subtle, but I was a young man desperate to find his friend. She was gone, and she hasn't returned since. I asked why she would become a priestess, and I was told she had been called. All those who turn to the priestess way of life have a calling and know that is what they are from a young age. I wondered if I hadn't really known her, if her passion for the gods was greater than her friendship with me. But it wasn't about me; it was her skill. Her visions had called her to be with others who were the same.'

'You guess at her calling as you guess at her true skill,' the priestess said.

'She had told me she would leave, that there were others and they needed her.'

'She would not have told you any such thing,' the priestess said.

'A laundry girl with a prince. She hoped to be your lover.'

'She was ten,' he snapped, standing. 'And only eleven when she disappeared. She was a scared child,' he continued.

'Does she still live?' the empress asked. 'She would tell you the truth now of what they are.' She pointed to the priestess. 'Call her here.'

'They have no name, once they join the priestesses. But it is enough that I know what they are, that they are the source of all the visions and prophecies.'

The priestess before them glared, and then she sighed. She knelt slowly before the throne again and touched her head to the floor. 'I will tell you what you want to know.'

'This is true?' the empress asked, standing quickly to join her husband.

'It is kept from everyone. Not a soul outside the priestesses know of what we are.'

'Someone does.'

'I have had visions of your future.'

'How can we believe what you have to tell us?' the empress asked.

'Your son will lose himself.'

'What does that mean?' the empress asked. 'Could you not tell us something real?'

'He will find himself with the throne.'

'It is as though she talks in riddles,' the empress sighed.

'It may be that she does not have the skill to decipher what she sees.'

The woman's face hardened at the emperor's words. 'I see it all,' she said. 'I don't have a child's simplicity to tell you what I think it means. I tell you what I see.'

'You see the end of this fight?'

She nodded. 'But I have seen different versions. It will depend on others and what they do. People will follow a path, if you lead them. Your son is led down one, but if he could be convinced to travel another, the future may be different.'

'Do you hope for one outcome over another? Would you influence his path if you could?' the empress asked.

'Perhaps I already do.' She smirked. 'Or perhaps I would rather let it play out and see what happens. I see only what the gods choose to show me.'

'You saw that the hidden princess had to die,' the empress said.

The high priestess smiled and inclined her head in a slow nod.

'I fear they have both died,' the empress whispered.

'Your love for them will not influence the outcome of this. No matter his love for you, he will do what he will do.'

'Someone has influence over him,' the emperor said.

'He has been shown a particular path.'

'You were chosen when the last high priestess died,' the empress said, stepping forward.

'I was, by the gods themselves.'

'Who will be chosen when you go?' the empress asked.

'It is not my time. And despite your fears, you will not share our secret.'

The emperor nodded once. 'I have kept it this long.'

The priestess turned, her white skirt flaring up with the movement, and she left without ceremony.

The empress sat heavily on the throne. How could all this have been happening around her and she hadn't known? 'They poisoned me, and you knew,' she said softly, realising he had kept this to himself, and that stories told by a child so long ago had led to war. 'You know what they have is a form of magic,' she continued when he said nothing. 'That the girl you loved was exactly what you fought against. What you wanted your own daughter killed for.'

'She allowed me to be a boy,' he said, turning to her, his eyes pleading for understanding. She stood slowly. 'Not a prince, not an heir to the throne—just a boy.'

'You were never just a boy,' the empress said.

4

Lis woke from a dream where she was hot, dry and burning. It reminded her of the dreams she'd had when she'd first come to the Palace Isle, or at least when the prince had moved her into the residence. She threw the covers back and swung her legs around at the same time. She blew out a long breath, thankful that for the first time since she had left her little island home, she was alone. Yang was always nearby, but he had taken to sleeping on his own, and she was sure he was better for it. The fight on the Palace Isle had taken a lot from all of them.

She stood cautiously, feeling a little shaky on her legs, and slowly stepped the short distance to the shuttered window. She pushed it open and breathed in the cool night air. The difference with this dream was that she was burning. And burning with the crown prince. Lis hadn't been hurt by the flames, but she was hot and dry. In some way, she was scared of what he would do to her, yet she knew that she was responsible for the fire and not him.

A shiver ran across her skin. The dream could be another sign that they needed to come together, and in many ways, she could see the sense of it. If they worked together as they had, they might be able to win. Although she wasn't exactly sure who she would be fighting.

The cloudless night was bright with the full moon and sparkling stars. She felt a moment of longing for her little island. On summer nights, she would lie out in the field and watch the sky, wondering just how far away it was and whether there was anyone out there.

Thinking back on it now, she had felt a sense of loneliness even then, despite having her family and Peng at the time. But Peng hadn't been what she had thought. He had left her so easily for her sister, and when they discovered the child Ting carried had magic, he had been ready to leave her too. She hadn't seen him since.

Nor had she seen her sister since she had arrived at the school, and Wei-Song had been less than forthcoming about her welfare. She looked back to the doorway for a moment and then back to the sky. If Ting was still on this island, she would have searched out Lis the moment she had arrived. Wei-Song and Yang had wanted to protect her, but they wouldn't have stopped Ting visiting.

Lis rested her head against the window frame. Ting must have returned to her father or to Peng. Either way, she was no longer on the island. Was there a risk to the school because someone else knew where they were, or had they had found a way to protect themselves?

The cool breeze over her skin was a relief, as she was still hot from the dream. Could the phoenix be connected to what she had dreamt? Was this another dream she shared with the prince? If he had survived.

'You don't think of him as a man,' a quiet voice said behind her.

'Who?' she asked without turning.

'Remi.'

She turned to the child standing in her nightgown in the doorway. 'Did you call the crown prince by his first name?'

'It doesn't matter what I call him,' the child said.

'I have no right to call him by his name,' Lis said.

'But you have.'

'Have I?' Lis asked, turning to back to the girl as she entered the room and made herself comfortable on the edge of the bed.

She nodded once. 'When you were at your weakest.'

'When he tried to kill me?'

'When you thought you were ready to die.'

Lis wanted to turn from the child again, but she forced herself forward and sat beside her. 'He called me Lis often.'

'He knows how he feels.'

'Does he?'

She shrugged then.

'How can you know so much and so little at the same time?' Lis asked her.

'It is a curse and a blessing.'

Lis wanted to laugh at the way she said it in her sing-song voice, but Lis was sure the child felt it more deeply than she wanted to admit. 'How old are you?'

'Old enough to know that what I see is real, even if I don't fully understand it.'

'Did you know I dreamed of the phoenix?'

'We talked of it, and you were concerned as to what it meant, so it was likely that you would.' Again, she sounded much older than her years.

'Why did you come?'

'I dreamt of a death.' She shivered.

'Mine?' Lis asked tentatively.

The child shook her head quickly. 'I don't want to talk of it.'

Lis wrapped her arm around the child and pulled her close. The child leaned into her, and Lis could feel the gentle shudder that accompanied her tears.

'What is your name?' Lis whispered.

'I am destined to have no name,' she sobbed.

'But you have one now.'

She shook her head against Lis.

'What if I were to call you…'

'No!' she cried, pulling back. 'Don't say it. You will doom us both.'

'With a name?'

The child nodded vigorously, and Lis believed she thought it was true. She pressed her lips together as she pulled the child back against her. 'Then you remain as you are.'

The girl sighed against her, and Lis looked back to the open window and her small view of the night sky. As she sat in silence, watching the stars move across the sky, the child fell asleep. Lis rolled her over and laid her down before curling against her and pulling the covers over them both. She had thought of Remi as a man, when she had woken in this room not so long ago. She had realised the connection, felt the loss of him, and she wondered what had changed in the last few days for her thinking to return to what it was, for Remi the man to become the prince once more.

Lis felt the same burning sensation again and tried desperately to put it out. If she was the cause, she could end it. Then she focused on a face in the crowd, the little girl who had seen her future. The child nodded slowly. Lis relaxed, allowing the flame to take over, and the world went dark.

Lis opened her eyes, unsure for a moment where she was, and an image of the prince flashed before her. She sucked in a breath only to find he was not in the room, and the child stirred beside her.

'It is a dream,' the child murmured.

'But is it real?'

'Maybe,' the child said, sitting slowly and stretching her arms above her head. 'You have to find him.'

'The prince?'

The child nodded and pushed herself from the bed.

'You don't think there is more I could learn before heading out to meet my death?'

'I wouldn't send you out to meet your death,' she said, 'but it may be that you die during this.'

Lis stared after the child as she padded out of the room. Did she have any understanding of what she saw, or what influence she had? Lis wondered who the prince might have surrounded himself with and what they were trying to influence him to do. They weren't concerned with his welfare or that of the Empire. They only wanted power for themselves, and they were going to use him to get it.

She sighed and threw the covers back. Despite all that had occurred, the child was right—she would have to find him. Together they could do so much to prevent the magics taking over. All she had to do was find him without being discovered herself and killed, then convince him they could work together and hope he didn't just kill her.

The following morning when Wei-Song came in with her breakfast, Lis wondered how she could ask her for what she needed. Then she remembered her sister doing the same.

'Where is Ting?' she asked.

Wei-Song paused too long bent over the tray before she stood up and turned around to face Lis, who was still sitting on the bed.

'She isn't on the island, is she?'

Wei-Song shook her head.

Lis waited. When Wei-Song didn't answer, she moved over and sat carefully at the table. The movement still caused her pain, and she wondered how she was going to make it back to Remi when she struggled to make it across the room.

'It was better for her to return to your father and her home.'

'She was well enough?'

Wei-Song nodded slowly, watching the water she poured into the cup rather than looking at Lis. Lis reached out and took her arm.

'She was well,' Wei-Song said.

Lis released her and picked up the cup. 'I need some help.'

'Anything,' Wei-Song said quickly.

'I need to know just what I can do, what the prince and I may be able to do together. And then I need to find him.'

'He will kill you,' Wei-Song said, sitting beside Lis and taking her hands.

The only thing of certainty the child had seen was that they had to work together. She had seen what had happened and lived what could happen when they worked against each other. And due to the child's continued reassurances that it was the only way, Lis knew he lived. 'I need to help him.'

Wei-Song indicated the plates before her. 'You need to get your strength back so you can hide.'

Lis nodded and squeezed her hands. 'You will help me?'

'As will I,' Master Yangshing said from the doorway.

Yang sighed behind him.

5

'I can't see the point of this,' Remi mumbled. He stood in the middle of the courtyard of the hidden princess compound. Nothing seemed to matter as it had before. Not now that she was gone. Chonglin had tried to reiterate just how strong they were, and that they could take control with little effort. 'I know what I'm doing. I have faced the soldiers before.'

'But in the end, you didn't really fight the soldiers,' a water bearer said, his face scarred from the battle with Lis.

Remi tried not to sigh. He didn't want to be here. Not now. He no longer had the will to fight, and despite their repeated attempts to convince him there was still a chance, that they would gain the control they had promised him, he no longer needed it. And with Lis gone, they should have taken over the Empire with little effort.

While he had lain unconscious, nothing of the kind had occurred. They had hidden away. He wondered if they were as strong as they claimed to be. They could have skills he wasn't aware of, but if that was the case, they could have used them.

As Lis had done. When the fight had started, he had no idea what was to happen or how he could even draw the strength to fight against her. And she had skills he'd had no knowledge of. Although when he thought about it, he had know what she could do. She had built a cage of vines and flowers on this very ground not so long ago.

But he'd had no idea she would be able to throw her skills, or that she could use them to trap and slow others.

'You need to focus on what you can do.' He thought the words had come from the priestess, but she was nowhere to be seen.

He nodded and focused on the heat surrounding him, the flames licking easily over his skin. He pulled the flames to his centre. The ball appeared between his cupped hands, and he moved his hands around the heat, growing it larger. He pushed it towards the man before him, who deflected it easily, driving it into the ground to his side where it left a scorch mark on the pavers.

'You need to think about where you are directing it.'

'I am,' Remi said through gritted teeth, bringing another fireball to life.

'Don't just throw it, *direct* it.'

Remi huffed as he pushed the next fire ball forward. The man dodged again.

Anger built in his chest, and the fireball that formed in his hands sparked and spluttered. The man before him raised his eyebrows. Remi focused on him, particularly his chest, and without any effort behind the throw, he released the ball, which honed in on its target directly. As the man sidestepped, it went with him, and despite his dodging it managed to hit him in the centre of his chest.

Remi grinned and crossed his arms. The fire didn't burn the fire bearer, but it had an impact. The man wheezed, winded by the blow.

'I am only standing before you.' He turned and looked through the straggly group. 'That man by the far wall. He is a fire bearer.'

Remi focused on the man, then formed another ball and released it. It moved in his direction, but it didn't have the force the previous attack had, and although it found the mark, it hit him with little impact on the lower leg.

'At least you didn't hit anyone else in the way. You need to practice. Find what drives you.'

'I know what drives me,' Remi spat, thinking of the anger he had felt earlier. But now that Lis was gone, he wasn't as focused as he could be, and he faltered. He didn't even care enough about these men to learn their names.

'You were able to defeat her, and she was stronger than we anticipated.'

Remi nodded once and formed another fireball. He tried to direct the same level of frustration he had with the other, but it didn't reach the target any better than the last attempt. He shook his head and formed another and another, with no better marksmanship.

Exhausted from the constant magic, he sank to his knees.

'You need to find a way to use it without using all of it,' the fire bearer said, turning his back on the prince and walking over to someone else. He watched the man twirl the air around them for a moment and then realised they were hiding their conversation from him. Remi wondered just how much he knew of their plans and how big a part he played in them.

He shook his head and climbed to his feet. He worried over nothing. If he wasn't needed by these men, they would not have sought him out, and he would not have isolated himself from all he knew. The wind bearer glanced at him over the shoulder of the other man, and Remi turned away. He walked back through the black gate, the silver characters still hiding, and he ran his fingertips over the gate as he walked past. A slight buzz of magic moved through his fingers, and he stopped. But the gate still appeared as it had, refusing to give up its secrets.

He didn't linger. This might be all that was left for him now. He had been so focused on losing Lis, but he had lost the Empire as well. No matter if he sided with these men or not, or against his father or not. The emperor would not accept him now. His side was chosen for him.

Before he realised it, he was again in the small room staring at the painting of Lis on the wall.

Lis flexed her fingers and pushed her hand forward, but nothing happened. She gulped down the rising fear and tried again. 'It won't come,' she said, letting her hands drop by her sides.

'You can't force it,' the master said.

'I need to be able to do this; I need to know that I can get to him before they get me.'

'You gave so much. Give yourself a chance to heal.'

'It has been a week,' she said, looking at Yang, who was leaning against the wall.

'You took a serious beating,' Master Yangshing said. 'And your emotions and magic are connected to all that has happened.'

'I know what I need to do.'

'But that doesn't make it easier.'

Lis nodded slowly and tried to allow herself to relax. As the master raised his hands, she copied the movement, pulling her hands in together in front of her chest, her fingers long and tall and pointing upwards. She closed her eyes and drew in a deep breath. She tried to keep her mind clear, focusing only on her breath rather than all she would need to know and face in the coming days. For they couldn't continue as they were, and the longer she left the prince alone with the magics, the more scared she was of what he would become.

She blew out a soft breath and hid. She opened her eyes as Yang clapped slowly, and she glanced across at him, feeling the magic working over her and keeping her hidden.

An awed gasp drew her attention, and she discovered the child hiding in the shadows. She sidestepped. Yang lowered his eyes, and the girl continued to look at where Lis had been. The child had gifts of her own, but this wasn't one of them. The master gave a subtle shake of his head, but Lis crept towards the child, whose wide eyes grew wider as she looked at where Lis had disappeared.

As Lis leaned forward to tap the child on the shoulder, she suddenly turned and reached out to grab Lis's hand. Lis reappeared and smiled. 'You could see me.'

'No,' she said, 'but I had a flash of a vision of what you would do.'

'Will I be able to sneak into the Palace Isle, even hidden, if they know what is coming?'

'How will they know?' the girl asked.

'Because we know there are others with your skill, and they are sharing their visions with the magics. Someone will know.'

'Once you reach him, it will be enough.'

'Will it?' Lis turned back to the master. 'I can't even raise my barrier. If the prince or any of them attack, I'll be lost.'

'You will do what you need to,' the girl said.

'I know you are trying to help, but you can't see it all.'

'I have seen enough to know. You only have to find him.'

Lis shook her head slowly, and the master waved her forward. When she'd needed to protect herself from the prince, she had found the strength to do so. She had once shielded many more than that. But she'd had help. She looked at the weary Yang. Wei-Song had never looked so serious. If only she had been able to protect them better in the last fight.

There had been a fear, she remembered as they moved through the fight. Too many, too close. If one of them had come within the barrier, she didn't know what might have happen.

'What will happen if he comes within the barrier?' she asked.

'You need to be able to raise it first,' Master Yangshing said, balling his fist. She could sense the magic in it. She tried to refocus on why they were there and held her breath as she pushed forward, but it wasn't enough. The magic he threw at her knocked her to the ground.

Yang rushed forward, but she waved him off.

'I have to work this out,' she mumbled, climbing to her feet.

'It doesn't have to be done now,' Yang said, stopping midway across the room. 'It is too soon.'

'I have to get to him before it is too late,' Lis said, feeling an overwhelming helplessness.

'Before he comes to us,' Wei-Song murmured.

'He won't. He will stay close to the palace, close to the throne. It is where he thinks he needs to be. Hiding.'

'And we can guess where,' Yang said.

'It doesn't matter where. We know he is on that island, and I need to get back there.'

'You will find it when you need it,' the child said.

Later that evening, Lis stood alone in her room, trying not to think too much on how she had failed during the day. No matter what they had tried, she couldn't muster the barrier, and she wondered how long it would take before she was ready to find Remi.

'You need to go now,' the child said hurriedly, sliding the door open. 'They won't forgive him.'

'Who won't?' Lis asked, sitting carefully at the little table. Her body still ached far more than she wanted to admit, partly in fear that Yang would want to help her more. But she couldn't take any more from him. He was still struggling from his use of magic in the fight, and he had spent far too long trying to heal her.

'The people, the ministers, the emperor.'

Lis had expected it would take some time for the people of the Empire to forgive their prince for what he had done. Yet she was more relieved every time the child mentioned him and their future. It reassured her he had survived. 'He does live?' she asked.

The girl nodded. 'But he may not survive much longer.'

Lis had been so worried she had killed him. She wondered if he feared the same, and whether he could ever feel about her as he had before he'd learnt what she was and the magic had taken him over.

She tried not to sigh. She felt so tired.

'You have to save him. You have to work together.'

'I can't,' Lis said, resting her head on her arms across the table. 'I've got nothing I can use to save him.'

'You dream of him,' the girl said, standing over her. 'You are the only one who can fix this. You are the only one to save the Empire.'

Lis shook her head without looking up. She wasn't anyone to try and save anything. She had only succeeded in nearly killing the prince. They hadn't defeated anyone. And she had felt so strong, so sure of her magic, allowing it to be what it was. But she had nothing left. She tried to form a barrier around her hand, but it wouldn't take.

The master had told her it would take time, that she needed to heal before the magic returned to what it was. 'He doesn't want me,' she murmured.

'That doesn't matter. What matters is whether you want to be with him, whether you choose him.'

Lis sighed again. It was not nearly as simple as the child thought. Despite all that she saw, she still saw the world from a child's point of view. Lis had known she cared for the prince just before she'd tried to hold him in her barrier. That she wanted him to live, whether with her or not.

6

Lis threw her arms around Yang and pulled him close, surprising them both. 'I need to do this,' she whispered.

'Sure,' he said, pushing her back to look at her properly. 'He will be only too happy to see you and not want to kill you at all.'

'I can still hide from him,' she said, turning away and wondering how good an idea this really was. She walked down the last of the path on her own and smiled to the boatman as she climbed into the little boat.

'Are you sure?' he asked her, his hand on the rope.

She nodded once. Lis was the only one sure that the prince could be saved, other than a child who didn't really know it, but was certain she had seen it.

The boatman pushed them out into the water and pulled another rope to shift the sail around, and they moved out from the little island. Lis hid and then waved at Yang. He lifted his hand—like a farewell, she thought—and then he turned away and headed back to the school.

Lis tried not to sigh. It was only because he worried, she told herself. And it would take far longer than she would like to reach the Palace Isle. Despite there being no one in sight and no boat on the horizon, the boatman pointed them in the opposite direction to their destination. They would be taking the long route to ensure there was no chance they could be traced back to the school. She wondered why this man, with no magic of his own, was so willing to assist them.

'The princess said you could sense us,' she said softly, and he barely nodded. 'Is it magic?'

'No, just an awareness of the world around me.'

'You don't fear the risks?'

'The risk for others is far greater.'

'What if you were discovered to be helping us?'

'Do you mean if they discover I like to sail my little boat around on my own?'

Lis laughed softly. Maybe he was safer than she'd thought. She had lived so long in fear of discovery. But now she worried she wouldn't be able to stop this from destroying them all.

She had curled at the end of the boat and drifted to sleep during the many hours it had taken them to reach the Palace Isle. She was awakened by the boat bumping against the pier, and then the loud voice of a soldier.

'What are you doing here? No one is allowed to enter the Palace Isle.'

'I pick up those from other islands without a boat and ferry them about.'

'You don't have any passengers now,' the man said. Lis moved as carefully as she could towards the dock, but as yet the soldiers weren't allowing him to tie up the boat. She wondered if she would end up in the water.

'I usually pick up an old couple from Second.' He looked towards the gate and, as the soldiers turned with him, Lis leapt the small distance to the dock and tried not to squeal with delight.

'No one is coming or going from the Palace Isle.'

'What has happened?' he asked.

'Where have you been, man? There is magic trying to destroy us.'

'I don't want to wait around here then,' he said, turning the sail and directing the boat from the dock. Lis watched as he sailed away. Then she turned and looked up at the large red gates of the Palace Isle. They looked so much bigger closed against the world, and she knew there was little chance of her sneaking in. On top of the wall by the gate, soldiers looked out over the world, and the soldiers who covered the dock walked back and forward.

'No one will come,' one of them said. 'We will just walk about here in the sun.'

'Would you prefer it if it rained, or snowed?'

The man shivered and went back to walking the edges of the dock as he stared out across the water.

Lis hadn't realised until she was on the island with the school just how much she had missed the water. She had been isolated in her palace of one type or another, and the rivers that ran through the palace grounds were not the same as the broad expanse of the ocean she had looked out on her whole life.

She tried not to sigh. She was trying to get away from it again, and it might be that she would be locked away for a very long time with no view at all. If she survived the day.

'I can't believe he did this,' the soldier murmured. Lis was sure he was speaking of the prince. They had such a clear idea of the man he was, yet he had behaved so very differently. She nodded slowly. She had also lost the man she'd thought he was, but perhaps with the right influence she could help bring him back. The child had certainly given the indication that she could. All she needed was a way through the gate.

As she moved along the dock, there were not as many soldiers as she'd first thought. She stepped up to the shiny red lacquer and ran her hand over it. The large pointed bolts glinted in the sunshine, and she wondered if they served a purpose other than decoration. She sighed and then stepped back. Was that a hint of silver glowing through the red?

She looked around, but none of the guards appeared to have noticed anything. She stepped back and pressed her hand to the gate. Then she sighed again across the surface, and a string of characters appeared in a line running down from where she had sighed, each character as big as her hand. She heard movement behind her, so she stepped to the side.

'What the…?' one of the men asked, coming forward.

'Who wrote that?' another soldier asked.

'It just appeared.'

Weapons were readied as the men stepped closer together around the gate, their backs to each other, looking out at the world. Lis was pressed between them and the gate.

'What is going on?' the hunter, Hui Te-Sze asked. He appeared through a smaller door in the gate, access Lis had not realised was there.

'A message,' one said, pointing at the gate without turning.

'The phoenix will rise,' the hunter read from the gate, and Lis realised the small gate was still open.

She crept closer, aware he might hear her. She thought he looked in her direction.

'Who wrote this?' he asked.

'It really did just appear on the gate,' one of the soldiers implored.

The hunter moved slowly forward, and Lis wondered if he might guess she was nearby, or someone like her. He ran his hand carefully over the silver characters. Lis waited for them to disappear, but they didn't. She stepped through the gate and then pressed herself to the inside and looked over the Palace Isle before her. There were soldiers everywhere, but no one else.

The damage from her fight with the prince was still clear across the square. Alongside rubble from some damaged buildings, the road and courtyards were charred and marked by fire and blood. Small gardens grew in some places, and Lis smiled at the idea. But it hadn't been her intention when fighting. She hadn't been sure she could fight; she had only tried to protect herself and others, and keep the prince from hurting himself.

She didn't know whether she should just walk into the grounds where she thought they would be or try something else. He had to be here. She couldn't have killed him—she wasn't strong enough for that. She sighed before she realised it, and when she made to step away from the gate, she found the hunter standing beside her. He tilted his head in her direction, and she froze.

'Princess?' he asked softly, a wobble in his voice.

She bit her lip as he leaned toward her, as though listening for her breathing. She needed to find the prince before she let anyone else know she was alive and on the Palace Isle.

He bowed his head and slowly made his way across the square. It was the hunter who had talked the general into allowing her to fight that day. And in that trust, she'd found more strength and ability than she'd known she had. Only she didn't have it now. And despite all that had gone on between them before, she was sorry she wasn't able to reassure him now.

She made her way towards the ruins of the residence first and wondered why, in all the months since it had fallen, no one had done anything to rebuild. It was a strange reminder of what the emperor had said they had no need to fear. The Palace Isle looked a very different place from what she remembered. Other than some soldiers, there was no one in sight.

She continued past the space where she had once lived and towards her little palace, but she veered off so she could check Remi's first. There was no sign of life when she pushed the door open, and the desk was still covered with reports that had gone unread. She couldn't tell when the advisor had last been here to add more to the pile. She moved over and lifted the top one, only then looking around to ensure there was no one else there. She hid the report in her hand before she started to read it.

It covered the sightings of magics in the area, but nothing of any use. Lis wondered if he had read it. She allowed the report to fall back onto the desk, then moved around the room for a better idea of what he had been thinking before he left and where he might have gone. But there was nothing. It was no different than when she was last here, when he had tried to burn her and Mu-Phi had bowed low to her prince.

Despite Mu-Phi's hatred of her, Lis was sad she had died as she had.

Lis took one last look around the room and then headed back out into the street. There was no one around her own palace as she drew close. When she pushed the gate open, she stopped, surprised by the lack of soldiers inside the wall. It had always seemed so full to her, and it was strange that there was no one there now. She walked around the garden she had never really entered before, taking in the flowers and the small pond she hadn't even known existed. She stood over it now, watching a lone fish swim in lazy circles before it disappeared into the dark water.

She turned to the house, unsure if she wanted to enter it or not. Taking a deep breath, she stepped slowly across the path and waited for the crunch of gravel to bring soldiers from inside. But no one came. It looked just the same, yet so very different. It felt cold and empty, and she looked for Yang and Wei-Song in the corners of the room.

She sat at her desk and looked over the papers. Someone had been through them, had pushed them from the desk and piles they'd were in. She wondered who it might have been. Someone looking for her, or looking for information? The hunter would have taken more time and been more respectful, she thought, and the prince might not care where she had gone. If he lived.

It was something she worried for. Particularly when the hunter appeared so sad. Could he know where the prince was?

Lis already knew where they could hide—the hidden princess palace. It was the only place he could stay nearby and be hidden from the rest of the island. She shivered at the idea of him taking the other magics to such a place. But then, in a way, it was theirs as well. If the war hadn't started, could the world have been a different place? Could they still have lived in harmony?

Lis walked towards the hidden princess palace. The streets were eerily quiet and, although she was hidden, she jumped at the slightest noises. It took her longer than she remembered to reach the gate that once would have marked the princess palace for what it was. But as she looked over the faded lacquer and the lack of characters or plaque, she doubted that it ever had. They must have been truly hidden from everyone, disappearing into a corner of the Palace Isle without anyone ever knowing where they went. Although someone had known. She just didn't know if it was the priestesses or simply tutors.

She rested her hand on the gate, but she didn't try the latch. She would have to find a way into the compound without alerting the magics she was there. The other gate had been melted closed by the prince himself. She stepped forward slowly. She was about to put her hand to it when it swung open, and she pressed herself against the wall.

A man rushed past her, dusty and still splattered with blood. She glanced into the training area to see others sparring with each other. The prince nowhere in sight. She wanted desperately to find out what they might have done to the grounds, or whether the prince hid amongst them. She also wondered what they might be planning to do next. She hovered for a moment, then heard footsteps coming back along the street. She moved to the side as the man marched past her and slammed the gate shut again behind him.

She couldn't hear anything beyond, and she wondered if the magic that hid the compound also hid what was done inside. She wasn't going to be able to reach him as easily as she had hoped. Not on her own. She sighed, then headed back to the square and the soldiers she knew were there.

7

The emperor sat back on his throne, the empress beside him. She at least smiled a little; he looked like he wanted to take her head from her shoulders. Lis tried to stand amidst the men she had fought with not so long ago. Although it felt like an age had passed, and now she wanted to cower behind General Zho-Hou and the hunter from the wave of anger that flowed from the emperor.

She gulped down her fears and stepped forward. She wished Yang had been well enough to travel with her. The child had seen that Remi needed her, and the certainty that he lived had sparked something significant in her chest. She had to do what she could to save him.

'Is there any word at all?' the emperor asked.

The general shook his head rather than answer, and the emperor stood slowly. The three of them dropped to their knees at the same time and touched their heads to the floor.

'He must be somewhere. They all must be somewhere on this island. Have you searched every inch?'

The hunter sat up slowly. 'Your Eminence, there is no sign of them.'

He glared again at Lis. 'You have some special skills. Can you hunt them out?'

'Perhaps,' she said, her voice shaking. 'My skills are not what they were since the fight,' she added quietly. 'I have an idea of where on the island they might be, but we can't…'

'You expect me to leave them there?' he interrupted.

She shook her head. 'They will be very difficult to capture. They have more skill. If we arrive at the gate, they could kill us all in the narrow streets before we could even determine whether the prince still lives.'

'He lives,' the empress pressed.

'He will be too well protected,' Lis said.

'We could go above them, hit them from the wall,' the emperor suggested.

'You can't see them from the wall,' Lis said.

Hui Te-Sze caught Lis's eye and then grinned. 'We could draw him out,' he said.

'How?' she asked.

'Oh,' the general said beside her.

The emperor stepped forward.

'He does not know that Lis lives,' Te-Sze said. 'None of us did but Yang.'

'You want to draw him into another fight?'

'Your Eminence, the boy loves the girl. If we allow the news of her return to filter through the men and the Palace Isle, he will learn of her and try to see her.'

'How can he love her? He tried to kill her. He very nearly did.'

Lis tried to tell Te-Sze it was a bad idea with her eyes.

'He does love her,' the empress said.

'They barely know each other.'

'I think they have spent far more time together over her time on the island than we have in all these years.'

The emperor scowled but didn't look at his wife. Lis sucked in a breath. What if they were wrong? But then, she had always known there was more feeling on his side than hers. Only now that she knew she felt the same, she would need to do all she could to keep him safe and save him from the dangers of the magics.

'Will it be enough? What will happen when you find him?' the emperor asked.

'We just need to know he is safe,' the empress said.

'It is not enough,' Lis said. 'If you try to hold him, he will fight his way out.'

'He might not,' the emperor said, 'if you are there. If these men are right.'

'He may try to fight me,' she said, 'and I'm not ready. I'm not strong enough.'

'We will put you somewhere safe, where he can't harm you but he might try to sneak in to see you.'

She nodded once.

'And then he shall face his punishment,' Advisor Gan said, striding into the room. 'As shall you.' He held out a sharp finger in Lis's direction.

'This is a private meeting,' the emperor snapped.

'This concerns the entire Empire,' a minister said, following the advisor into the throne room along with other ministers of the Empire.

'I thought you had run away,' the emperor said.

'We continue to advise, Your Highness, and we advise the death of the crown prince, once he can be separated from the magics. They would be easier to face without him,' Advisor Gan continued, looking towards the general, who nodded once.

'Kill the crown prince?' the empress asked softly.

The little man bowed before the empress, and Lis realised he had not shown the same respect to the emperor when he entered the room. She wondered what his punishment would be.

'What do you propose we do in relation to the continuation of the line?' the emperor asked. 'The Rei Dynasty has ruled this Empire for countless generations. It is our Empire.'

'Until your son became the enemy. Do you have any other children hidden away?'

Lis looked up at the empress, who continued to stare

disbelieving at the advisor, and Lis caught the eye of the emperor before he sighed.

'We feel it might be time for the representatives of the people to rule.'

Lis sat back at the overwhelming emotion in the room as it washed over her. The fear, the uncertainty, the nervousness. These men were claiming they should rule over the emperor, and Lis didn't think they would survive the day.

'I put you in these positions,' the emperor snapped, swinging around and marching back to his throne. 'You represent my interests, not the people. You are men of rank, a rank I gave you. From wealthy families, as favours to keep you close, to ensure you wanted to keep your families safe. Do you think the people of this Empire will let you decide their fate?'

Several men nodded. Others looked around and exchanged glances.

'I was born to this role,' the emperor went on. 'The gods put me here, not you. Only the gods can remove me.'

'Even the priestesses have run away from the Palace Isle,' the little advisor said. 'No one will return to you. Do you really think you can save us by playing games to bait the crown prince?'

'Do you think you can take on the magics and remove them from the Empire? I'm sure there are some priestesses still hiding somewhere on this island. And they haven't left us; they have returned to the Sacred Isle, which is part of this Empire, to see how they can assist us with their prayers from there.'

Lis wondered just what the emperor knew of the priestesses, or what he might have guessed.

Gan looked over the ministers but said nothing.

'Well?' the emperor prodded. 'Are you to stand in the square and fight my son and his magics?'

Several of the ministers dropped to their knees. But others remained standing, some looking to Gan for guidance.

'Do what you think you can,' Gan said. 'And then we will

revisit what the man is.'

A part of Lis was relieved, but when the emperor waved her forward, she realised things were about to get a lot worse before they got better.

As Lis stepped forward, the empress stepped up to join them. She reached out for Lis, who was thankful for her comfort, although there was a nervousness around the woman she hadn't felt before.

'You want to save him,' the emperor said quietly, and Lis noted the little advisor leaning forward. 'You will do what is best by him.'

Lis bowed her head to him.

'Despite my concerns, he is my son, and the only heir to the Empire. I trust you,' he added softly, and Lis wasn't sure she heard him correctly. 'I know you put this Empire before your own needs, and that is what we need in an empress. You have not wed yet, but he is your husband. I trust you will do what is necessary.'

'I will do whatever I can,' Lis said.

Murmuring started amongst the ministers, and the little advisor huffed. Again anger rolled off the emperor, but he maintained his calm features, his attention focused only on her.

'Work with the general,' he said as the general stepped forward and bowed low. 'Find a way to bring him out. Or we may have to face him again, and I'm not sure the ministers could win that fight.'

Lis bowed again and followed the general towards the door, the hunter only a few steps behind. The ministers maintained their stance, but as Lis left the throne room and hit the warm sun at the top of the stairs, she heard them following her out.

She stood to the side and hoped they would continue past, but the advisor stopped, his face showing the anger he felt at the situation. 'I don't care what the emperor thinks you are, or what you might be able to do. You are a girl. And a magic at that. You will suffer the same fate as the crown prince.'

Lis opened her mouth to respond, but the words were slow to come. In that time, he turned with a flourish she didn't think a man of his size was capable of, then moved down the stairs and away, the ministers trailing behind him.

'I think he sees himself as the next emperor,' the hunter said, his voice unkind. It reminded Lis of the fear she used to hold for him.

But as she looked up at his scarred face, she knew he was no longer such a threat.

'What do you need me to do?' she asked.

'I want to put you somewhere we can watch and keep men close, but where he could reach if he tried.'

'What if he can't? What if he is no longer here?'

'He is. And if he was hurt as badly as you were…'

'Or worse,' Lis murmured. 'Are you sure he is alive?'

The hunter surprised her by placing his hands on her shoulders and looking her square in the face. 'Of course, he lives. There is some strange destiny the two of you share. If you could survive that…whatever it was, then so could he.'

Lis nodded slowly.

'Your Highness,' a soldier called, running towards her. Then he dropped to his knees and bowed low before her. 'I feared you lost.'

She recognised him instantly as one of her guard, one who had stood for so long in her garden, keeping her from others and safe at the same time. He had also fought beside her as they'd left the little palace on the day she had faced Remi. She smiled at the idea that she could use his name. Such a strange thing to be able to do, and yet it meant so much to her. She wondered why it had been so easy for him to call her Lis right from the beginning. But then, he had chosen her.

'As did I,' she said to the soldier. 'But all is well, and I am returned. Have you seen the crown prince?'

He shook his head, and Lis could feel his confusion. She understood what these men had faced by standing against someone they had respected so much.

'Do you think he survived?' she asked.

'I didn't think either of you had,' he said quickly as he climbed back to his feet. 'I shall gather your guard,' he announced, looking briefly at the general. 'Where are you staying?'

Lis looked at the hunter for an answer.

'We will keep her close,' he said, 'but it may be that we are to find refuge in the servant's quarters before we can find suitable accommodation.'

'The laundry girls had a good-sized room, and they have all gone. Shall I show you the way?'

'We can find it,' the general said. 'Go find your men and let them know the good news.'

He bowed again to Lis, and then the other two men, but not as deeply, before he ran down the stairs and away from them.

'The laundry could be as good a place as any, and the ministers would not expect us to hide you there. I worry what harm they may do to the Empire before we can bring you back together,' the general said.

'The Empire survived the magic war,' the hunter added.

'Come,' the general said kindly, indicating the way. Lis walked between the two large men, hoping the news would spread quickly.

The laundry, when they reached it, consisted of a large open courtyard, strung with lines and surrounded on three sides by covered walkways. On the fourth side, a small garden sat against a high wall. They entered the space along one of the walkways, and it had an abandoned feel; sheets and clothing lay haphazardly across lines and in the dirt. The smell of soap reminded her of the baths.

She was tempted to pick up the fallen clothing, but she continued along the covered walkway. On the far veranda, she realised the shadows hid a door. The general pushed it open, and they entered a large dormitory-style room with a raised platform. Sleeping mats were lined along one wall, and the rest was open space. She imagined it full of laundry girls of a night, all lying down together.

'We can bring in a table,' the hunter said, 'and a kettle…'

'It will be fine,' Lis said, trying to give him a reassuring smile. 'But where will you be?'

He looked around the room. There were some high windows along the far wall, but it was a space designed for sleep only. He turned back to the door and sighed. 'There are other rooms,' he said.

Lis walked ahead of him out onto the veranda and continued along the walkway. There were two more narrow doors on the third side of the building. She opened the first and found a narrow room, with space only for the bed and a small table against the wall. A coat hung on the back of the door, and the bed appeared to have been left in the middle of the night, the covers thrown back and half on the floor. A single shoe sat in the middle of the floor.

The next room was similar, although a little larger. The bed was also similarly dishevelled, and clothes lay on the floor as though someone had pulled together all they owned and then only packed some of it.

'Perhaps I would be better here,' she said. 'The two of you could be in the larger space; it would be more comfortable.'

The general laughed. 'We are soldiers. We aren't used to being comfortable. Although there is a small window there. I would rather you in the other space. If the prince arrives, it would be easier to contain him rather than trying to get into a room.'

'Are we sure he isn't going to try and kill her?' the hunter asked quietly.

'Are we sure any soldiers won't try to kill him?' Lis asked.

'I will talk with them,' the general said as the first of the hidden princess guard rounded the corner of the courtyard. Lis smiled at the sight of them.

'Clean this up,' the general called over the group, and they moved into the courtyard. 'I want all the washing and the lines put back how they should be.'

A couple of the men looked at each other and then bowed to the general.

'We need to keep the princess safe, but we need to ensure this place looks like a laundry.'

The men bowed as one and then got to work. Lis moved back into the large room, listening to the men move around the courtyard. She waved one hand over the other, and a single cake appeared in her hand. She held it out to the hunter and then, closing her eyes, she tried again. A bowl appeared, but it was empty. She sighed and screwed her eyes closed as a heavy hand rested on her shoulder.

'Save what energy you have,' the hunter said, glancing at the general who stood by the door. Lis could not only read the concern on his face, she could feel it. At least her senses weren't dulled. But if she needed to protect herself or others, she had no idea what she could do other than hide.

Lis stood out in the evening light and looked over the washing blowing gently in the breeze. She knew the soldiers were close. She could sense their uncertainty—or was it their vigilance? Either way, she couldn't see them, and she wondered if Remi would sense them as well. She sighed. In many ways, she wished Wei-Song were here, and Yang, yet she didn't want them anywhere near the mess this might easily become.

The general and Hui Te-Sze were so sure they could take him unawares. If his magic was still anything like it had been, there was no chance. He was stronger than Lis. She only hoped that her choosing to return to him, choosing to help him would be enough. The child had been so clear that Lis needed to return to the Palace Isle and to Remi.

She felt both exposed in the open courtyard and too closely watched for Remi to take the chance. And it was all a gamble. He may not be interested in seeing her again. Everyone, from the general to the little girl she had left behind at the school, felt that he would do anything he could to get to her.

She walked back around the covered walkway as the sky grew darker and the shadows longer. If she'd had a little palace like this, she might have been happier. She looked across at the garden by the wall and wondered if there would ever be a time she could simply sit amongst the grass and flowers.

She moved into the oversized room, designed for so many laundry girls and now only occupied by herself. The general and the hunter had retired to their little rooms. They had promised to stay alert, yet she questioned whether they would really have the time to reach her if Remi was determined to kill her.

That was, if he came. She sat slowly on the edge of the sleeping platform. She had insisted on a simple mat rolled out. They had moved a small table into the space, and it looked strange in the vastness of the room. She waited, looking into the dark corners of the room as they grew deeper. She didn't know what she would say to him. She didn't know how she could make this any better.

When the room had darkened to the point that she couldn't see her own hands, she lay down on the mat as she was and stared up at the ceiling. Would she ever sleep? And if he didn't come, or took days to learn she was there, she would be a mess by the time he did arrive.

She must have drifted, for she was suddenly aware of someone close by. She stayed stock still, but her eyes were open. There was no light, and then someone was leaning over her.

'General?' she asked in a whisper.

'I was just checking,' he murmured.

'I'm still here. Do you think this is a good idea? What if you are seen?'

He murmured something else before his quiet footsteps disappeared across the floor and out. She sighed into the darkness and then sat up. Someone else was already in the room. As the door clicked quietly closed behind the general, Lis pushed the cover back and slipped from the platform to the floor.

She stood in the middle of the room and waited. Her hands hung by her sides, and although she was tempted to pull her barrier in tight around her, she didn't think it would work, so she didn't try. She closed her eyes and could almost hear the quiet breath in the corner. She waited for the light, but it didn't come.

'Will you speak to me?' she asked. 'Or do you just want to see that I'm alive?'

He stepped out of the shadows then, looking tired and worried and lost. She stepped forward without hesitation. Relief washed over her that he had survived the fight, and she felt the same from him. She paused only momentarily before him, and then she threw her arms around his neck and pulled herself against him. He rested his head on hers and wrapped his arms around her. For a single moment she felt calm, comfortable and complete.

And then he pushed her off. But as the empty feeling surrounded her with the air that filled the gap between them, he took her hands.

'I thought I had killed you,' he whispered.

'I thought *I* had killed *you*,' she returned, trying to calm her heart rate as it took off and tears threatened to run over.

'They want me dead,' he said, tipping his head towards the door.

'No,' she started, but she could hear the footsteps getting closer and sense the soldiers. 'You knew they were there.'

'Of course,' he said, his hands still holding hers firmly. 'But I had to see if you had really survived. The priestess…'

Lis waited in the silence for him to continue. What did he know of the priestess? Had he stayed with her, or she with them? Was she the connection, the way the magics knew of the visions? But as her head reeled with the possibilities and her mouth failed to voice any of them, the door swung open with a bang, and she moved between Remi and more soldiers than she'd realised had been standing guard over her.

8

Remi didn't move as the men entered the room. He knew they were there—he knew exactly what this was—and he rested his hands on Lis's shoulders. There was a certainty to her, a confidence he hadn't expected. Her relief at seeing him had filled the room, and he had known in that moment that he had made the right decision to find her.

It hadn't been very hard. They had made it easy, and that was why he had known they wanted him to find her and that it was a trap. The priestess didn't know what he had discovered, or at least he didn't think so, but it wouldn't be long. And she would know where his allegiances lay when she learnt he hadn't snuck in and killed Lis.

He couldn't. Lis had filled his thoughts. When he'd thought he had killed her, he had only thought about what he might have done differently, despite her not wanting to be there. And now she had come back. He only hoped it was for more than to pull him into a trap and have his father kill him.

She rested her hand on his and stepped closer to him. Her back was almost against his chest, and he knew she had chosen to return to help him. He wanted to pull her out of the way, ensure she was safe from the possible danger of these men, but then he knew they would do everything they could to protect her first.

'General,' Remi said, surprised at how level his voice sounded. There was a slight gravel to it, as though he had burnt himself during the fight. 'What can I do for you?'

'You could come quietly.'

'To stand before the emperor and die.'

'That is not what we intend,' Lis said, 'but you can't return to the magics.'

'What would you have me do?'

'Why did you come?' the general asked, stepping further into the room.

Remi remained silent.

'Could you step away from the princess, Your Highness?'

'I still have a title then,' he said, anger creeping into his voice. He had thought his father would have disowned him. 'And the princess appears to have a hold on me.'

'Perhaps you should go with him,' Lis said, releasing her hold and turning to him.

'To sit in a prison cell and have gods know who try to kill me? The soldiers of the Empire will want to take their revenge, and the magics will fear my returning to you.'

Lis looked back at the General. 'Perhaps he could wait here until he is presented to the emperor.'

'Is he to take my head directly?'

Lis grumbled under her breath and looked up at him with disappointment. 'We are trying to protect you.'

'Protect me?' he asked, trying to sound disbelieving, but he couldn't hide the smile. 'You have set a trap for me.'

'We pulled you away from the magics to where you are meant to be.'

'The laundry?'

'Seriously, Remi, you want to joke about this after all that has happened?'

He stepped forward quickly and, despite the movement amongst the guards, he pulled her close and kissed her.

He half expected her to step back out of his reach, or fight him in some way, but she didn't. Instead, she pushed herself towards him.

'You called me Remi,' he murmured when he released her.

She smiled and then gave him a shallow bow. 'Forgive my not greeting you appropriately.'

He laughed as the room filled with soldiers. Hui Te-Sze sighed, and Lis smiled enough to light the room.

'Why are you smiling at the idea of my demise?' he asked her, but he couldn't remove his own smile. And he was reluctant to let her go.

'He will let you stay here,' Lis said.

'How can you be so sure of my character?' the hunter snapped.

She was far more confident than he remembered her. Lis smiled warmly at the number of men in the room. 'Because you know that if you remove him to the prison, I will remain there with him.'

The hunter sighed again. 'You will not be alone. At least two men will stand inside this door.'

Lis nodded before Remi could say anything. Did she fear him still?

'Can you fetch more bedding?' she asked, and one of the soldiers disappeared without a word.

'What do you propose?' the general asked.

'Only that we sleep. If we are to face the emperor in the morning, I would rather be well rested, and I haven't had the opportunity as yet to sleep.'

The general bowed before her.

'Another favour, General,' she said as he turned to head outside. 'Can you keep this from the ministers? If only for tonight.'

He bowed again and departed without a word. The large number of soldiers followed, leaving Hui Te-Sze and the two guards inside the room. A soldier moved past the exiting crowd with two rolls of bedding, which he carried towards the sleeping platform before stopping. He looked back at the hunter and then at the princess.

'Put them there,' she said, pointing to the floor by the table. The relief was evident on his face, and it filled Remi's senses, going some way to calm him. He hadn't realised until the man had returned that his own tensions were rising.

'Are you to stand by the door as well?' she asked Te-Sze, who shrugged in response. 'Forgive me, but it has been a long day.' She bowed to Remi and then climbed easily onto the platform and disappeared under the covers.

Te-Sze looked pointedly at the rolled bedding by the table. Blowing out a slow breath to calm himself, Remi unfurled them, slipped his shoes off and climbed in. He felt the distance from Lis, but he smiled up at the ceiling. Not only was she alive, but she had been relieved to find him alive.

In some ways, he felt he could take on the world, particularly his father and the ministers, if she was standing beside him. Otherwise, he feared his control on his magic might not be as strong as he would like.

In the quiet room, he could only hear the gentle breaths of the guards standing in the dark. He wondered what they might do if he tried to pass them. There might be some in the ranks who didn't want to kill him on sight, but he was sure they were in small numbers compared to those who did.

He was angry with himself for having been so easily swayed to believe that he and Lis couldn't work together. Some of the magics might have been working to save his brother and the Empire, but too many of them wanted only what would benefit them. And he had fallen too easily into their way of thinking.

As the edge of the covers lifted, he baulked, pulled from his thoughts as he wondered which of them was going to drag him out and have him killed in front of his own men before his father was even aware of his capture.

But the movement was slow and quiet, and as Lis settled against him with her head on his shoulder, he was overwhelmed by her. He moved his arm out from between them and wrapped it around her shoulders.

'I didn't mean to wake you,' she whispered.

He shook his head, too afraid to speak. And he rested his hand on her shoulder.

9

The empress stood beside her husband and tried not to move. Despite the emperor's efforts, the ministers murmured amongst themselves. The hidden princess stood calmly before the soldiers. Despite her trying to look serious, the empress was sure the girl smiled.

Remi stood beside her, his hands shackled before him. Although the room was hostile, he looked much calmer than she would expect. She had heard such terrible things about the fight in the square, the words and threats he had thrown around along with his fire.

The emperor cleared his throat, and the noise finally subsided amongst the ministers. 'You have come forward willingly, I understand.'

Remi nodded, although he moved his hands to draw attention to the shackles.

'You are aware of the danger you have posed to the Empire of Rei-Een.'

'I was misled,' Remi said.

The emperor growled, and the empress was sure he would leap from his seat and stride across the room to knock the boy down himself. She wasn't quite sure how he would react to such a thing from his father.

The general and the hunter shuffled behind the princess, but after a subtle look from her, they both stood still. Remi's eyes were fixed on his father, and the empress couldn't help but look across at the ministers.

'Now that the prince is in custody,' Advisor Gan said, 'we…'

'When were you raised to minister?' the emperor asked without looking at the little man.

He snapped his jaw shut and glanced at the minister beside him. The man he had glanced at cleared his throat and then stepped forward from the group.

'We have allowed Advisor Gan to speak for us,' the minister said. 'But you are right, Your Eminence; we are the officials of the Empire.'

The emperor waved him forward, and the man cleared his throat again. The empress was pleased to see he had the confidence she had remembered of him. He bowed low to the emperor and then looked at Remi.

'I believe the crown prince has done much for the Empire as a hunter and as a soldier. This should be considered when you decide on his punishment. But as far as the people are concerned, he is no longer the crown prince of the Empire. He is no longer the heir of Rei-Een.'

The empress was sure her heart stopped. Across the room, she could see the flames leap to life behind Remi's eyes. At the same moment, Lis looked up at him and the soldiers behind him stepped back. She could see the haze of heat around him. Lis rested her hand on his arm, and it dissipated. He blew out a slow breath, but his focus never moved from his father.

The empress stepped forward, waiting for the emperor to turn his disappointment on her. She was sure that he blamed her for this mess, and she both wished that Wei-Song were present while feeling grateful she wasn't.

The emperor surprised her by reaching out and taking her by the arm, pulling her closer to him. She was momentarily relieved by the action, but then Remi stepped forward and the room became unsettled.

The ministers talked amongst themselves, the soldiers murmured, and Remi inched further from the group behind him. The emperor's grip on her arm grew tighter.

'We must do something,' she whispered.

'And we will,' he answered. Still holding her tight, he stepped forward. 'There will be no question as to whether my son is the heir to the Rei-Een Empire.'

'We aren't questioning anything,' the minister said. 'We are telling you what the people want.'

'Have you asked them?' The emperor faced the group, pulling the empress with him.

The man stammered and looked back at his fellow ministers. Some shook their heads; others looked at the ground. Still others amongst the group looked defiant, and the empress wondered for the first time if she would survive this.

'He has worked against the Empire,' someone called from within the group.

'He has magic,' someone else said.

'As do many,' the hunter said, stepping forward and standing beside Lis. 'We were never able to defeat the magic. Maybe we shouldn't have tried. But in working against it, we have only made it stronger. We have created a divide within the Empire, and it is time to heal the wounds.'

Lis smiled up at him, but he kept his focus to the front.

'I am not a threat to the Empire,' Remi said softly.

'You fought your own men,' Advisor Gan said loudly. 'You fought against the hidden princess...' But his voice faded away, as though he was suddenly aware that she had magic and had worked in favour of the Empire. 'Why is the girl not in chains?' he asked sternly, looking back at the emperor.

'Because she is the hidden princess,' the empress said.

'And she did far more to stop this than any of you have done,' the general said, standing on the other side of Remi. 'Without the hidden princess, many more men would have been lost, as would your prince.' He sighed and, without a word of approval, he reached out and unlocked the shackles around Remi's wrists.

The ministers, as one, moved back a step.

'We need to focus on what we can do to stop this. It will not stop with your punishing the prince, or your ideas of deposing the emperor,' the general said, stepping towards the ministers. Several shook their heads while others looked between each other. 'We need to stop those who actually want to destroy our Empire, and we need the crown prince and the hidden princess working together to do that.'

'She has magic. We heard she had been killed in the fight—how is it that she is standing here before us now?'

'A good healer and good friends,' she said softly, but the empress noted with pride how her voice carried through the room.

'And when she brings her magic friends here and joins with the others, we will all be doomed.'

'Did you not listen to me?' the general asked into the room. His voice was thick with his frustrations.

'You have been bewitched,' a minister called out.

'Enough!' the emperor bellowed, and the room fell into silence. 'Take him away,' he snapped at the general. 'I would talk with the ministers together. Leave the hunter.'

The empress was relieved that Remi didn't put up a fight as he turned and followed the general from the room, with Lis following behind. They had both bowed slightly to her and the emperor, but neither had acknowledged the ministers or the advisor. She blew out a slow breath, relieved that nothing had happened. She only hoped he could forgive Lis for tricking him into coming to her. But then they had all been sure, other than Lis, that he would have done anything to track her down.

She only wished she had been there. Lis seemed calmer amidst all of this, and despite what Remi had tried to do to her, she had stood by his side. This might end as the empress had hoped it would so long ago.

'You have not talked with the people, and yet you are determined to speak on their behalf. Do they have any idea what occurred here? Does anyone?' the emperor asked.

A minister from near the back stepped forward. His headpiece appeared tired and faded, and the empress wondered where they had been staying in the time since the fighting.

'We were elected to act on their behalf,' the man said, more confidently than the empress was sure he felt. 'We have been making decisions for generations on what they need. The magic has spread throughout the Empire. We need to ensure it is stopped before it grows to what it was before and there is more than just fighting in the street.'

'I think what we saw was more than fighting in the street,' another said, stepping forward. 'Where are they now? That is the question we should all be asking.'

The emperor sat back slowly on his throne.

'Will the prince tell us where they are?'

'What would you do if you knew?' the emperor asked. 'Would you take them on, take up a sword?'

Murmuring started again amongst the group.

'I fear the general is correct. We are going to need to trust some of those with magic to stop the others from taking control of the Empire.'

The murmuring increased as the empress turned to her husband with surprise.

'There was a time,' the empress said carefully, 'when we worked with magics, when we lived together.' The emperor nodded for her to continue. 'If it had not been for the visitors, we may have continued that way. I think we can find a way back to living together.'

'How can we seriously return to what the world was?' Advisor Gan asked. He strutted forward, and for a moment the empress was sure he thought himself equal to the men around him. But he had been a highly valued advisor to the emperor for many years, and it might be that he was entitled to feel the way he did.

'You are the one, Your Eminence, who was sure the magics had to be stopped. You were the driving force of the war.'

The emperor nodded slowly, and the empress felt the weight of the movement. It was hard for him to admit he'd been wrong; this would be even more than admitting an error. This would be admitting a war should not have happened. The ministers had clearly gotten the same sense from his subtle movement, for the level of murmuring increased tenfold.

'What of your first born?' the advisor called above the noise, and the world fell into instant silence. 'What of Prince Ta-Sho?'

'We may never know what truly happened to him,' the emperor admitted. 'It may be that finding a way forward is more important. No matter what we have done or experienced in the past.'

'You want to forgive them, and then what? Hand over the Empire?'

'That is not what I'm saying.'

'How could you protect the prince for all these years?' another minister asked.

'He didn't show any signs of magic. The hunters didn't sense him,' the empress said, stepping forward to be more involved in the conversation. 'This is something very new to him, which is the reason he struggled with what he was and how he fit into the world.'

'He was very quick to side with the magics against us,' the minister said. 'There didn't seem to be any doubts there.'

'He was misled as to what he was, and as to what the princess was.'

'And what is she exactly?' another asked, apparently braver than he looked due to his colleagues stepping forward.

'Different from the others,' the empress said. She didn't want to use the word Hidden, and she certainly didn't want to use the name of the order. Too many of these men had been involved in the magic war and knew the danger they might pose.

'How can we be sure she will continue to fight for us?' another man asked.

'The hidden princess has already proven herself too ready to fight for the Empire. She would not fight against it.'

'She was prepared to fight the crown prince,' he said.

'She was trying to protect him,' the hunter said. The first words he had spoken. 'She knew what he was battling with, and she wanted to ensure he was safe.'

'How do we know the girl is safe?' someone else asked, and although the empress scanned the group, she couldn't determine who it was.

'Because she stopped the prince, almost killing herself in the process. She insisted on standing up for the Empire. And she has done all she can to help bring the prince in, despite the threat to both him and herself.'

The murmuring started again amidst the ministers, and the empress was sure there was not just discussion, but some argument about what they had heard. It might be that they did not all feel the same. But the advisor stood silent, his hands clasped before him and a sour look upon his face. He would not be easily swayed, the empress determined, and she was disappointed that a man she had thought loyal to their family would be so quick to give them up.

The hunter must have had a similar thought. Resting his hand on his sword, he bowed towards the emperor and made to leave.

'I'm not sure we are finished here,' he said.

'I don't think we are going to get very far. I'll check on the princess and decide what we shall do with the crown prince while we consider what can be done with the magics.'

'I think we have far more to discuss. But I think the ministers could take their leave.' The emperor looked older and more tired than the empress had expected, and she wondered if he would consider allowing the ministers to take Remi into custody. Although she doubted it would end there.

10

Remi watched the general walk ahead as the soldiers surrounded them. Despite the number of men, he didn't feel threatened. He knew they would do whatever Lis asked of them. He recognised many of the men from the hidden princess guard. They tended to pay more attention to her than to him, and at first he had thought it was because they feared her. But they were watching out for her, ensuring she was happy and comfortable walking beside the prince who had tried to kill her.

The disappointment leaked from him in a sigh, and the swords moved in their sheaths as Lis turned to him.

'What is wrong?' she asked.

He shook his head. 'Where are we going?'

'Back to the laundry,' she said. 'I think. What do you think, general?'

He nodded solemnly but kept moving ahead.

'You don't want to lock me up?' Remi asked, regretting the move as the general stopped.

'Would you rather we put you in the prison? Would that make it easier for your magic friends to find you?'

He shook his head, noticing that Lis watched him too closely. 'Are you scared of me?' he asked without thinking.

'Should she be?' the general asked for her, and Remi shook his head.

'Maybe the general should stay with you in the big room, and I take a smaller one,' she said softly.

'You are scared,' he said, reaching for her arm, but she pulled it back out of his reach.

'I'm not scared,' she said, her chin held high and her voice too loud. 'I'm sure it is not right that we stay together.' Her cheeks blushed brightly.

'You didn't mind…' He stopped when she looked away.

'I was relieved that I hadn't killed you,' she said as they continued towards the laundry. After some time in silence, she asked, 'How long do you think until they try to find you?'

'I don't know that they will,' he said.

'They need you for their plan, don't they?' the general asked.

'They might have got all they wanted,' he said.

'They might have got wind of the princess being alive, and where she is,' one of the soldiers said. 'You are more a danger to her now than you were as a hunter.'

'I didn't try to kill her,' he said to the man.

'And yet you very nearly did,' the man snapped back, the anger behind his voice surprising the prince. 'You were supposed to protect her, to keep her hidden until she could be your wife. Yet you only brought harm and fear her way, siding with the magics who want her dead.'

'That will do,' the general murmured from the front, and Lis gave the man a friendly smile.

Remi's heart skipped. He shook his head to dispel the feeling and tried to remember how he had slept with her against his body, her head on his shoulder. His tensions eased. When he refocused on the world around him, he noticed she was watching him again, and he smiled. She bowed her head and looked away. Did she think he could be a threat, that he was scouting her out for the magics? She had seemed so relieved the night before, so comfortable standing between him and an army of men.

'Was it simply the relief?' he asked.

'Sorry?' She turned to him as they continued towards the laundry.

'That you were so accepting of me yesterday—was it only because of your relief that I wasn't dead?'

She shook her head. 'I knew you weren't yourself,' she murmured, watching the street ahead of her rather than him. 'It is so quiet,' she said.

When the general turned back to say something, a fireball flew towards them. Before he could act, Lis was standing before the general, her hands raised, and the soldiers surrounding them. Another fireball hurled towards them, but it stopped midair and dissipated.

'Keep moving,' the general said through clenched teeth.

Huddled together, they moved through the open space and into a narrow pathway.

Lis swayed to the side, the general put his arm around her, and they ran faster. Remi was swept up in the movement of the soldiers rather than any forward momentum of his own. He tried not to let Lis out of his sight as they moved forward and the group ahead of him disappeared through a gap between two buildings. They were close to the laundry, but Remi wasn't sure it was going to do them any good. It appeared the magics had them as another fireball sailed overhead.

His main concern was reaching Lis before any more magics showed up. She wasn't as well recovered as he had thought, and although she appeared as strong as she had been that day, it certainly wasn't the case. If she couldn't protect them with her barrier, she might not be able to protect herself at all.

He pushed a couple of the younger soldiers out of the way, trying to get to her—she always seemed to be out of his reach. As he made his way forward in the group, he soon found that they had stopped. Lis was leaning heavily into the general.

'Can I take her?' he asked.

'Where would you take her to?' the man asked, his arm tighter around her shoulder. Lis, with her eyes closed, didn't even move.

'I simply meant take her weight,' he whispered. 'What can you see?'

'Nothing. I don't suppose you could use some of your hunting skills and see if there is anyone around?'

Remi nodded and pushed to the front of the narrow space between the buildings. He wondered briefly why they had come this way, but then it could have been just to keep them out of sight. Not that they had seen anyone yet. He tried to keep within the shadow of the building and closed his eyes. There was something in the distance, but he wasn't clear on what exactly it was. No one was using any magic at the moment.

But the fireballs had been a good indication that there were fire bearers around. Perhaps the priestess had seen something that had led to them realising the princess was still alive. Because she hadn't seen that before—or if she had previously, she hadn't been willing to share that information with Remi. She may have felt there was an advantage to his not knowing, that it gave her power over him.

He blushed at the idea of her and looked back just as Lis opened her eyes. She seemed to stare for a moment before closing them again. He didn't think he could be separated from her again. A breeze blew over his skin, making him shiver, but it wasn't magic. Whoever had been out there had disappeared. But they might be waiting to follow them.

'People will know where we are,' he whispered. 'It wasn't hard for me to learn where you were hiding; it won't take the magics long either.'

'But we will be ready for them,' the general said. He lifted Lis easily into his arms and nodded to a soldier, who headed out into the street before them. Nothing happened, and the general followed with the princess in his arms.

There was no sign of magic or magics on the rest of the journey to the laundry, which still looked like a working laundry when they reached it. Remi wondered what had happened to the girls who had worked here. Like the rest of the island, they had gone. Would they ever come back?

Despite the earlier idea of the princess moving, the general carried her into the large room and then waited while Remi raced forward and unrolled her covers. The general laid her down carefully and then covered her up.

'What is it?' Remi asked, sitting on the edge of the platform.

'She isn't healed enough yet. She can hide, but a barrier to protect us all was simply more than she was able to handle.'

'I'm sorry,' Remi mumbled, more to Lis than the general. It was the fight between them that had caused so much of the trouble and taken so much from her.

They sat in silence around the sleeping princess. Remi could hear the soldiers outside walking back and forth across the doorway, and he was grateful they hadn't followed them in. He was pleased the men had continued to keep her safe and watch over her, but they had quickly formed a dislike to him, and he wasn't sure if he could turn it around. Or even if he deserved their respect.

Lis murmured in her sleep and then rolled over. The general sighed and ran a hand over his ragged face. He appeared to have aged so much since Remi had last seen him, and Remi was sorry he hadn't really focused on the man the day before.

'Has it been so bad?' he asked softly.

The other man nodded.

'I really thought I had killed her,' Remi said.

'We all did,' the general murmured. He ran a hand over her forehead, brushing away a loose hair. 'I was so sure she was gone. I think the healer did far more than he had before to bring her back to us. Enough that she worries for him. Any talk of bringing him back from wherever he is hiding is quickly shut down.'

'She has always done all she could to protect him,' Remi said.

'And so she should. He is a good friend to her. She is lucky to have been surrounded by those she has been.'

'Does that include me?'

'No,' he said matter-of-factly. 'You left her.'

'It wasn't by choice,' Remi said. But in many ways, it was. He had been fed all sorts of information, and much of it he had felt in his heart wasn't the truth, yet he had followed it anyway. 'I never wanted to hurt her,' he whispered instead.

'You have said that before, and yet you nearly killed her.'

'You sound like Wei-Song,' Remi said, louder than he intended. Lis groaned and opened her eyes.

The general glared at him. 'Rest,' he said.

'Did they follow us?'

'We don't think so,' Remi said, and she turned towards him. He waited for her to smile, but she didn't. Her eyes closed again. 'Maybe I should move into one of the other rooms,' he said, but she reached out then and took his hand.

'There aren't any other rooms,' the general said. 'Despite what we think and whether it is appropriate or not, it may be best you stay close to her.'

Remi looked at him with surprise. Then he nodded slowly. If they were discovered in the night, he would rather be close to protect her.

11

A soldier ran into the room and stopped, bowed to the emperor and the empress and then rushed towards the hunter. He stepped up to Hui Te-Sze.

'Magics have attacked the princess,' he murmured.

Te-Sze looked at the emperor and then turned to the man beside him. 'And?'

'She held them back.'

'How many?'

'We didn't see them. It took a lot out of her.'

'Your Eminence,' the hunter said, stepping forward. 'It appears that the princess and the crown prince were attacked on their way back from their audience with you. I would like to see how they are.'

'You have just been told,' the emperor said. 'If we don't find a way to end this, there will be more attacks.'

'I fear their attacks will be focused on the prince and princess.'

'I thought they understood Remi to be on their side,' the empress added.

'I fear they have doubts now that he has returned to the princess.'

'If they stay together,' the emperor said. 'She may not want him.'

'She has returned because of him,' the hunter said.

'But is it enough?' the empress asked, stepping down from the platform beside the emperor and crossing the floor with surprising speed. 'Can they stop this together?'

'The prophecy seems certain that they will. Now that she has chosen to be here, it will be different.'

'I do hope you are right,' the empress said.

'May I take my leave?'

The emperor nodded, and the hunter moved quickly from the room and across the Palace Isle towards the laundry. He tried to be aware of his surroundings in case there were more magics about, knowing he might also be a target. Yet he raced to ensure the little princess was safe. He knew she would do all she could to keep the prince and the soldiers from harm, and she wasn't ready for a battle of any kind. She might not even be ready for a single fireball.

The compound was dark when he reached it, and he moved confidently through the open hallways and straight into the large room that had once housed so many laundry girls.

A soldier drew a sword but stopped midway, recognising him for who he was. He bowed. At least they were ready. There was only one soldier inside the room, but he was sure many more watched from the shadows outside, as they had done the night before. Only he didn't think all those trying to get to the princess would be as thoughtful of her safety as the crown prince. If he was the crown prince any longer. Despite his father's wishes, the ministers were too keen to have him removed.

Te-Sze drew in a breath as he focused on the prince in the dim light, sitting cross legged on the platform and watching over the sleeping princess. The general was nowhere to be seen. The prince glanced up at him, nodded once and turned his attention back to the princess.

'Is she well?' Te-Sze asked, stepping closer and trying to keep his voice low.

The prince nodded once, then shook his head. 'She does too much,' he said.

'She does what she can to keep us all safe, when we should be protecting her,' the guard by the door said quietly.

'She is not as strong as she could be,' the prince admitted sadly. 'And it is my fault.'

'No,' she murmured in her sleep. Te-Sze wondered if she had heard what was said, or if she dreamt of something else.

'She is too good for me,' the prince continued. 'But you always knew that,' he added with a sad smile.

'I thought you too good for her,' Te-Sze admitted. 'It wasn't so long ago I wanted you to run her through. And then where would we be?'

Remi smiled and then looked back at the sleeping woman.

'She is not what I thought she was,' the hunter admitted, 'and neither are you.'

'I'm not sure what I am,' the prince said. 'I may be more dangerous for the Empire than I would like to admit. The ministers may be right.'

'I doubt that. And your father is determined they are not.'

Remi sighed. 'What will he do?'

'I don't know,' the hunter said. 'I don't think he knows yet what he will do, but your mother will speak for you.'

The prince nodded slowly.

'I wonder if the Empire will ever be what it was again,' Te-Sze mused.

'What it was before the magic war, or before this? I don't think it will ever be quite the same. The hidden princess traditions are gone. You may very well be looking at the last one.'

'What will happen then? What will you do if they take away your crown?'

'I was never destined to be Emperor,' Remi said.

The hunter thought he detected some sadness there. But he was unsure if it was because of the state of the world or because of

Remi's brother. Te-Sze waited before he asked again, 'What will you do?'

'Leave. Find somewhere they will accept us for what we are, who we are.'

'We?' the hunter asked.

Remi glanced down at the princess. Te-Sze knew the prince had loved her from the start, but he had always thought the princess would return to her father and her island, if given the chance. He wondered now if that was the case. She had returned for the prince. What would she do for him if he could no longer remain on the Palace Isle?

'I'll check on the men. I think you should get some rest, but keep an eye out, or your senses. We don't know what they might try.'

Remi nodded, never taking his eyes from the princess. The hunter sighed, then bowed and left them to it. He would most likely keep watch over her all night. He wondered if the prince had been impacted by their fight. If his magic was subdued and he had only handed himself to his father so easily because he wasn't able to fight them.

Despite what he had heard during the day, Te-Sze knew that Prince Remi was the right man to rule the Empire, only several things had to change before that could happen. He nodded silently to the men he passed. Without checking on the general, he disappeared into his own small room.

The high priestess tried not to sigh as she looked at the dark water of the pond. Chonglin stood beside her, sighing loudly. She was disappointed that the prince had been so quick to disappear with the rumours of the princess's survival. And although they had sent men to check on what he did and where he might be, she wondered if they had lost him.

Her visions had been intermittent and unclear. Partly because of where she was, she thought. She longed for the cool white stone of the temple. But the Empire believed them all gone, and although there were only soldiers on the island, she didn't want anyone making guesses as to what she did.

'His father has forgiven him,' a magic said, rushing up to them at the pond.

'How can you be sure?' Chonglin asked.

'He wasn't wearing shackles, and he walked with the hidden princess and her men as though he was part of the group. He even walked beside her for most of the journey.'

'Did the fire work?' the priestess asked.

He nodded. 'Just as you said, she could deflect it, but she had nothing left and the general carried her back.'

'Not the prince?'

He shook his head.

'Interesting. I wonder what she has told him.'

'Why did he go to her?' the man asked. 'Is he finding information?'

'He was certainly searching for something,' she said.

'He was turned once…'

'I don't think he can be again. He went to her to ensure she was alive, and she is. He will not be parted from her again.'

'And what will that mean for us?' the younger man asked. 'You said we couldn't defeat them together.'

'They haven't quite come together yet, and she isn't able to do anything in her current state. Attack them now, and you might have a chance of destroying this partnership before it takes hold.'

'They are surrounded by soldiers,' Chonglin said.

'And you have magic.'

'We are a lot like the princess—worn out. I fear we would lose more badly if we were to attack now. We know where they are. Go and rest,' he said to the younger man. 'We can defeat them when we are stronger. Who else was with them?' he asked after the man.

'The general and a group of soldiers.'

'The healer? The little princess?'

He shook his head.

'Better and better,' the priestess said. 'I will take your advice, but if more of the Hidden arrive on the Palace Isle, we may not be able to stop them all.'

'It will be over long before then,' Chonglin said.

12

Lis walked slowly through the hidden princess compound. She was certain she could sense someone, yet she was unnerved as she couldn't see anyone. Taking a deep breath, she turned around slowly. Still no one. She could smell sweet grass, and the flowers that bloomed on her little island. She turned again and found herself in the throne room. She knew she was dreaming, but she also knew something was very wrong.

She tipped her head towards the emperor on his throne, his fingers curled tightly around the arm of it, the skin white and stretched. His other hand pointed beyond her, and she turned to follow his finger to find Remi standing before him. His hands were chained, but the chains disappeared when she shook her head.

Murmuring surrounded them, but she couldn't see anyone else. The shadows moved in closer around them and then leapt back as flames consumed the prince. She could feel the anger and uncertainty ebbing from him.

'Remi!' she called, but he didn't look at her, didn't appear to know she was in the room. Only him and his father.

The emperor released his iron hold on the throne and stepped closer.

'Stop!' Lis cried, but he didn't stop or turn, or appear to hear her.

Remi continued to burn, as though out of control. Flames like a monster licked over his skin, as she remembered seeing in the main square. Maybe together, they could tame the monster. She stepped closer, the heat from the flames slowing her steps. Her skin burnt, and she was sure she blistered, but she continued towards the prince, knowing only that he needed her.

Despite the heat of the flames, she stepped up to him and closed her arms around his neck. He looked at her with panic in his eyes, and then the flames vanished.

She opened her eyes and patted along her arms. She wasn't burnt; in fact, she was quite cool. She sat up slowly. The moonlight shone through the high windows, marking out rectangles of light across the floor. She was still in the laundry.

She looked around slowly and nearly squealed with fright at the prince sitting beside her, his head resting forward. After a moment, she realised he had fallen asleep watching over her.

She reached out a tentative hand, and his skin was cool to the touch. 'Remi,' she said softly.

He looked up and then shook himself a little.

'How do you feel?' he asked.

'What are you doing?'

'Watching,' he murmured.

'You need sleep,' she said softly.

'I'm worried something might happen,' he said.

She reached forward and brushed a loose strand of hair from his face. 'You can't watch over me forever.'

'I can try,' he said softly, capturing her hand in his and pressing it to his face.

The guard by the door coughed quietly, and Remi released her hand. She let it linger against his skin for a moment before she pulled it back.

'Do you still burn?' she asked softly, and he gave her a quizzical look. 'I dreamt of you burning.'

'Did I hurt you?' he asked quickly.

She shook her head. 'They are going to find us,' she said.

He nodded once.

'I'm not strong enough,' she whispered, feeling the uncertainty of what might happen if they were attacked. 'And I think they know it.'

'Together we will be fine,' he said, patting the bedding. She lay back slowly.

'Neither of us are what we were,' she murmured, watching him, and he nodded slowly. He looked so tired. She moved across a little and patted the bed beside her, but there was a noise by the door. A muffled noise, and then something heavy fell to the floor. She wanted to call out, but the prince put a finger to her lip. When she glanced at him, he looked around the darkened room. He slipped from the platform, and then the white dress of the priestess appeared to glow in the moonlight as she stepped into the moonlight.

'You switch sides so easily,' she said, her voice soft and friendly. 'Is your bride willing to accept a man so fickle?'

Lis remained where she was and said nothing. Despite the concerns of everyone around her, she trusted him. Yet Remi stepped closer to the high priestess. He shook his head a little, as though trying to clear his head.

Could she turn him so easily? Lis wondered. Did she have power over him?

'You are still needed,' the priestess said. 'You have work to do as a magic.'

'I am not what you want me to be,' he said. He stood tall and confident, yet Lis noted he had moved another step closer to her.

The priestess smiled up at him, and Lis realised in that moment that the priestesses were all the same, that they all had visions and worked for their own agenda, not that of the gods. Had they been behind this all along, or did they only want to save themselves? They were another form of magic, another form hidden from the Empire for so long.

Lis felt a moment of loss, as though she was working against so many without the energy to face even one of them. Her heart stuck in her throat, feeling useless and helpless, and then the prince was wrapping his arms around the woman before him. She threaded her hands up through his hair, pulling it loose about his face and directing him towards her.

A sharp pain sliced at Lis's chest as their lips touched. She wanted to scream, but her voice wouldn't work. Then a flash of light filled the room. Remi burned, and the priestess staggered back. Her hand on her chest, she looked up at him as the flames licked over his skin, lighting the pale horror on her face.

'I would have thought you would have seen what would happen if you came here,' he said softly, and Lis thought for a moment that he carried a sword. But she hadn't seen once since he had returned to her.

The world turned into chaos as the priestess dropped to her knees. The blood slowly leaked down through the white robes she wore, and soldiers pushed on the door as they called out. Remi burned brighter than he had before.

He had kissed her, but then he had killed her. As the soldiers managed to push the door open, Lis moved from the platform between the strangeness in the room and those filling it. She felt more drained than she had before. She staggered forward, and the general called out.

'She worked with them,' Remi said, his voice calm despite the flames that appeared to be consuming him.

The priestess dropped to the side, looking far less refined than she had ever appeared. Her blood marked her clothes and slowly spread across the floor.

Lis reached out and took Remi's arm. The heat danced over her skin. It was hotter than she had expected, but she kept her hand there. The flames raged around her and, like in her dream, she was lost to them as much as he was. As he turned to face the men behind her, a sword of flame held tight in his hand, Lis stepped into the heat of him, wrapping her arms around his waist and closing her eyes to it.

The magic ran through him directly into her, and it gave her a strength far greater than his pushing the magic on her ever had. She pulled it to her and felt her own strength returning, but she didn't want to take too much and leave him vulnerable. On the edge of her senses, she could hear the soldiers, the concern, the worry, the uncertainty as to what to do.

The heat intensified around them. But it no longer burned. She knew it grew hotter, but she couldn't feel the heat. Then the flames died down around her and the silence grew heavier, and she wondered if they had burned away to nothing.

As his hands closed around her shoulders, holding her closer, she peeked out between her lids and found the soldiers on their knees. She pushed away from Remi and turned to them.

'It wasn't what I intended,' Remi said softly. Lis looked back at him, then down over the body of the priestess. 'She gets in my head.'

'You kissed her,' Lis said before she could say anything else.

'She twists my thinking, convincing me that it is what I want—that she is what I want.' He turned back to Lis, taking her by the shoulders. 'You are what I want,' he whispered. 'It was the only way to get her out of my head.'

'Where did you get the sword?' Lis asked.

'Where is it now?' the general asked. Lis looked back and noticed Hui Te-Sze in the doorway, standing behind all the others who still knelt before them.

Remi shook his head.

'It was made of fire,' Lis whispered.

He closed and opened his hand but shook his head. Then he looked at her closely. 'You stepped into the flames,' he said. 'Why would you do that?'

'You needed me to,' she said. 'I knew it wouldn't burn me.'

'How did you know such a thing?' the general asked.

Lis shook her head. She wasn't sure if it was the dream or something else, but she knew it was where she needed to be. Where Remi needed her to be.

Remi rested his hand on her shoulder, and she sighed. 'I feel like we have been here before,' she said softly. 'Only I never dreamed of this.' She looked up, and he nodded towards the men still kneeling before them. 'Why?' she asked.

'We can see what you are,' the general said.

'And what is that?' Remi asked.

Silence followed. Lis looked at the priestess again, wondering just what she had thought she could do to take Remi back to the magics and turn him against the Empire. The sword was bright in her memory. 'Do you fear what he can do?' she asked.

'That isn't it,' the general said, clearly lost for words.

'The two of you were destined to come together,' the hunter said from the doorway.

'You sound like Yang,' she murmured, trying to indicate that the men should stand again, but they remained where they were.

'He might have known more than he was willing to share.'

'What did you see?' Remi asked.

'The phoenix,' one of the soldiers whispered, and they all leant forward and touched their heads to the floor at the same time.

'The phoenix,' Lis said, turning back to Remi. 'That is what it is.'

'What?' he asked.

'The fire that surrounds you.'

'It threatens to consume me.'

She shook her head, but then she had thought the same thing.

Hui Te-Sze moved through the soldiers and bowed low to both of them before he sighed and knelt directly before Lis.

'You don't need to do this,' she said, leaning forward to take his arm.

'I do,' he said, waving her off. 'There was something around the prince, something that could have been seen as a creature of fire. And although I sensed that the priestess did something to him, I couldn't sense any magic about her.' Lis opened her mouth to give her opinion on the priestesses, but the hunter held up his finger, and she pressed her lips together. 'When you held him in your arms, he changed. The flames pulled together and the phoenix was revealed.'

'A phoenix?' Remi asked. 'You are saying that I am a phoenix?'

'No, Your Highness. I am saying that the two of you together are *the* phoenix. The great and wise creature of our history, returned to save us all.'

'It is a myth,' Lis said.

'We all saw it, Your Highness,' a soldier said. Murmuring started amongst the group.

'We did, Your Highness,' the general added.

'I'm not sure I'm comfortable with that title. We are friends,' she said, squatting down before the hunter. 'You were to call me Lis.'

'You are the hidden princess of Rei-Een,' he said, bowing low before her, 'and the phoenix.'

Lis shook her head and stepped back to stand beside Remi.

'Do you think this is what they meant by us working together?' he asked.

'I don't understand,' she stammered.

'We need you to show the ministers,' the hunter said.

'How?' she asked.

'The crown prince burns, you step in and…'

'Who do you want him to kill?'

'You only need to show them. They will understand. It will end any concerns they have that he should not be the crown prince.'

'And how do we do that?' Lis asked. 'Do you know how you did that?' She turned to Remi.

He shook his head.

'You can't hide it. This could be just what we need to save the

Empire.'

'Leave,' Remi suddenly said, stepping around Lis and pointing to the door. 'Let us work this through.'

The group stood as one, bowing again, and backed from the room. The soldier who had been knocked to the floor when the priestess arrived was hauled to his feet and carried out. The door closed behind them and then almost immediately reopened. Two men moved quickly in to collect the body of the priestess, part dragging her across the floor. A thick trail of blood showed the path they had taken.

The door closed, and Lis sat heavily where she was on the floor. She had seen something around Remi before. She had sensed a creature, and she had dreamt of it. But she hadn't thought she was in any way a part of it. How could they be something that could save the Empire when she would have to be standing between Remi and whatever danger threatened with her arms around him? It didn't make any sense.

She jumped when he rested his hand on her shoulder again, and he withdrew it quickly.

'I'm sorry,' she murmured.

He sat beside her and pulled her against his chest. 'You have found a way to save us all.'

'Hardly. I have only found another way for them to try and attack us, you. How can we be a phoenix?'

He didn't say anything, just held her tighter.

'If we are, they will want proof. The magics will try harder to defeat us, and I haven't got the energy…'

'You have,' he whispered, pressing his lips to the top of her head.

'I took it from the fire,' she murmured, then pushed out of his arms. 'You kissed her,' she said.

'She got in my head,' he said again. 'She creates this wanting for her that I can't resist.'

'She did this before,' Lis said slowly, unsure why the idea hurt her as much as it did.

He swallowed loudly and nodded.

'I have no right to ask anything of you,' she said, standing slowly.

He reached out and grabbed at her hand. 'You are the hidden princess. You don't need to ask—I would willingly give.'

She nodded once and pulled from him. But he was on his feet and, despite the fact that she wanted to be there with him, she stepped out of his reach. Her heart beat fast, and he worried her as he stepped with her. And then her back was against the platform, and he closed his arms around her.

'I chose you,' he whispered. 'I need you. I didn't choose her in any way. I was magicked into believing I wanted her.'

Lis tried to shake him off, the lump forming thick and large in her throat. There had been too much confusion between them already. A fear of what the priestess might have made him do worried her more than she could admit. Would a woman of the gods really be so determined to have the crown prince do her bidding?

His hands closed around her face and he forced her gaze up to his eyes. 'I choose you,' he whispered. 'Again, and again, I always come back to you.'

Then he bent towards her, and as much as she wanted him to, she pulled back. Almost in that instant, he burned bright and hot. She could feel the confusion and the hurt that fuelled the fire.

'I chose you too,' she said softly, placing her hand on his chest. An uneasiness settled on him. 'But I just saw you willingly kiss someone else. Whether she magicked you or not, I can't...'

The flames seemed to consume them for a moment, and he pressed his lips to hers. An overwhelming clarity filled her. The flames continued to burn around them, and in some distant place in her mind she sensed the fire leaping and spreading around them. But she also had the sense that this had happened before. That she had been in this safe place, surrounded by Remi and his fire, and his lips pressed against hers. She had never been so content and so scared at the same time.

A shout drew her attention, and she reluctantly pulled her lips from Remi. She still felt the same comfort, his arms around her, her own around his neck and her body pressed against his. Then she remembered the priestess, and they took a step away from each other.

Another shout and she turned around, the heat still overwhelming yet not burning. Had they formed some other creature? But the soldier before her shielded his face with his arm as he called out for her.

The flames died away, and Lis realised that the building they were in was well alight. Remi released her and stretched out his hands, and the flames died away. The fire marked the walls, and the platform smoked. Her bedding was nothing but ash.

'Are you hurt, Your Highness?' the soldier asked.

'No,' she murmured, her head still light from the strange feeling of being wrapped in Remi's flames. 'Did you see the phoenix?' she asked, stepping forward, but the man stepped back away from her and bowed. 'What did you see?'

'I'm not exactly sure,' the man murmured.

Lis could feel the blush coming to her cheeks. What did he think he had seen? They may be linked and promised, but they weren't married yet. And the prince certainly wasn't behaving as he should. She looked back at him standing silent behind her. He had never behaved as he should when it came to her.

'It was as through the phoenix stood between us, protecting the two of you. Although the flames spread, and when I saw the smoke...'

'It is separate from us?' Lis asked.

'I don't know what I saw,' the man murmured. Lis wondered if he had seen more than he wanted to and wasn't sure how to say it. 'I will send for more bedding—or do you think we should find somewhere else?'

Lis took a moment to look around the room. The damage was superficial, but she wondered if this would be a risk whenever they came together or one doubted the other. They couldn't spend their lives burning the world around them. She sighed and nodded, and the man disappeared.

The blood still marking the floor made her wonder if it might be a good idea to find somewhere else, but she wasn't sure where that might be. The prison, she remembered, was made of stone. That might be more durable and less flammable. And it was away from the smell of blood that seemed to fill her senses suddenly. It was as though the priestesses were to cause her trouble for eternity. She put her hand to her nose. 'Maybe we should leave,' she murmured.

'Do you want me to leave you?' Remi asked.

She shook her head as the hunter entered the room, 'I think we should keep you together. Despite the danger to others, I think you might be safer together.'

'Safer?' Lis asked. 'We could have killed everyone here.'

He shook his head, a slight smile curling up the corner of his lip. 'I shall send someone to clean up the mess, but you need to sleep. It was not so long ago that the two of you were thought to be dead.'

Remi opened his hand, and a small flame leapt to life. It jumped from his hand to the puddle of blood that marked where the priestess had died, then burned along the trail. It slipped beneath the door, and Lis heard a shout on the other side. She rushed forward and opened the door as a young soldier stood and watched the flame run along the covered walkway. Then it disappeared. He carried an armful of bedding, and he stood and stared at Lis.

'Bring that inside,' the hunter muttered.

He moved past Lis and then stopped by the platform, where only remnants of the other bedding remained.

'Here,' Remi offered, pointing to a place against the far wall. There was no charring or hint of the drama of the night, and the man dropped the bundle, bowed low and disappeared. Remi bent down and started straightening out the bedding. Lis looked from the place the blood had been to the hunter and then back to Remi.

'Sleep,' the hunter said, bowing low, and then he too left them. As he closed the door behind him, Lis realised there was no longer a guard on the inside of the room.

She was still staring at the door when Remi took her hand. She jumped, but he held her tight and led her to the bed. She lay down and allowed him to pull the covers over her. Then he sat against the wall, his legs out before him. And without a word, he gently ran his fingers through her hair.

'Are you not going to sleep?' she asked.

'She wasn't working alone,' he murmured.

'Remi,' she said softly, sitting back up and moving to sit beside him. 'You can't do this alone.'

'You need to sleep,' he said.

'As do you.'

'What if I burn the building to the ground while I sleep?'

'I don't think you will.'

'What if the phoenix takes control? What if it tries to protect us?'

'Surely it knows these men work with us.'

'Are you certain?'

'I'm not certain of anything at this moment.'

'Then let us sleep and see what happens.'

She smiled up at him and moved back down the makeshift bed, holding the covers for him to lie beside her.

'Are you sure?' he asked.

'No,' she admitted, 'but I think we stand a better chance together, whatever is to come.'

He nodded once and lay down beside her. She rested her head on his shoulder and closed her eyes as his arm closed around her. The same feeling of contentment washed over her. She opened her eyes briefly to make sure they weren't burning, and in the darkness that surrounded them, she allowed herself to sleep.

13

Wei-Song watched the child playing on the beach. She squealed and ran away from the waves before following the retreating water back across the sand, splashing and then running away. She had never appeared so relaxed and childlike before, and Wei-Song worried it was a sign of something worse to come.

The master stood beside her, smiling at the child's antics. She wondered what Yang would have made of the behaviour, but she saw little of him. He spent a most of time in his room, possibly sleeping. Wei-Song worried he had spent more energy than he could spare to bring Lis back from the nearly dead. And she was sure that he missed her. She had been tempted to follow Lis, but the child had said they needed to maintain some distance, to allow Lis and the prince time to find each other.

Wei-Song thought it was a bad idea to let her go alone. The crown prince had been so different that day, throwing his fire around, trying to kill Lis. Would seeing her be enough to bring him back to where he was meant to be? Was it more wishful thinking than actual sight that had directed the child to push Lis to find him?

Wei-Song was increasingly isolated from the rest of the world. She didn't know how her mother faired, or what her father—no, the emperor—thought of what had occurred. Did he know that she lived, or even that Lis had survived? She looked up at the man beside her, still smiling at the child in the waves. This man was her father. Not that she had ever called him such, but she loved him as she loved her mother, and she knew with a certainty that he would do anything to keep her safe.

The emperor held no such feelings. Wei-Song may have felt something for the prince, but she wasn't quite sure what that might be. The child looked back at them and waved before running headlong back into the water. How could the child be so sure he could be saved? Wei-Song knew there was a connection between him and Lis, although she doubted Lis felt the same for him. Although she had been eager to head back to the Palace Isle and risk it all to find him.

He had seemed so disappointed to learn she was his sister, and that his mother had kept such a thing from him. She wondered if the prince doubted the empress would do the same for him. Lis had been right—he was lost. She only hoped Lis could help him be found.

Tired and wet, the child appeared before them. 'I'm hungry,' she said, looking back longingly at the water.

'That looked like fun,' the master said as he reached out a hand to take hers. Wei-Song was reminded of him indulging her as a child. When the others had worked hard between classes, she had been allowed some freedoms. Although, as she watched the child walk ahead of her along the path, hand in hand with the master, she wondered if that had been because of who her parents were rather than who she was.

As they walked, she wondered what else the child had seen and whether she could tell them if Lis had found Remi. She knew not to push, and that the child would share when she had something to share, but Wei-Song was finding it hard to wait.

As they sat at the table and the child filled herself as though she hadn't eaten in months, Wei-Song's mind still wandered. She thought of Yang, still hidden away in his room.

'What do you think Lis would have called me?' the child asked suddenly.

'I thought you couldn't have a name,' Wei-Song said, sitting her own bowl back on the table.

'The world is different,' the child said, pushing more food into her mouth. 'I can't remember the name my own mother gave me. And Lis wanted to give me a name. What do you think it would have been?'

'I can't guess,' the master said. 'What do you think?'

The girl shrugged and returned to eating.

Wei-Song and the master shared a look of confusion across the table.

'How is the world different?' Wei-Song asked carefully.

'The phoenix returned,' she said between mouthfuls.

'And what does that mean?' Wei-Song asked.

The girl shrugged.

'Can't you see what it will do?'

She shook her head, smiled broadly and then sat her chopsticks down. 'I can't see anything.'

'You can't see what comes next?'

'Nothing,' she said with an even wider smile. 'I saw the phoenix and then nothing—no history, no visions, no idea of what people want or think.'

'Why is that?' the master asked.

She shrugged again. 'Can I go and play with the others?' she asked. 'I know there are some of my kind who have magic as well as visions; I would like to see if I have any skills.'

The master nodded, and she skipped out of the room. She was like a different child.

'Do you think they have stopped?' Wei-Song asked.

'It appears so, but why? And what is the phoenix?'

'Lis saw something in the flames,' she said.

'Something around the prince?'

Wei-Song nodded. 'She saw it when they were fighting. She murmured about it in her sleep. She worried it would consume him. Do you think that it has? Has he been lost?'

'Lis would have returned to us if she could, if there was nothing for her on the Palace Isle. Maybe she has found a way to save him.'

'But there are magics and the like trying to end them.'

'She is stronger than you think.'

'I have a fairly good idea of how strong she is,' Wei-Song snapped, then bowed her head. 'I'm sorry, Master. I wonder that I should not have gone with her. What if something has happened? The Empire was attacked by magic, and they may not forgive her even if she fought with the Empire's men. What if the prince didn't survive?'

'They are both a lot stronger than we think they are,' the master said softly.

'I do hope so.'

'Your brother is a good man,' he said, giving her a smile. 'And Lis knows what he is. When they need us, we shall follow them to the Palace Isle and stand beside them.'

'I don't want to expose you to such a world,' Wei-Song said.

He laughed then and rested his hand on her arm. 'I was born into such a world. I have seen far more of it than you.'

She nodded and rested her hand on his.

Wei-Song headed out to the little stone terrace that overlooked the ocean. It was a quiet place that the master often used for quiet contemplation, and she needed some quiet time herself. The days since Lis had left had been harder than she imagined. She constantly worried if Lis had survived the Palace Isle and what she might have found there. In some ways, it was a relief to believe the prince was alive, but she wasn't sure how he would react to Lis. He had seemed to hate her enough to want to kill her, but he had been twisted by the magic then. Could Lis bring him back?

She slid open the door to the little terrace to find someone already there. She apologised as she backed up, then recognised Yang when the man turned. He appeared older, thinner and less robust for a man of his age. She stepped forward and bowed to him. He waved her away with a laugh and turned back to the view.

'I have heard the child has lost her visions,' he said softly, his voice croaky, and Wei-Song wondered again if he was well enough to be out or if he had in fact given too much of himself to Lis.

'It seems so, although it isn't exactly clear what has caused them to cease. She talked of a phoenix, and then they were gone.'

'A phoenix?' he asked, turning back to her.

She struggled to make eye contact now that the dark circles were so deep around his eyes. 'Should you be resting?'

'I have rested enough,' he murmured. 'Tell me about the phoenix.'

'I don't know that I can. She hasn't been clear. I don't know if it is a good thing or bad, if it is real or imagined, or what it might have to do with Lis.'

'She found him,' he said softly, looking out over the ocean.

'Is that a good thing? Or might he hurt her?'

Yang shook his head. 'He wouldn't.'

'Yet he has, so many times. He has nearly killed her twice, and both times you were there to save her. This time, we are here, and we don't know where she is or what she might be facing. We might really lose her this time.'

He turned and smiled at her before wrapping his arms around her. Despite her surprise, a calming effect washed over her. Then he slipped in her arms and she was holding him up.

'Why do you always try to make everything better?' she whispered as she lowered him to the ground.

'I'm a healer,' he murmured, resting his head on her shoulder. 'I'll be ok,' he said as she slowly pushed her energy through him.

'Just rest,' she said, holding him tight and hoping he would allow her to help him as much as he helped everyone else. Lis might need them yet.

14

Chonglin paced along the walkway by the pond. He shouldn't have let the priestess go alone, but she had been so sure she was the only one who could bring the prince back to them. He had disappeared with the rumours that the princess was still alive, and Chonglin had known then the prince wasn't quite as dedicated to their cause as he had claimed to be. But they had coerced him from the beginning. The prince had been sure there was a way to work with the princess, that they were to work together, and now Chonglin was sure that they were.

The priestess had not returned, and he wondered if she would return to the Sacred Isle and her sisters if she failed at the task she had set herself. She should have gone with them in the first place; it was better that the priestesses were well away from the situation. He worried more than she did that they risked being discovered, but then he thought there were more who knew that secret than he realised, or even than the priestesses realised themselves.

There was much the woman hadn't told him, and he probably didn't need to know what she did or with whom as long as it didn't interfere with what they wanted. The only important factor was making sure the magic was in control of the Empire. However that looked.

There was no one left on the island outside of officials and soldiers, and they didn't want to seek out any of them. Not yet. Not until he knew what the prince was doing. But there was no one to ask. Now would have been the time to be in league with the Hidden, so he could send someone in to discover the truth. There weren't even any servants left to glean for information.

He thumped his fist down on the railing. All those years of planning, of hiding from his own people, and they were no closer to what had been foreseen. Despite their strength in facing the soldiers, somehow the prince and princess had ended the fight while fighting each other.

He still wasn't quite sure what had happened. The magic was still thick in the air, yet they had dragged the half-dead prince away from the fight in the hope of fighting again. And they'd thought he had managed to kill the princess.

But now he knew that hadn't been the case at all. Somehow, she had survived what he had nearly not. Chonglin's ears had rung for days after, and despite all that, the prince was chasing after her, wanting to be reassured that she was still alive.

Chonglin had thought the priestess had found a way to keep the prince on their side, but when it came to the hidden princess, there was too much there. He wondered if things had been done according to tradition, had she had been chosen as a girl, would the prince still have had the same idea of her? Was it that he saw her as a man saw a woman rather than as a prince saw a hidden princess?

Whatever it was, she was the reason he had developed magic, and it should have been enough to make him hate her. Chonglin waved over the nearest man. 'Any word of the high priestess?'

He shook his head.

'Take some men, go carefully, and find her. Check the temple and the prison. And if you can find anything on our prince or his princess, that would be useful too.'

The man bowed his head and called to some others, who walked quickly out through the black gate. Chonglin looked up at the great wall surrounding the Palace Isle. He smiled as he watched a distant soldier walk along the top of it. They had managed to hide in the one place they could never be found, where they could not be seen. They were at the centre of magic in the Empire, when the Empire had tried so hard to stamp it out.

He wondered for a moment whether they could win this, with or without the prince, whether magic could take control of the Empire so completely. As a boy, his parents had longed for peace and the ways of old to return, but he knew it would never happen that way. They would never meet their true potential under the shadow of an Empire willing to destroy its own people for their differences.

The empress sat on the edge of the throne as the emperor stalked back and forth before it. It still felt strange for her to sit on it, yet he had led her there and sat her down himself that very morning, after she had woken in his bed. Another strange moment she had never thought to experience.

With the destruction of the residence, he had turned one of the many hidden rooms near his study into his own. Even then, it had been so long since she had been anywhere near his private rooms, let alone in his bed. He had visited her chambers when they were younger, when they'd had a need for children.

After Wei-Song, he had only visited her once. She could still remember the cold, empty look he had given her as he'd left that night. And yet, she had done everything she had been asked to do. Or at least she had let him believe that. Yangshing had been only too happy to help her.

Although Lis hadn't mentioned Wei-Song since her return to the Palace Isle, the empress was sure she had survived the fight in the square. Remi and Lis had been so determined to kill each other that day, and now they stayed together. What might they do to each other?

A soldier ran into the room, and the emperor stopped his pacing. He bowed stiffly and then looked between them.

'What is it?' the emperor asked.

'There has been a fire,' he stammered.

'The prince?' the empress asked, leaping to her feet.

The man nodded and then shook his head.

'Tell me,' the emperor said, his voice surprisingly calm.

The young soldier took a deep breath. 'They were… it is hard to explain, but there was a fire in the laundry. They are both unharmed.'

'Did the prince cause the fire?' the empress asked. She had seen the fire in his eyes the previous day.

'I think so, but it was the high priestess who provoked him.'

'The high priestess?' the empress repeated.

'I thought they had all left for the Sacred Isle,' the emperor said.

The soldier shook his head. 'She is dead,' he said in a whisper.

'The high priestess?' the emperor asked, turning to look at the empress.

'Another will be chosen,' she said. 'It may be best that they stay away for now.'

The soldier nodded slowly.

'Should we put the prince somewhere more secure?' the emperor asked.

'I'm not sure we can move them.'

'What do you mean?' the emperor asked, turning back to the soldier.

'They are protected.' The man shuffled, looking uncomfortable, and the empress wondered just what he had seen.

'By what?' the emperor asked, and the man dropped to his knees.

'A phoenix, Your Eminence.'

'A phoenix,' the emperor laughed.

'*The* phoenix, it seems,' the man said, lowering his head to the floor. 'I saw it myself.'

'It is a sure sign that the gods watch over them.' The empress sat slowly back on the throne. Could the gods be watching over them? Could they be sure that Remi and Lis were the future of the Empire? All those prophecies and stories of what was to come, she had never really put much on them. But now it seemed they were true.

'Did this phoenix start the fire?' the emperor asked.

'It isn't clear exactly what happened,' the soldier said softly. 'But the general felt you should know.'

The emperor nodded and waved him away. He stood slowly but didn't leave the room.

'I wonder if… the general wonders whether it might be of benefit to share this information with the ministers.'

'They will want proof,' the empress said, wondering if a phoenix would allow itself to shine in the throne room and who else might die if it did.

'The princess wasn't sure how that could happen, but she agreed,' he said, bowing again to the empress.

'Let me talk with them,' she said.

The emperor shook his head. 'Did the phoenix harm the priestess?'

'No, it was the prince…' The man looked about. 'She had bewitched him.'

'Bewitched?'

'He was not himself. And then he was, and she was dead.'

The emperor sighed. 'This will be another charge for the ministers to use against him.'

15

Remi sat against the wall in the dimly lit space and watched Lis practice her magic. She had pulled enough magic from the fire that had burned between them to heal what had been lost. She appeared to be back to what she had been when she had faced him in the square. Despite the anger he had felt then, watching her now made him smile.

The soldiers remained outside the room. He wasn't sure it if was a trust in him or in Lis, but either way they were left alone. They had spent the night curled together. He questioned what his mother would think, but he couldn't be parted from her. Not now that he knew she was alive and well, despite what he had tried to do to her.

'They will interrupt us for breakfast,' he said as she turned and changed her outfit yet again. She smiled back at him and waved her hand towards the table. It filled with bowls of rice and vegetables and meat, the smell overwhelming, and he realised just how long it had been since he had eaten properly. He crawled forward and then stopped. 'You kept this from me,' he said softly, disappointed that she hadn't been able to trust him before.

She stopped then, the smile slipping.

There was a sharp knock at the door, and then the hunter entered. He looked at the table and smiled. 'You are recovering,' he said, bowing low to Lis, and then he did the same to Remi. Remi couldn't remember when the hunter had last showed him such respect, other than during the night.

Lis nodded in his direction, but the smile didn't return. 'Join us,' she said, holding out her hand, which now contained a plate of cakes.

Hui Te-Sze grinned. 'I do love your cakes,' he said, taking the plate from her and sitting at the table. He looked at the plates before him and then at Remi. He opened his mouth to say something and then looked at Lis, still standing where she was.

'I thought you were friends,' the hunter said, and before Remi could apologise for his thoughtless comment, she was out the door.

Remi made to stand, but the hunter held up his hand. 'I understand there are still many secrets between you,' he said softly, lifting a cake to his nose. 'But all she has ever done is for you.'

'Even standing against me?'

'Especially that. She has always been sure that she could save you from yourself. She feels she is to blame.'

Remi shook his head.

'Give her some time,' he said, looking towards the door. 'The men will watch over her.'

'I don't think I can be apart from her again,' Remi said. 'It is my fault that the world is what it is. I have allowed the magics to become as strong as they are.'

'They were always stronger than we could manage; it is why they were killed during the war. Now we need to find a different way.'

'How do we do that? They are still determined to kill Lis, and they want me on their side. They won't be kind about the high priestess.'

'Was she working alone?'

'I doubt it,' Remi murmured, picking up sticks and starting to eat. 'She is good,' he said as he pushed more into his mouth.

The hunter nodded.

'You knew of this skill too,' Remi said, wondering who else Lis trusted over him.

Te-Sze nodded once. 'She looks more like herself today, despite what occurred in the night.'

'Neither of us understand what or how that happened. But it helps that we have something we can share, something that may be able to help us end this.'

'You need to work together,' the hunter said. 'We have always known this.'

'But it isn't always that easy. There is a certain level of trust, and we seem to be able to destroy that with each other so quickly.'

'She trusts you,' Te-Sze said, reaching for another cake.

'Does she? I question her too often.'

'I worried she would never again be what she was,' Te-Sze said. 'That too much had been taken from her that day in the square. I was so sure she was gone. I think only Yang knew the truth of it, and he kept it to himself to help protect her.'

'Did he think she needed protection from you? She fought with you.'

'She did, although he might have been right. She might be strong, but she needs looking after.'

'I want to do that,' Remi said quietly.

With a sharp knock, the general entered the space. He looked around for a moment and then back towards the door. 'Where is she?'

'Walking,' Te-Sze said. 'Give her some time.'

'The emperor wants to see you.'

'Not the ministers?' Remi asked.

'Not yet. He wants to know what you are first.'

'I'm not sure we know what we are,' he murmured, climbing to his feet. 'Let me talk to her.'

The general bowed before him and walked towards the table, and Remi moved out into the open space of the laundry. It was surprising that the sheets still swayed in the breeze, some brightly coloured skirts amongst them. He wondered for a moment if Lis could change whatever she touched.

He glanced around but couldn't see her, and then he wondered who else might be able to wander through the laundry and steal her away. In the shadows of the covered walkway, he saw a soldier. The man nodded acknowledgement and then indicated the washing with a tip of his head.

Remi stepped forward. He felt the sadness radiating from between the sheets before he found her standing still.

She looked off into the distance. 'Will we do this forever, do you think?' she asked without turning around.

'Keep things from each other?'

'Hurt each other,' she said, turning to face him. She looked calm, but her cheeks were wet.

'I trust you more than anyone,' he said, stepping forward. 'I understand why you don't trust me.'

'I do,' she said. 'At least I do now. I'm not constantly worried that you will run me through. But I am worried you will leave, turn your back on me.'

'Never,' he said softly, stepping forward and taking her in his arms. 'Is this because she kissed me?'

'You kissed her,' she said, and then she shook her head. 'You think that I keep secrets from you.'

He shook his head again and pulled her closer. 'I was just painfully aware of how hard it must have been for you that you needed to keep things from me. Don't try to read more into what I say.'

'I don't know how to not be afraid,' she whispered, burying her face in his chest. He rested his chin on the top of her head.

'You came back to find me, all on your own, not knowing what you would face.'

'You needed to know that I chose you,' she said, looking up at him.

He took her face in his hands and ran his thumbs over her cheeks to wipe away the tears. Then he pulled her closer and kissed her before she could protest.

Someone coughed behind him. He reluctantly let her go and turned to the general.

'The emperor is waiting,' he said.

Remi nodded and took Lis by the hand. They headed to the throne room, surrounded by soldiers.

Holding tight to Lis's hand, Remi led her through to stand before the emperor and bow low. His mother, he noted, sat on the throne while the emperor stood before it. A memory of another prophecy came to mind, of two sharing the throne, and he wondered how many visions had been misinterpreted.

'Do you keep a hold of her in case she escapes or runs away again?'

Remi bristled at the comment. 'What do you want of us?' he asked.

'I was told there was an event in the night.'

Remi waited. His father was pushing for something, and he could only guess at what that was. He had appeared a little more protective before the ministers, and Remi looked about now in case they were waiting to take him away.

'We were attacked,' he said.

'By a woman?'

'I don't think a priestess could be referred to as just a woman. They have far more skills than you could know.'

'I have some idea. I thought they had all left the Palace Isle.'

'Not the high priestess; she was working with the magics.'

'Are you saying that the priestesses are corrupted?'

Remi glanced at Lis as she squeezed his hand. Was his father trying to provoke him?

'What do you want from me?' Remi asked, trying to keep his voice level.

'I doubt you could give it to me.'

'What are you doing?' his mother whispered loudly, but the emperor gave a subtle shake of his head, and she sat back.

'The ministers are sure you are a menace to the Empire. I tried to convince them otherwise, but now you have killed a priestess, the high priestess, in the night.'

'She was in my room, trying to…'

'Your room?' the emperor interrupted. 'I thought it was the hidden princess's quarters.'

Remi looked at Lis then, and she gave a subtle shake of her head, but he could feel the heat rising and trying to push though his skin. He knew that his father was trying to provoke him, but he wasn't sure why.

'You have no idea of what a prince should do,' the emperor said, his voice too loud.

Remi snapped. The fire pushed through his skin, and those around him stepped back. Lis maintained her hold on him, although he could feel the tension in her arm. He glanced at her as the fire moved along her arm. Panic hit, and the fire burned hotter. His father grinned, and he lost control.

He could hear muttering behind him. His mother stood, grabbing at his father's arm. The look of delight at Remi's loss of control turned to one of concern, but he was lost the fire now and couldn't bring it back. And then Lis had her arms around his waist, holding him tight, but the flames still raged.

'Where is this phoenix?' his father asked in the distance.

'Lis,' he begged, and she reached up, put her arms around his neck and pulled him close.

'I'm here,' she whispered before she pressed her lips to his.

The fire burned hotter around them, but there was something different about it, more controlled, and he looked up and sighed. He could feel it this time—the creature that had been inside of him needed Lis, or at least that connection to her, to be in a place everyone could see.

Lis's arms closed tighter around his neck, her face beside his, and he realised he could no longer feel the floor beneath him. The world was hazy around them. He buried his face in her neck.

'Are we flying?' she whispered.

Remi could feel the wings slowly beating beside him, up and down. He longed to be outside, but instead he kissed Lis on the forehead, then the cheek and quickly on the lips before he took her by the shoulders. 'Breathe,' he said.

She nodded as though in slow motion, and their feet touched down again. As the fire around them disappeared, she stepped back from him and bowed.

'Did you get what you wanted?' he asked his father.

16

Despite his father's wishes, Remi was determined not to perform in front of the ministers. Lis wasn't sure they could do what they needed to when required. So far, the phoenix had been seen three times, twice in her room after the death of the high priestess, and then before the emperor on demand.

She had been so nervous. He had clearly been pushing Remi, and although Remi had tried to resist it, he couldn't. The fire had raged out of control first. She had felt the heat of it, as had the soldiers behind them. She didn't think it was a risk worth taking for anyone else. Surely there was another way to bring it forward.

The first time, her holding him had been enough to tame the fire. But the third time it hadn't, and she had thought they would both be lost. Otherwise she would not have considered kissing Remi in front of anyone, although it appeared to be happening more often. She blushed at the idea of it. She would like the chance to kiss him more often, but they weren't living free on her island, as she had with Peng; she was living amidst royalty on the Palace Isle. She was the hidden princess, and if things were as they were meant to be, she wouldn't even see Remi, let alone have the chance to kiss him.

'What are you thinking?' he whispered in her ear. Although he smiled when she turned to face him, she could feel the uncertainty flow across his skin.

'Too much to share right now,' she returned. 'But I do agree with you. We don't know what we have.'

'If the ministers see what power you have…' the emperor started.

'They might be even more determined to destroy us,' Remi said.

'They know what the phoenix is and what it represents.'

'But it isn't the best way to reach it. We don't know what we are doing here.'

'They may be willing to work with you.'

'They would rather see us dead,' Remi snapped. 'We need another way to get to them.'

'Perhaps we can find a way to get the magics on our side,' Lis suggested.

'Not possible,' the general muttered.

'Lis is thought to be the one to bring both sides together. It might be an idea.'

'In what way?' the emperor asked. 'They want control—are you going to give it to them?'

Lis shook her head. She wasn't sure how she could bring them all together, but it was worth trying.

'What would they want?' the emperor asked.

'Schools,' Lis said without thinking. That was something she would have wanted if she could have chosen a different life, a chance to learn just what she could be. 'A place to learn control,' she said, looking to Remi, and he nodded once. 'But I'm not sure I am the right person to do this.'

'You were destined to be that person.'

'But not yet. Not until I am Empress. I'll be lucky to survive to be the crown princess.'

'Don't say that,' Remi muttered.

'They might have disappeared for the moment, but we know where they are, and we know what they want. With or without the high priestess, they will come for us, for me.'

'Do we draw them out?' the emperor asked.

'We aren't strong enough to face them,' Lis said.

'You have a phoenix,' the hunter said.

'But we can't use it,' Remi said.

'We can't sit here on our hands waiting for them to come to us.'

'We can't do this alone,' Lis said, looking towards the empress. She shook her head ever so slightly.

'Would she come?' Remi asked.

'I don't think she should. And she won't risk her family.'

'Who?' the emperor asked, stepping forward.

'Wei-Song,' Lis said.

'Yang would come,' Remi added softly.

Lis shook her head then. She didn't want Yang in the middle of this. She had never wanted him involved in this. He was a healer, not a soldier. Although she wasn't quite sure what she was, at this point. They might have discovered something new in working together, but she wasn't sure how they could use it. Would it be enough to show themselves and have the whole world bow down before them, as the soldiers had done? She shivered at the idea.

'What is it?' Remi asked softly.

'I'm not sure what we can do,' she said. 'I don't want to drag them into this.'

'We are all a part of this.'

Lis nodded slowly. She hadn't been sure she could stand against the magics last time, and this time they would be even more determined for blood. They could attack at any moment. 'Did they have others behind them?' she asked.

'Who?'

'The magics. There was fighting in the streets on the other islands, yet only a relatively small number of magics fought here. Are they hiding, or waiting?'

Remi shook his head. 'I don't think I was aware of all that went on. Only what they thought would benefit them for me to know.'

'Did you not question more?' the emperor asked. 'I taught you better than that.'

'You might have,' Remi shot back, 'but I wasn't exactly thinking clearly.'

The light flashed behind his eyes, and Lis put a hand on his arm. He blinked and looked at her slowly, then smiled and released his breath. The fire died down.

'Could we go to some of the other islands and find out?' Lis asked.

'The Empire is in an uproar,' the emperor said. 'The people already question the crown prince. On what basis could you say you were there? Any hint of an investigation, and they are going to assume it is the magic war all over again.'

'Wedding parade,' the empress offered.

'Pardon?' the emperor said, turning to her.

'No,' Lis said before she had the chance to think about it too much, and Remi appeared more disappointed than she had ever seen him.

'Tradition would have the hidden princess and the crown prince travel the Empire after their wedding to meet with the people.'

'We aren't to be wed for years,' Lis said, trying not to look at Remi.

'These are difficult times; the people need to see you together.'

'I'm not ready,' Lis whispered. 'I'm not trained to be the crown princess, or an empress. I am a country girl with magic, fighting with soldiers. The people won't want me.'

'Yes, they would,' Remi said.

'We would be attacked.'

'I also think it is an excellent idea, Your Highness,' the hunter said, and Lis turned a steady gaze on him.

'Am I to offer them cake as we go?' she asked.

'Your cakes are good,' Wei-Song called behind her. Lis swung around, raced across the room and threw her arms around her friend.

'So, we are winning this on cake,' Yang said, standing in the shadows beyond the doorway. Lis released Wei-Song and stepped forward to throw her arms around him.

'You should have stayed away,' she whispered, holding him close.

'I wanted to, but you know Wei-Song once she gets an idea in her head. You look much better,' he added once she released him and stepped back.

'I just needed some things to fall into place.' She looked back at Remi standing in the middle of the room, still flanked by the soldiers. She had worried he would be angry or uncertain about Yang, but he didn't appear to be.

'Have you heard what might be to come?' Remi asked as Wei-Song moved into the room.

She took the time to bow to the emperor, who stood awkwardly from his throne, and the empress, who wanted to race forward. Lis could see her itching to move, but she stood silent beside her husband.

'The visions have stopped.'

'She has had no more?' Lis asked.

'She saw something of you coming together, and then nothing.' Yang said.

'Not a vision since. She is a very different child,' Wei-Song added with a smile.

Yang followed a few steps behind and bowed to the emperor, the empress and then Remi. 'Is there a plan?' he asked.

'No,' Lis said.

'Yes, a wedding parade,' the empress said, far too chirpily.

'You realise you are throwing your own traditions away,' Lis said. She tried not to sound disappointed, but she failed. And she wasn't quite sure why she felt that way.

'It is a good reason to get you onto the other islands. I only hope you will get the chance to discover what you need.'

'The soldiers will travel with you,' the general said.

'As would a hunter, and a healer,' Hui Te-Sze said, looking at Yang.

'And your maid, of course, would be useful,' the emperor added.

'Is there is no other way?' Lis asked.

'Not unless you are so determined not to marry me,' the prince said, the disappointment rolling from him. 'If it is not what you wish, we shall consider something else.'

'Why would she not want to marry you?' Te-Sze said with a sly grin. 'You are nearly there already. Did you not just kiss the man before the emperor?'

Lis felt her whole body colour, the heat almost the same as what Remi had produced earlier.

'Lis,' he said softly, taking her hands. 'If you are not ready, we can come up with another plan. I could go undercover and appear as though I want to get back with the magics.'

'That isn't safe,' she said, shaking her head. 'They know you have left.'

'But…'

'I chose you,' she said. 'I choose you. I don't want to destroy all the Empire's traditions. I'll go down in history for all the wrong reasons.'

He laughed then, the sound comforting. 'I think the history books will be discussing far more than the date of our wedding.'

She smiled and nodded once.

'It is settled. We shall send news of the changes. Do you think we could send Advisor Gan out to tell the people, or should we surprise them?' the emperor asked.

'Maybe the latter,' Remi said. 'Let's not give them too much time to prepare.'

'We will need enough time of our own. There are dresses to make, hair pins and the like to organise.'

'I am sure there is much we can do,' Wei-Song said, and she gave Lis a wink.

Lis turned slowly, and her dress changed to a brilliant red.

'Something a little more like an empress,' Wei-Song whispered.

She turned again, and the material looked as though it floated. The brilliant red background was now covered in a pattern of golden phoenixes. The empress stepped forward, in awe, looking over the fine material.

'If only we had organised the crowns as well.'

'I may be able to help with that,' Remi offered. He waved his hand over her head, and those around her stared openly. She put her hands up but couldn't feel anything. She glanced up, and instead of beads falling towards her, there were flames.

'I can't wear this on the whole journey,' she said. 'I might set the carriage alight.'

'But you would draw out any magics,' Yang offered.

'And what of the prince?' the empress asked.

Lis rested her hand on his arm, closed her eyes and breathed out slowly. His clothing changed to match hers. He swirled his finger, and a matching crown of flames hovered above his head.

'You must at least allow me to do your hair,' the empress pleaded.

Lis could only smile and then focused on the emperor. He didn't look as pleased, and Lis wasn't sure what she could do to make him more so. 'Do you think we should wait, Your Eminence?' she asked.

He shook his head slowly.

She put her hand on Remi's arm and returned their clothes to what they had been, the crowns disappearing at the same time. She bowed low before the emperor. 'Forgive me,' she said.

'There is nothing to forgive. It is what we need,' he said. 'And yet it goes against all I wanted.' He stepped forward and surprised Lis by taking her hands. 'I have no one to present you to.'

She smiled then. 'You have a whole Empire.'

'You have us,' the general said. 'The men would be honoured to be amongst those before such an event.'

'When the sun has filled the main square tomorrow,' the emperor said. 'Line them up before the throne room steps, and we shall have the couple sent out before evening to start their journey.'

Lis bowed low, and he turned without another word.

'I hope we have somewhere to stay,' Yang said.

'A larger palace than your last one,' the general said.

Lis laughed.

'Do you have another option?' the general asked.

She shook her head, and they moved as a group towards the laundry.

Yang looked back at her several times to ensure they were headed in the right direction, and Wei-Song poked at him repeatedly.

Lis walked silently with Remi in the middle of the group.

As the light faded from the small windows in the dormitory room, Lis leaned against the platform, singed as it was. Yang walked in circles around the large room, his arms stretched out like a child. Two young soldiers arrived with armfuls of bedding, which Remi was quick to direct. He and Yang settled by one wall, Lis and Wei-Song by the other.

Despite the time away from each other and the plans for the following morning, there was little chatter between them. They settled quickly, although Lis was sure she lay awake for a long time. The room dropped into darkness, and someone snored quietly.

She was sure she heard movement, and she held her breath. She strained in the darkness to sense who it might be, but she couldn't see anything. They had doubled the guard on the door, and although Lis had said they could be inside the room, they waited outside.

With the movement of her covers, Lis expected Yang to be setting up at her feet, although he hadn't done such a thing since they had left the palace across the island. She was sure he had done far more for her when they'd been at the school, but she hadn't been aware of any of it.

'It is cold,' Remi whispered, sliding in beside her. 'I have got too used to being close. And from tomorrow, it will be given that we share.'

Lis could feel her face grow hot. Once they were wed, it wouldn't be simply sharing covers.

Remi wrapped his arms around her and pulled her close. 'Are you nervous?' he asked.

She nodded into the dark. 'Do you think the people will be accepting?'

'They will love you,' he said, kissing her forehead.

'Do you think we are doing the right thing?'

'You don't?'

'I'm not sure.'

'Are you not comfortable with this?'

'Nothing of this match has been what it should have been, or what was expected. I fear the people won't forgive me for changing so much of the world.'

'It is a brighter place for having you in it.'

'You didn't think so not so long ago.'

'Maybe the world has already changed for the better by having you in it.' He kissed her forehead again and lay still. The only indication that he was still awake was the tight hold he had on her.

17

Lis woke with a jolt, alone in the large room. It felt dark and cold. She stretched and headed to the door. Perhaps the others were getting ready, given what today was to be. She wondered for a moment if she really could wear a crown of fire. Smiling to herself, she pushed open the door and was surprised to find the courtyard before her empty. There were no soldiers, no men, no prince.

'Hello?' she called out. Surely, they wouldn't have left her alone. She headed towards the throne room.

The whole island was oddly quiet. Not even a bird chirped. No wind even to indicate the rest of the world still existed.

She stopped well before she reached the steps of the throne room. People were lying across the flagstones. She picked up her skirt and ran. Her hidden princess soldiers lay at odd angles across the stones, as though they had been cut down while they'd stood in neat rows. Blood seeped out across the world, the bitter scent of it causing her to put the back of her hand to her nose. She looked up at the steps and then raced forward. Yang lay dead partway up the stairs, reaching out to Wei-Song, who had also been cut down. The empress was next, almost at the top of the steps.

Lis looked about wildly. There was no one else around, and no sign of magics. She took a deep breath and headed inside the throne room. Sun filtered through the windows, high up along the walls, and the dark polished floor squeaked beneath her bare feet. There was no one there. She turned slowly, trying to determine where they could be, but as she turned to face the throne again, the emperor sat slumped to the side, his golden tunic soaked with red. She stepped forward blindly, and her foot snagged on something, causing her to trip.

Landing on her knees, she came face to face with the staring eyes of Remi. She gulped down the overwhelming loss that threatened to break through her skin. In his arms was a woman. Lis reached out and brushed a blood-matted clump of hair back from the woman's face, only to reveal her own. She sat back screaming.

She opened her eyes, unable to breath in Remi's tight embrace. A soldier raced through the door.

'What has happened?' the soldier asked, stopping suddenly and then bowing.

Lis shook her head, looked up at Remi and then promptly burst into tears, burying herself in his chest.

'It was just a dream,' he whispered, waving the soldier away.

Lis nodded, but it had felt far worse than just a dream. It had felt so real. She wondered if there was any meaning behind it. She couldn't remember what she had been wearing when she'd found herself; it could have been a vision of what was to come. The visions may have stopped for others, but might they have started for her?

'Can we send someone to check on the emperor?' she asked, running her hand across her face.

'Of course,' he said softly, and she heard the rustle of someone else climbing out of their bed.

'Is it morning yet?'

'Not quite,' Wei-Song said. 'Was it so bad? Were you burning?'

'No,' Lis whispered, clinging tighter to Remi. 'Everyone was dead.'

'Who?' he asked softly.

'Everyone. The soldiers, Yang, Wei-Song, you…'

'We are all well,' he said, running a hand over her hair.

She nodded again and tried to focus on the firm, comforting realisation that he was there with her. She squeezed her eyes closed, but all she could see was blood. She sat up slowly, and he rubbed gently over her back.

'Sleep,' he murmured, but she couldn't. Then Yang was back in the room and climbing into his bed.

'The emperor is sleeping soundly.'

Lis nodded slowly. It worried her that this might be an indication of what was to come. Like all the dreams she'd had of a burning world, when she had flown with Remi—was that the phoenix? Was she destined for something greater, as everyone seemed to think?

She spent the rest of the night sitting beside Remi, trying not to revisit the images that haunted her. Every time she closed her eyes, she saw her own lifeless form, and it scared her. As the morning light started to brighten through the window, the general appeared in the doorway. She stood carefully, so as not to wake those around her, and padded across the room.

'Has something happened?' she asked.

He shook his head. 'I just wanted to ensure you were well. You don't appear to have slept very well.'

'Bad dreams,' she murmured, thankful that the sheets still blew back and forth across the lines before her.

'You know this is where you are meant to be,' he said, indicating that they move away from the door. 'He needs you.'

She looked back then, and nodded. 'I need him too,' she admitted.

'I had feared him lost,' the general went on in a hoarse whisper. 'And as much as I thought we shouldn't be using your magic or placing you in danger, you were the only one to save him.'

Lis nodded again. 'Do you think this is the right thing to do?'

she asked. 'Will the people see it for what it is and not think we are hunting through them as my father did?'

'Maybe if they know you have some magic, it will help.'

'Unless they are like Peng and don't want the magics to return—then it will cause more trouble.'

'We may not know what the Empire will be. But I trust the two of you will do the right thing by the people, whatever that might be.'

'Thank you, General Zou-Hou. We would never have survived this long without you.'

'You are much stronger than you realise.'

'I hope you are right.'

As they rounded the corner, Lis's heart stopped. Not only her own guard, but all the solders still on the island were lined up before the steps of the throne room. The emperor and empress waited at the top of the steps, and he was dressed in the golden clothing of her dream. She held tighter to Remi's arm.

'You should have been carried here,' he whispered.

She shook her head. She looked over the men before her and wondered if everyone else had really disappeared from the island. Would they ever return?

They moved between the rows of soldiers and up the steps to the waiting emperor, Wei-Song and Yang behind them. The emperor looked uncertainly at Wei-Song for a moment and then cleared his throat.

Lis bowed low to the emperor and empress, then turned back to face the rows of soldiers and bowed low towards them. The world was still and quiet. Remi bowed to the soldiers and then to his parents. They repeated the ritual, and then he came to stand beside her and took her hand.

The emperor stepped forward. 'I present to you my daughter, the crown princess, Lisabet of Rei-Een.'

Lis bowed again to the soldiers as they cheered. She looked

back at Remi then, and he beamed.

'Now we shall send you to visit the Empire.'

Lis only then realised that not all of the men lined up were soldiers. At the front of the group were most of the ministers. Advisor Gan, grumbling, was also present, standing a little to the side.

'Prepare the fleet,' the little man bellowed, and Lis looked back to Remi. What might this man try to do once they were away from the emperor? But then, she would have the hunter and soldiers with her.

'Come,' the empress said, directing them inside the throne room while the men started to move away from the steps.

'That didn't seem too bad,' Remi said. And she realised that she still held his hand very tightly.

'When will we sail?' Lis asked.

'In the morning,' the empress said, leading them through the secret door behind the throne.

'The emperor had said we were to leave before dark,' Lis said, following the empress through the silent narrow walkway. 'Where are we going?'

'There is something you must do before you go.'

Remi pulled Lis to a stop. 'Mother,' he chastised. 'This is hardly the time.'

'There are some traditions that must be followed,' the empress said, opening a door in the wall.

A long room stretched out before them, and Lis was momentarily reminded of the room she had been assessed in during the Choosing. The walls were covered with screens, and a large bed sat in the middle of the room. Lis froze in the doorway. She could sense others in the room, behind the screens.

'No.' Lis said simply, refusing to enter the room. 'We have broken enough tradition. What is one more?'

The Imperial Healer stepped out from behind a screen, and Lis wondered how anyone could watch such an event.

'Sit down, Your Highness.'

She reluctantly followed the man to the bed, and as she sat down, he knelt at her feet.

'I have heard that you share covers with the prince already.'

She nodded once.

'Provide your wrist,' he said, and she looked back at Remi as she held out her arm.

He carefully placed his fingers to the skin and closed his eyes.

'What have you been doing?' the empress whispered angrily.

Remi only looked at Lis, and the heat of his gaze covered her skin. She wasn't quite sure what they wanted from her, but she was sure this was not something she wanted them involved with.

'She is not with child yet. We shall stay,' the Imperial Healer announced.

A level of excitement rose from behind the screens, and she was sure she would be sick.

'Not today,' Remi said.

'This is not for negotiation,' the empress responded, moving towards a screen.

'Then all you do is delay our departure,' Remi said, sitting on the edge of the bed.

Lis glanced at him, but he stared straight ahead, his hands clasped in his lap. She tried to keep her back straight, but the uneasiness in the room made her shiver.

After too long sitting in silence, the empress sighed.

'The crown princess is not with child,' the Imperial Healer announced. 'We might assume any child she does bear to be his…' His confident voice petered out, and he sighed.

With a disappointed murmur, several other healers appeared from behind the screens and filed from the room. Lis breathed a sigh of relief. The empress gave Remi a scowl and then followed after them, locking the door behind her.

Lis leapt up at the sound of the bolt. 'They can't leave us here. There is much to do.'

Remi clenched his hands together, a nervousness she hadn't noticed until then radiating from him.

'What is it?' she asked.

'You told them we have lain together already,' he said, looking awkward.

'No, I said…' She stopped. 'Oh.'

'Oh indeed.' His nervousness shifted, and he grinned at her.

'We need to be planning,' she whispered. 'What are we to do once we reach Second? Are we only to parade through the streets? Can we talk to the people? Are we to stay for days?'

He reached out and took her hand. She flinched, unsure why, and took a step back. He stood and stepped with her. He pulled her back towards the bed, sitting quickly, and she sat heavily beside him. He appeared to be blushing just as much as she was.

'I can understand this is difficult,' he said. 'That you are not ready. But she is not going to let us out anytime soon.'

'But we did this so we could have a reason to get to the other islands. We need to consider what we will do. Or are we to land on each dock and try to recreate the phoenix?'

He shook his head.

'It is not that I don't want to be your wife,' she whispered. 'I chose to be here,' she added, looking around the room, thankful that her abilities allowed her to sense anyone who might have tried to continue hiding, or his mother standing by the door. She sighed. 'This isn't quite what I imagined,' she said.

'What did you imagine?' he asked kindly.

'Somewhere quiet and alone and comfortable, like we are of a night. There is a lot of pressure here.'

'It is quiet, and there is no one around now.'

'But everyone knows what we are doing.'

'Our lives are never going to be our own again. Yours hasn't been since you arrived here.'

She nodded. 'What if I'm not enough? What if I can't make you happy? Or can't give you the sons that you need?'

'Is that your concern? That you won't be what I need you to be?'

She nodded once, and he surprised her by taking her face in his hands.

'You are already far more than I ever hoped for. You keep me grounded.'

He pressed his lips to hers, and she allowed him to lay her back across the bed.

The next morning, they boarded the largest ship of the Empire, both dressed in navy blue with silver trim. It had appeared she had come full circle when they dressed, for they were in the same colours the royals had worn the day she had been chosen as the hidden princess. She longed for her hair to be free, but it was neatly pulled back with pins gifted to her by the empress. Elaborate and expensive, all with blossoms. A small silver crown was nestled into her own hair amidst the pins, and despite Wei-Song's assurances, she wasn't sure they would be able to recreate the look. She watched Remi's back, his hair smoothed into a bun beneath his own silver crown.

She remembered Remi from the afternoon before, his hair loose and free around his face, and she smiled. She wondered if they would have the chance to be so relaxed with each other again. Despite her happiness to see their friends again, she knew they would always be surrounded by people. She was grateful in some small way that the empress had provided them the time together, and she was even more grateful that the healer had been confused and not watched over them to ensure the act occurred.

'Lis,' Yang called, coming to stand beside her, and she blinked herself back to the reality from her dream of the day before. 'I apologise, Your Highness, for my informality.'

'Don't you dare,' she whispered loudly. She noticed Remi turned just slightly, to listen more closely to what was said. 'You have always called me Lis. If you change now, I might have to create a title for you.'

He grinned and bowed a little. 'What plan do you have to win the hearts of the people?'

'I'm not sure it is a plan. Maybe trying to show that things are as they should be.'

He raised his eyebrows.

'Provide some normalcy,' she said.

'Where does the magic come into it?' he asked.

'Let's just see what kind of reception we receive. The Palace Isle has been so quiet; I can only hope there are more people on the other islands of the Empire.' Remi said, turning to join the conversation.

Advisor Gan made himself comfortable at the front of the boat. Lis was sure he wasn't the best person to have on this trip. He wanted both of them in cuffs, but perhaps it was a risk the emperor took so he could have some discussion with the ministers away from the little man.

Lis wondered just what the advisor might say when he reached the people. She looked across to find him watching her. Stepping forward, she slipped her arm through Remi's. It wouldn't take them very long to reach Second in a ship this size. She tried not to sigh. They could be zigzagging across the Empire for weeks.

Tradition dictated that the islands of the Empire were visited in a particular order for the wedding parade. Second, Third, Fourth and then Fifth; then the Sacred Isle, and then other outliers. That included her own family island. She longed to see her father again. She was worried for Ting and Peng. She was not as keen to visit the Sacred Isle. The priestesses might already be aware of what had happened to their high priestess, and she didn't know whether they continued to have visions. If the high priestess had been working with the magics, it might well be that they all were and this visit may not be able to sway them as they hoped.

As they neared the main dock of Second, Lis realised there were far more people waiting to look at them than she had expected.

'In my parents' time,' Remi said, 'They would have sailed past and waved. Are you sure you are ready to face the people?'

She nodded, but her heart thumped in her chest. This wasn't just about her. The people knew what Remi had become and what he had done in the main square of the Palace Isle, so she feared him in greater danger. Particularly as the ministers were so sure the people wouldn't support him as their crown prince.

As the boat touched against the dock and the gangplank was pushed out, a cheer went up from the crowd. After a moment too long hesitating, Advisor Gan rushed forward and out before the people. A strange hush moved over the crowd, and Lis could feel the tension.

As he straightened his coat, Remi took Lis by the hand and led her forward.

'You should wait,' the general said, standing by the gangplank, his hand on his sword.

Remi shook his head and led Lis down to the people, just as the advisor announced them. Remi squeezed her hand, and they both bowed to the crowd.

There was a moment of stillness, and then the crowd, as one, dropped to their knees before them.

'We thank you for your kind welcome,' Lis said, stepping forward.

A murmur spread through the crowd, and a small child broke free, racing towards Lis. She could hear the soldiers running down behind her, but she stepped forward and took the child by the hands. A hush fell on the people, and Lis smiled at the girl.

'Is it true that you have magic?' she asked. The awe in her voice made Lis smile, and although Remi stood straight like a rod, she nodded once.

Advisor Gan grumbled loudly, and Lis looked towards him just as the general elbowed him sharply.

Lis held out her hand, and a small stalk grew up from her palm. A bud formed on the end, and a little leaf sprouted from the side.

Then a bright yellow flower bloomed. The child squealed with delight and clapped her hands.

'It is yours,' Lis said with a nod. The girl reached forward carefully and closed her hand around the stalk. She then turned back to the people and held it up.

They stood in silence and then, without warning, the girl took Lis by the hand and dragged her closer to the crowd. She glanced back at Remi, who looked a little uncertain, but he stayed where he was. The general followed her without hesitation.

Lis gave him a shake of her head, and he stopped. She was sure Wei-Song called out cake from the ship, but she did nothing other than let the child guide her. She looked down to see the girl still held the flower tight in her hand.

'This is my mother,' she said.

Lis bowed to the woman before her, who appeared confused as she looked between her child, the flower and Lis, then back again.

'This is the princess,' the child said, as though her mother didn't know.

'The royal family never gets off the boat,' she stammered.

'We wanted to meet with people, to see how the Empire is faring after so much turmoil.'

'You have married earlier than expected,' a man in the crowd said. 'Traditions seem to be lost.'

'The empress would agree with you,' Lis said, realising that she was surrounded, and she looked back through the crowd for Remi.

'You are both so young,' another voice said.

'Is the prince really returned?' someone else asked.

Lis nodded, and then he was standing behind her.

'We wanted you to see that we are united,' he said, his voice clear and loud, and many people nodded. 'I was lost for a time, but the crown princess saved me.'

'She fought against you,' a male voice called out.

'And now we fight together.'

'My grandmother had magic,' the little girl said, and the crowd dropped to silence again. 'But we aren't allowed to talk about it.'

Lis dropped to her knees beside the child. 'We would like a world where magic can live in harmony with everyone.'

The little girl nodded, and a spark jumped in her hand. The anger in the crowd pushed at Lis, and she pushed the girl behind her. 'She is not to be feared,' Lis said.

Her mother burst into tears, and another woman wrapped an arm around her shoulder.

'I am sure there are others out there with various forms of magic,' Remi said, and Lis could see the uncertainty in the crowd. 'We worked together once.'

'Can we again?' someone else asked. 'Is it really possible, or is this a plan to flush out those with magic, to start to another war?'

Lis felt the heat before it flashed across Remi's skin, and she moved the child quickly from between them, although she reached for the flames. Lis put her back to him and reached out for him. As soon as she touched him, she felt the phoenix clear around them, and then she realised the child was still pulled against the front of her.

With panic, she looked down, and the child grinned up at her. She released Remi and the fire dissipated, and she wrapped her arms around the child in front of her. 'Are you hurt?' she whispered.

The child shook her head. 'I like fire,' she said.

'Just don't burn anything down.' Lis looked back at Remi, smiling down at her, and he nodded once.

She then realised that the people were kneeling before them, giving them a space although the mother of the child in Lis's arms was inching forward. Lis gave the child a nudge, and she ran to her mother. Lis looked back at the soldiers lined on the dock, also on their knees. The only other one standing was Advisor Gan, and he stood with his mouth agape.

18

As they stepped aboard the boat that night, Lis wondered how long it would be before news of their visit reached the other islands. The people had looked with awe at the two of them and listened to what they had to say, but the people of Second were not very forthcoming.

The little girl might have admitted that her grandmother had magic, and she had raised a spark, but no one else was admitting such a thing. Many of the families they had seen would have had husbands or siblings who worked on the Palace Isle. They would have heard a lot of what had happened during the fight and were possibly keen to remove the prince from his position.

But they hadn't shown the fear that Lis had expected, and she could only hope their visits to the other islands would be just as friendly. It would only take an hour or so to reach Third from where they were, yet it was decided they would spend the night on the ship. Someone had suggested their staying on the island, but the general thought they could be better protected on board the ship. The soldiers camped on the dock and, despite her concerns, the people brought them a range of dishes to keep them well fed.

Advisor Gan didn't touch what was offered by the people. He was sure they weren't as accepting as the princess thought they were and would try to poison them. He only ate from the supplies on board the ship.

Their planned travel was going to take them away from the Palace Isle for some time, and Lis wondered what might happen while they were away. It could be the perfect opportunity for those waiting to take it.

'Is it worth us stopping back at the Palace Isle as we sail to Fourth?' she asked Remi that night. She felt that so far, this journey had been far easier than either of them had thought possible. 'Might the magics try something with us away from the Palace Isle for so long? Could they see this as a chance to take control? Should we have left the general? And who is watching over the emperor while we are gone?'

He nodded slowly.

'Remi? Are you listening?'

'I am. But I'm thinking at the same time. Do we really think this will bring the people to our side?'

'You are questioning it now. They saw the phoenix,' she added.

'They nearly saw a prince lose control.'

'But you didn't lose control.'

'Because you were there. What if something happens—what if you are busy and I can't keep my frustrations or anger in?'

'What was it today?' she asked, sitting beside him and resting a hand on his knee. A different fire leapt behind his eyes. 'What caused you to lose control today?'

'I feared for you.'

'Then don't.'

'That is easier said than done.'

'I can look after myself,' Lis said, standing up. She moved across the small cabin to the doorway. 'I have my barrier. I took you on.'

He grinned then and was across the small space, his arms on either side of her head, against the door. She smiled back and then pushed gently with her barrier, sending him back across the room.

The knock on the door startled them both, and Lis was still

smiling when she opened it to Advisor Gan.

He bowed low and then pushed past her into the room. Remi sat on the end of the bed. Lis closed the door and leaned against it. She wasn't quite sure what this man wanted. Or whether he would ever be what he had been before.

'You must have worked with magics before the war,' Lis said, allowing her thoughts out into the world. 'You would have seen the world as it was.'

He nodded solemnly and then turned back to the prince. 'I have seen what you are,' he said. 'But apart, are you a threat to this world? Will they turn you as they did before?'

Remi shook his head.

'You might have claimed her as your wife, but I know that you see the world differently from your father. You might not honour such a union.'

'I think I have done enough to prove that I will do anything for Lis.'

'You might have followed her around. You might have bedded her before you wed…'

'That is not the case,' Lis murmured.

'But you would not let those who should have witness the consummation. This must be a legal marriage if she is to be empress.'

'There is no question to its legality,' Remi spat, and Lis could sense the flames again. She shook her head, and he took a deep breath. 'We are not just here for a tour; we are here to find a way to bring the Empire back together and make it as it was. Can't you see that the Empire is dying? If we leave things as they are, it will be lost.'

The advisor sighed and looked at Lis. 'I don't trust that you are doing this for the Empire.'

'Who would we do it for?' she asked.

He shook his head. 'I shall do as I am bid by the emperor. But I keep the ministers' concerns foremost in my mind.' He bowed ever so slightly and then closed the door behind him with a bang.

'Do you think we made a mistake?' Lis asked. 'The ministers might take this as an opportunity to depose him.'

'I think my father is stronger than you realise. As is my mother.'

'I hope you are right, or we may return from this journey to a very different world.'

'I am hoping we change it.'

Lis sat beside him. 'I don't think it is going to be that easy,' she said, thinking about the people they had left. 'They may not fear us as they did, but they aren't going to embrace magics as they once did.'

'Maybe we just need to show them the phoenix.'

'I think there will come a time when that too will mean something very different.'

Lis had assumed that the people of Third would greet them as those of Second had. But when the dock came into view, there were very few people out to see them.

'Maybe this isn't a good idea,' Lis said softly, standing beside Remi as she watched the approaching dock. She was sure that amidst the trees, there were more people watching them arrive than they could see. She wondered if word of their visit to Second had done more harm than good. 'What if they fear us?' she asked.

'There is a little school at the far end of the island. Let's walk the length of the island. We only saw a small part of Second. Maybe being amongst the people would be of benefit.'

Lis nodded slowly.

'That could take all day,' Advisor Gan moaned. 'You do realise how big the island is?'

'Yes, thank you, I am well aware.' Remi looked at the general. 'We'll take some men with us, and Wei-Song and the healer,' he added, looking back at them across the ship. 'You can continue sailing to the end of the island and send out a small boat for us when we reach the shore.'

'I don't like this,' he said, 'but I will do as you wish.'

Remi was quick down the gangplank and held his hand out for Lis to join him. Advisor Gan had to push in front of a soldier to be next off the boat. There were only a couple dozen people, and Lis tried to smile into the crowd as the advisor stepped forward.

'The Empire would like to announce the crown prince and princess of Rei-Een. Their royal highnesses would wish to know the people.'

The crowd bowed low before them, and Lis smiled. 'We would like to see your island,' she said.

'Which part of it?' someone in the crowd asked.

'All if it,' Remi said with a nod towards the man.

'Send for a carriage,' someone else called out.

'We can walk,' Lis said.

Advisor Gan actually groaned.

'I have never visited Third,' she said, ignoring the little man. 'In fact, other than my little island, I had only ever been to Fifth,' she said to a woman who smiled at her. 'I'm sure the islands of the Empire are similar in so many ways, but then I'm sure there are many more differences I'm not aware of. There is only so much to learn from books.'

The group bowed again and indicated along the narrow road that led from the dock. It initially took them along the water, and Lis was reminded again how much she had missed the water. She stopped and looked out at the blue-green ocean, with nothing to break the surface until it reached the horizon. 'You don't get views like this on the Palace Isle,' she said.

'Do you miss your little island?' the woman who had smiled at her asked.

Lis nodded.

'Is it very different being the hidden princess? Or the crown princess?' She looked down at her feet.

'Yes,' Lis said honestly. 'It wasn't a place I ever thought I would be.' She glanced back at Remi, who was talking with Wei-Song a little way back down the path, the soldiers dotted between them. 'But I'm where I am needed,' Lis said with a smile.

'My cousin lined up for the Choosing,' the woman said, looking along the path. 'I was disappointed that she wasn't chosen, but then when we heard what was happening on the Palace Isle, I was pleased it wasn't her.'

Lis nodded, unsure of what she could say. If her cousin had been selected, things might have been very different. The prince might not have developed his magic, and Lis might be married to Peng. She looked back again then. Wei-Song hadn't mentioned Lis's sister at all other than that she'd needed to return to their father. Lis didn't know how she was or whether the baby was close. And given the choice, she might have preferred to be far away from the Palace Isle herself.

'But you are here now,' the woman continued. 'And married already.'

'Times are different from what they were. And with the fighting, this might be our chance to try and bring the Empire back to what it was.'

'You mean bring magic back,' another man said, joining them as they climbed the small rise from beside the water to amongst the trees. Lis didn't think she had ever seen such tall trees up close before. There were trees higher up the mountain on Fifth, but these were close enough to touch. She reached out for one.

'Your Highness,' a soldier called, coming around the bend in the path.

'Look at the size of this,' she said, finally putting her hand on the trunk. It was tall and broad, the branches jutting out, and she was nearly lost in the depth of them.

'Please be careful, Your Highness,' the soldier pleaded, and she cried out as a branch snagged her arm.

'Where is she?' Remi asked, joining them. 'What are you doing?' he asked as she came out of the tree with her hand on her arm.

'Let me look,' Yang said, stepping forward quickly.

'It is just a scratch. Have you ever seen anything so huge?' she asked, looking up at the sky.

The soldier groaned.

'What have I done?' Lis asked. 'Am I not to touch them?' she asked the woman beside her, who broke into a smile.

'You don't behave as I expected a princess to behave,' the woman said quickly.

'You have no idea,' Yang offered.

'I am excited,' Lis said in way of explanation.

'You will want to climb one next, like a child,' Yang said.

She glanced at Remi, who grinned. 'Can I?' she asked.

'Not today, Your Highness,' the soldier said. 'We have much ground to cover.'

Lis nodded solemnly and stepped forward.

'You didn't answer my question,' the man beside her said. He was less friendly than she remembered. 'Magic.'

'We would like the world to be what it was, only more supportive of the magics to ensure they are more comfortable with their skills.'

'You want to make them stronger?'

'No, just give them the chance to be who they are.'

'But magics want to take over the Empire. They fought in the square. With the prince,' he added, looking more uncertain of the people he was with.

'They haven't been treated as they should,' Lis said. 'It can be different.'

'And the prince?' he asked.

'Has found some control,' she answered for him.

The trees opened up before them, and they arrived in a village. It was different from what she had seen on Fifth. The houses were neat and whitewashed, their black tiled rooves sparkling in the sunlight. A market was set up at the far end of the street, and although there were people moving between the stalls, it wasn't loud. No one argued over prices or jostled over what was for sale as they did in the market on the Palace Isle. Lis paused for a moment, remembering the enthusiasm when Mu-Phi had described them to her.

As they drew closer, the little movement there was in the market stopped. People bowed as they passed, but no one spoke, and then a girl ran forward and dropped to her knees before the prince.

'Your Highness,' she said, touching her head down into the dirt.

'Please,' he said, reaching forward.

As she looked up at him, Lis recognised her from the line. She had been quiet, and Lis had no idea of her name. Although she wasn't sure she could name anyone else who had lined up with her during that time.

'Please, stand up,' he repeated kindly.

The young woman smiled and glanced at Lis. 'We did not expect you, Your Highness, nor for such a reason as to present your wife.'

Lis nodded and smiled in her direction. 'Your cousin has been most helpful in guiding us here,' she said.

The girl looked to the woman who had been talking with Lis and then glanced back at Remi. 'I can organise a carriage,' she said quickly.

'The prince and princess wish to walk,' her cousin answered before Lis could thank her.

'Walk? To where?' she asked, then seemed to remember her audience and bowed again.

'I have sailed past Third recently and noticed a school at the far end. We would like to explore and meet as many people as we can while we make our way towards the school,' Remi said. 'Our ship will meet us at that end of the island.'

'There is no dock,' a man said.

Remi nodded. 'They can ferry us out by rowboat.'

'From the beach?' a woman asked. 'The princess will get her feet wet.'

Lis laughed at the idea. 'It has been some time since I have had the chance to put my feet in the ocean.'

Remi coughed politely, and she smiled at him, taking his arm. 'Although I doubt the prince will even allow my feet to touch the sand.'

He placed his hand on hers and smiled down at her. 'If you wish to swim to the ship, who am I to stop you?'

The silence around them seemed overwhelming.

The girl smiled nervously. 'I see you chose the best princess,' she said softly, bowing to Lis. 'I remember you with your hair flowing free,' she said softly. 'I envied you. But I didn't imagine you would be chosen.'

'Hush,' someone scolded from the small group around them.

'Neither did I,' Lis admitted. 'And I was sure the prince had made a terrible mistake, but I'm pleased now.'

Remi surprised her by kissing the side of her head, and the crowd led the way towards the market. They looked over the goods before following the track beyond the village. The woman who had talked with them paused and bowed.

'Thank you,' Lis said, taking her hands.

'I wish you luck, Your Highness, but be careful. Not everyone wants the magic to return, and some don't want to share the power.' She glanced back at the crowd standing in the market, then bowed to Lis again. She headed back to the group, and the girl who could have been Empress led the way along the path towards the next village.

The people of Third were quiet and polite, but Lis was sure there was something else beneath the surface. If they didn't have the soldiers with them, things might have been different. An old woman at a village they passed through close to midday insisted that they stop for lunch. Lis didn't want to admit that her feet were as sore as they were. Despite the comfortable pace they made, she wanted to sit and watch the world pass her by. They accepted the woman's hospitality, and she happily poured rice wine for the soldiers.

Yang insisted on checking the scrape on Lis's arm from the tree. Although it was sore, she hadn't thought very much of it. As she slipped her fine cloak from her shoulders, the old woman was quick to take it from her. She looked it over and nodded.

'I can fix this,' she said, carrying it away inside.

'I would rather eat first,' Remi murmured, and a young woman came out of the house with a tray of food. She put the bowls down on the table before Remi and Lis and then disappeared back into the house. It was another moment before she appeared with more for Yang and Wei-Song. Yang waited for her to go inside again, then put his hand over Lis's arm. The gentle sting stopped, and Lis rolled her shoulders.

'I know you are keen to behave as a child,' he chastised her, 'but stay out of the water. With your luck, you will be taken by a sea monster.'

She laughed, and the girl behind her sucked in a breath. The bowls slipping from the tray, and one of the soldiers grabbed it before it all tumbled to the floor. 'Are you alright?' he asked her.

'You cannot speak to the crown princess in such a way.'

'Someone needs to,' Remi answered for him.

Some of the soldiers laughed. 'She is not your typical princess,' one of them said.

'Really?' Lis asked.

'Yes,' Wei-Song chimed in.

'I am trying to portray an image here,' she said.

'Yet you would rather run barefoot through the waves,' the older woman said, coming out of the house.

Lis nodded.

'I knew your mother when she was but a child,' the woman said, and Lis moved across the bench to make room for her. 'She was very much like you.'

Lis smiled at the idea of her mother, but she couldn't say anything. Remi reached out and took her hand.

'I can see that he chose you for the woman you are,' she said, smiling at Remi.

He nodded once. 'I'm afraid that I saw no one else in the line after I saw Lis.'

'Destiny has a strange way of working.' She handed the coat back to Lis. It was perfect; she couldn't even tell where the small tear had been. Lis placed her hand over it and closed her eyes.

'There are many who use that term,' Remi said.

'You are Hidden,' Lis said.

The woman nodded.

Lis could feel the magic in the cloth. She wondered if that was something new, something more acute she had developed since she had pulled energy from the phoenix. But she hadn't felt the woman using the magic.

'You want to bring the worlds together,' the woman said.

Lis nodded.

'If we can,' Remi added. 'Not all with magic feel the same way.'

'And not all without agree with you,' the advisor muttered from amidst the soldiers. They turned to him.

'He will come around,' Lis said quietly.

'Or we will roast him,' Remi snapped, the flame jumping quickly to life in his hand. The girl squealed.

Lis had forgotten she was still with them. 'He is in jest,' she said, standing from the table.

'Your world is very different,' the girl said softly. 'I didn't know what he was, and we heard stories. Is he...'

'Dangerous?' Lis finished for her.

The girl shook her head. 'Cruel?' she asked.

Remi allowed the fire to die, and Lis could feel the disappointment radiating from him. It was almost as overwhelming as the fear from the girl.

Lis took her hands. The girl flinched and then focused on Lis. She was a woman, Lis had to remind herself. The same age as herself, yet she appeared so much younger—or was it that Lis had aged so much since the Choosing?

'He is the kindest man I know,' Lis said softly. 'He has done far more for me than I could ever expect.'

'You have magic too,' she said.

Lis nodded once. 'And it is because of that magic that the prince developed his. It is my fault he is what he is.'

'It is destiny,' the old woman and Yang said in the same instant.

'Now show us how you will bring the world together,' the old woman demanded.

Lis, still holding the girl by the hands, looked at Remi. Was this something they could do on demand? Would it make a difference?

Remi sighed and stood. Lis let go of the girl and indicated that she take a step back.

'I don't know how much longer we can do this,' he murmured.

'Let's try together,' she said, taking his hand.

He twirled her around to stand in front of him, his arm across her chest, holding her tight against him. As the heat buzzed around them, Lis knew that they had formed the phoenix immediately, or at least it had shown itself. The girl dropped to her knees, and the old woman grinned.

19

Lis stood on the deck of the ship, looking back at the pale lights of Third, drenched and shivering. Remi had tried to ensure she stayed as dry as possible, but she was already halfway to the boat from the shore before he could stop her. If it hadn't been for her skirts filling with water and threatening to pull her under, he was sure she might have tried to swim.

'You know I could dry you,' he said, wrapping his arms around her and feeling the heat just beneath his skin.

'You might burn me too,' she murmured, leaning into him.

'Did you have a nice visit?'

'Yes. There are more amongst the islands with magic than I expected. I suppose I wasn't the only one to hide. But will they be willing to come forward? What if they think we are trying to trick them, or that your father is using us?'

He shook his head and pulled her closer.

'He isn't, is he?'

'I know he has doubts about us and the power we hold, but he needs the Empire to succeed. He wants the Empire to be as strong as it can.'

'He was very determined to stamp out all magic not very long ago.'

'You are safe,' Remi whispered, kissing the side of her neck.

'Are you?'

'Do you mean in my father's eyes, or for you? Because I don't think you should feel very safe at all right now.'

'There is enough heat radiating from you to set the boat alight.' She pushed him back. 'You best take a breath, or maybe you need a swim.'

'You are wet,' he said, the seriousness back in his voice.

'And my feet are sore. It is easy enough for me to change, but perhaps it best I retire for the night before we walk across any more of the Empire.'

He laughed, then took her hand and looped it round his arm. Holding her securely in place, he headed for their cabin. Lis had changed her clothes with the ease only she had, and he was pulling at his own ties when there was a knock at the door.

He opened the door to Wei-Song and stepped back to allow her entry.

'I wanted to ensure you were well after the day,' she said to Lis.

'Tired but well enough. Are we sailing tonight, or in the morning?'

'We are closer to the Sacred Isle than our next destination. But I think it best we travel during the day. There may be magics out there who aren't as keen to see us.' Remi said.

'Do you think they have selected another high priestess?' Wei-Song asked.

'We will find out when we get there,' Remi said. 'But Fourth needs to be our first priority.'

Lis nodded and stifled a yawn.

'I just wanted to ensure you were safe,' Wei-Song said. 'I will take my leave so that you can rest.'

Lis nodded, and by the time Remi had seen Wei-Song from the cabin and bolted the door after her, Lis was already lying down and breathing slowly.

Remi pulled the last of his clothes off quickly and slipped in beside her. He wrapped his arms around her, holding her tight, and she sighed softly.

He was disappointed she had fallen asleep so quickly, but then she rolled against him. 'Do you think the phoenix will continue to work?' she asked.

'In bringing the people to their knees?'

'In a way. But I hoped it would unite them.'

'I only wanted to control the fire burning inside,' Remi admitted.

'What if it is your phoenix, and it has nothing to do with us?'

'I can't find it without you.'

Lis sighed again. 'My feet hurt.'

'Do you want me to rub them?'

'I don't want you anywhere near them. Just hold me and tell me we are doing the right thing.'

'As long as we are together, there can never be a wrong thing,' he said, kissing her neck again.

'I was tired,' she murmured.

'Now?'

'Not so much.'

The next morning, as the light pushed into the cabin through the small windows, Remi was cold. He had no covers at all. But when he reached for them, Lis was cocooned in not just the covers, but her barrier as well.

He sat up slowly and reached for her, but the barrier held, and he couldn't get close enough to shake her. 'Lis,' he called softly.

She murmured in her sleep but didn't move.

The boat rocked back and forth, and Remi wondered how long until they would sail back towards the Palace Isle. They should be on deck, looking back over the people and waving. He wondered how many would come to the shore to see them. Then he stood slowly with the knock on the door.

Yang stood there, looking a little worse for wear.

'Are you sick?' Remi asked.

'I don't like the water,' Yang admitted.

Remi went to ask why he had come when he realised Yang was watching Lis.

'I wanted to be sure she hadn't caught a chill,' Yang said.

'She changed quickly. I kept her warm,' Remi added, then bit his lip as the other man blushed. 'No different from what I did before, Yang.'

'I am sure some things have changed,' the other man admitted, pushing into the room.

'She has her barrier up,' Remi said as Yang sat on the edge of the bed and reached for her.

'Why?' he asked, running his hand over the invisible wall between them.

Remi shook his head. 'Maybe a dream,' he offered. But she had been quiet during the night, and she tended to call out when she had bad dreams. Not that she had recently. Not since they had wed.

Yang looked from her to him. 'What did you do?' he asked, his voice loud. Lis moaned in her sleep, rolling towards them. She appeared contented enough.

'She was worried last night that we might not be able to do what we hoped with this tour.'

'The people need to see that you are alive and working together. I'm not sure about the phoenix, but it makes a difference.'

Remi nodded. 'Lis,' he called louder. 'Yang is here.'

'I'm too tired,' she murmured.

'Lis,' Yang said, 'why is your barrier up?'

She sat up slowly, wiping the sleep from her eyes. She had slept soundly enough, but Remi wondered if she was indeed sick.

'No, it's not,' she said, moving across the bed to sit beside him. She rested her head on his shoulder as he had seen her do so many times before, only something prevented her from reaching him.

'Do you feel well?' Remi asked.

She nodded slowly. He reached forward, but he couldn't touch her again.

She shook her head and stood, then reached out and took his hand.

'What happened?'

'I don't know,' she said softly, yawning and stretching her hands above her head. Without turning, she made her clothes change. 'Do we need to be on deck?'

He nodded, unsure what he had done.

'Get dressed then,' she said a little more brightly, standing on her toes and kissing his cheek. 'Yang can walk me up. I'm ready for some fresh air.'

Many more than Remi had expected came out to watch them pass. But not all of those who lined the shores waved as enthusiastically as Lis did.

'What do you feel?' he asked, joining her at the railing.

'Confusion, uncertainty, joy,' she said, still smiling and waving. 'I'm not sure if this has been enough. If the magics attack again, we may never see these people again.'

'Look,' Yang said, pointing behind them. Several smaller vessels followed along in their wake.

'Are they coming with us?' Lis asked.

'Or making sure we are gone?' Remi said, unsure where the negative thought came from. He wasn't sure he had learnt as much as he had hoped on this journey so far. Some people had been friendly, but others wondered at the real reason they were there. He hadn't sensed any magic, but then he might have been somewhat distracted. Lis was still waving, although they couldn't see anyone on Third for the trees.

'Did you sense magic?' he asked, standing behind her. He threaded his arms around her, but he didn't feel quite right.

She shook her head. 'Sometimes, but it wasn't clear.'

'Are there more Hidden?'

'I think there are many kinds of magics all in hiding, hoping for a normal life.'

'Is something wrong?' he asked quickly. 'Is something worrying you?'

She shook her head.

'You are pushing me away,' he whispered, and she looked down at his hands, cupped close to hers but not touching.

'I'm not,' she whispered, but he couldn't get any closer.

He turned to Yang, who was also watching her.

'What is it?' she asked, but her voice was light, where Remi felt only concern.

'Yang?' he asked.

The healer shook his head. 'I can't feel anything. I can't get close enough.'

'Will you two stop?' she asked, moving along the railing to Wei-Song, who also watched the coastline.

'Can you see anything beyond the trees?' she asked.

Lis shook her head. 'It is beautiful. I forgot how much I missed the water,' she said softly.

'Too long trapped in a little palace,' Wei-Song said.

'I quite liked our little palace,' Lis said.

Remi couldn't tell if she was serious or sad, and he looked at the man beside him. Yang watched her too closely as well. He took the man by the elbow and dragged him across the boat, as far away from Lis as he could get.

'Tell me what you do sense,' he demanded of the healer.

He shook his head and looked back at the women on the other side. 'It is almost like she is protecting herself, but without knowing she is.'

'Is she more concerned about the state of the Empire than she said? Can she sense more magic than I can?'

'I don't feel anything,' Yang said.

The two women laughed, and Remi waited for Lis to turn and smile at him, but she continued to watch the coastline. As they came along towards the dock where they had been dropped on

Third, several people stood and waved, and she waved heartily back. Amongst them was the young woman who had lined up to be chosen. She appeared even younger now, waving from the dock, than she did had day in the line. He looked back to Lis—he had made the right choice.

They remained on the deck watching the world go by. Despite Yang's dislike for the water, he maintained his watch over Lis, and Remi was pleased he had come along. As they passed Second, there were far more people smiling and waving.

'Could it be a side effect of our fight?' he asked Yang quietly.

'She didn't show any signs of it before. And you haven't noticed anything since she returned to the Palace Isle. You have touched her?' he asked softly, the colour again rising to his cheeks.

She had wrapped her arms around him, shielding him from the soldiers. She had even pressed her lips against his before his father. And he had shared some more intimate moments with her, which had started with his running his hand over her bare skin. He felt the heat in his cheeks at the idea.

'Last night,' he murmured.

Yang looked at him expectantly.

'I touched her last night,' he said. Then he looked away, noticing that the smaller boats no longer followed behind them. 'Maybe she is right,' he said as the docks of the Palace Isle came into view. 'Should we check on the Palace Isle?'

'The people of Fourth will wonder why we didn't travel directly to them,' the general commented.

'Are you looking for a detour?' the hunter asked.

Remi shook his head. 'I just want to be sure things are how we left them.'

'Let us worry about getting the rest of the Empire on our side first,' the general said. 'We visit, you talk, you share the phoenix and the people will follow you.'

'I hope it is that easy,' Remi said, looking across at Lis.

20

On reaching Fourth, Remi was surprised that there was no one to welcome them, not even a curious face to see why they had come. Gossip spread quickly through the Empire, and he wondered if it was good or bad news that had reached Fourth ahead of them. They tied up at the dock, and the gangplank was lowered. Advisor Gan was sent down first, although he wasn't as keen this time.

Lis was next, her smile not quite as bright as before, but she was still confident the people would welcome them in some way. The arrow that sailed through the trees towards her was not what Remi was expecting. He wasn't quick enough to throw his flames and consume it, and it bounced harmlessly from her barrier.

'Lucky you had your armour on,' the general said, coming down to stand beside her, his sword drawn.

'I didn't realise I did,' she murmured.

Remi stood beside her, an angry heat trying to burn through his skin. Reaching towards her, he let it take control.

Lis not only didn't react to the heat of his fire, she didn't touch or hold or grab him. The fire burned hotter, and the phoenix remained hidden.

'I think you should try something else now,' the general murmured.

Lis stepped forward as though Remi wasn't burning and

stretched her hand out before her. The ground rumbled and the trees shook. Voices cried out in fear and pain behind the foliage.

As she stepped forward, the general followed her, and Remi's flames died away. But as the general reached out to touch her, she stretched out her hand towards him and he fell back, landing heavily.

'Lis!' Remi called, but she continued towards the trees, as though protecting herself was her only focus. He moved quickly after her and threw his arms around her. But the barrier was still in place, and he too was thrown back.

'She'll kill us all!' someone cried from amongst the trees.

Hui Te-Sze approached Lis from behind with his sword in hand, and Remi's blood ran cold.

'Wait,' he called. But as he climbed to his feet, Yang somehow managed to find the space between them. The hunter, thankfully, pulled back at the last moment. Yang stood with his hands up and his eyes closed.

Lis stepped forward once more and then turned back, looking over the group as though she were lost. Remi scrambled to his feet and then stood still. There was a moment of doubt as to what Lis might do, and then she dropped, Yang only just stopping her from hitting the ground.

Wei-Song rushed forward, but Remi couldn't move. The hunter sheathed his sword, and a soldier helped the general to his feet.

Yang managed to get Lis into his arms, and Wei-Song directed him back to the ship. Remi watched them go and then looked back to the trees.

'That could have gone better,' the general murmured, standing beside him and rubbing at his arm.

Remi could only nod as he followed him back onto the boat. As the last of the soldiers climbed aboard, he looked over the empty dock. 'Take it out to sea,' he said. 'The gods only know what will happen now.'

Lis tried to lie still and listen to the water sloshing against the side of the hull. She felt unsettled, and not just because they were further out on the water than she had ever been from land before. She wasn't sure what had happened when they landed on Fourth, and Remi had been nowhere near her since they had come back on board.

Yang had sat and talked with her for a while, then left only to be replaced by Wei-Song not long after. It appeared as though Lis couldn't be trusted, like she was back in her little palace, sick and not knowing herself what she wanted.

Only she was very sure this time that she didn't want to die.

She closed her eyes and stretched out her senses. They were all back on the boat. She vaguely remembered pushing out with her barrier, but she had no idea whom she had pushed. There had been an arrow. She could remember that. She felt unsettled, scared almost, and that worried her more than what she might have done at the dock.

They had left her alone to rest, but she couldn't, and she searched the ship for those she trusted. Remi had been outside their door for far too long. She could feel the fear ebb from him, and it only heightened her own.

She closed her eyes and tried to remember Remi on the dock, but she couldn't remember where he had been or what he had done. She wondered now if he was scared of her, what she might do to him, and she was taken back to the day in the square when they had nearly killed each other.

The sob surprised her, and she felt even more confused and lost than she had before. Then the door burst open, and he was standing there. She could see other faces behind him, but then he pushed the door closed and had her in his arms.

'You have to let us in,' he murmured. She couldn't quite feel his skin against hers. She wondered if she was dreaming. 'Lis,' he said. 'Can you hear me?' He held her back at arm's length, and she nodded.

'I don't know what you mean,' she said, wiping at her nose.

'You have your barrier up. I can't get at you. Yang can't learn what is going on.'

She shook her head.

'We won't hurt you,' he whispered.

'I know that. I didn't know I had it up.'

She breathed out slowly. She could still sense it, keeping her separated from him, from the world around her. 'Why?' she asked.

He shook his head. 'Can you let it down?'

'I'm trying.'

'I'm worried that the phoenix has done this to you. Maybe you can't take the heat of it. I burned beside you on the dock, and you couldn't even see me or feel the heat. Like you had lost your ability to sense me.'

'I sensed you outside the door. I could feel you on the ship.'

'What do you think it is?' he asked.

She shook her head again. 'Maybe we should return to the emperor, although I don't think he will be happy. I have made a bigger mess of this.'

'What of your father? What of Fifth?'

'Do you think it wise after what we experienced here? They are going to think we are coming to attack them.'

'Then let us sail past Fifth and around to your father.'

'We are supposed to visit the Sacred Isle first.' Lis could hear the whine in her voice. But she didn't know where it had come from. She longed to see her father, and her sister. She gulped down the tears that threatened to run over and nodded mutely.

He pulled her close again. She tried to focus on his skin, the strength of his arms around her, and assure her body she was safe, but the barrier held, although she felt it pull tighter against her skin.

He held her tighter than he had before. She could feel the fear and desperation in the tension of his arms, and again her own fears flared, pushing out the barrier to form a cushion between them.

'Rest. When we get closer, I'll come for you. I think we should stand on the deck together.'

'So that they can pick us off together?'

'It may not be the same as Fourth.'

It felt like only moments later that he was back at the door, indicating it was time to go up to the deck. She was shaky on her legs, but she changed and took his hand, then followed him up into the cool breeze. Wei-Song smiled, and Yang gave her a nod. The general looked a little wary, and she couldn't see the hunter. She could have reached out for him, but she didn't want to experience whatever disappointment he was feeling.

Instead she focused on the shores of Fifth, reminded of the day she had left her little island and sailed towards the Palace Isle for the first time, on what she had thought would be a quick visit but had instead changed her life forever.

There were a few people dotted along the beach. Lis raised her arm as she had done that day, and they waved back. She breathed a sigh of relief. But there were few of them, so she wondered where the other members of the island were and what they were planning. She turned away then, her chest tight and a sick feeling growing in her stomach.

'Lis?' Remi asked, reaching out to take her hand.

'War is coming,' she whispered. 'We can't stop it; we have only fuelled it.'

They sailed out beyond Fifth and then slowly turned around, heading out towards the vast ocean, and for a moment Lis hoped they could continue out that way forever. Then her little island appeared in the distance, and she moved to the front of the ship to watch it grow larger. No one came to join her. No one came near.

21

No one waited on the little pier for them, and it looked more run down than Lis remembered. Had it been so long since she had been home? She felt a moment of fear that the boat wouldn't be able to reach it, but it did, and she remembered just how deep the water was. She closed her eyes, remembering jumping from the end with her sister on hot summer days to her mother's cries of fear.

As she raced down the plank, she again wondered why her father hadn't come, and then she was running along the pier, along the path and standing before the house. Despite her little palace, the house didn't look as big as she remembered it. She had only been back once after she had settled on the Palace Isle, and she was sure it hadn't looked any different from how it did now. It was almost like the house itself was sad.

The field beside the house was awash with flowers yet to open. She half expected to see Peng standing amidst the field. A strange panic filled her chest. She willed the flowers to bloom with barely a glance and headed into the house. Remi followed not far behind.

She found her father in the main room, sitting over a table. He looked half asleep, the room a mess around him, too many empty bottles of rice wine to count.

'Where is Ting?' she asked. 'How could she let you get to this point?' When he looked up with sad eyes, she stopped. 'She was sent home from the island,' she murmured, not thinking about what their sending her away would have done to him. 'What of Peng? Where is he?'

Her father only shook his head. He didn't try to rise or greet her.

'Father?' she said softly, kneeling before his table.

He shook his head again, and when she felt the overwhelming loss sweep over her, she couldn't stop the barrier from pushing out further.

The table he leaned against moved slowly across the floor, and he was pushed back.

'No,' Remi said. When she turned, he stood with his hand out towards the door, and she saw Wei-Song waiting.

'Where is she?' Lis asked, climbing to her feet.

'We sent her home. The child feared for her at the school.'

'Feared for her?' Lis asked.

'That her child would die there and bring trouble to them,' her father half cried, half coughed.

Lis continued to stare at Wei-Song.

'She wasn't clear about what she saw, but she thought that if the child died, Ting would blame you.'

'If the child died? Your little vision girl saw clearly that the child would die, and that was why she sent her away. Did she also see that Ting would go with her?'

Lis felt the ground sway beneath her feet, and then she was sitting on the floor. The world was hazy around her. She looked back at Wei-Song, who shook her head. And then Remi was kneeling on the floor beside her. 'When?' she asked, wondering if her voice worked at all or if she had only asked in her head.

Her father mumbled something that she didn't catch.

'Where is Peng?' she asked.

'Gone,' he slurred, lifting another jug of wine, only it was empty. He threw it across the floor, and then the cup followed it.

'Why would he leave you? Where would he go?'

'To raise an army against the magics who killed his wife.'

Lis shook her head.

'He blames you,' he said, his finger sharp and surprisingly steady as he pointed as Lis.

'I was trying to save her,' she cried.

Remi groaned as the force of the shield hit him, and her father was pushed against the far wall of the room, the table and bottles following him.

'Stop!' the hunter shouted from the doorway.

Lis turned to him, and the hurt crashed in on her. Then Remi was holding her close.

'What has got into her?' the hunter asked.

'She hasn't been herself at all today. She was like this before we reached Fourth. She is protecting herself, but I'm not sure what from. Her barrier is up, and she can't or won't lower it,' Remi said.

'Get Yang to look at her.'

'He has tried, but he can't get close enough.'

Lis couldn't understand what was happening to her, and now she had attacked her father—but her sister was gone, and he was lost, and nothing in the world made sense anymore. When had she died? Why had no one told her? Or had her father been unable to share the news with the world?

She clung to Remi. Nothing made any sense. Her strong father was a mess, looking broken and scared. Had Wei-Song told her what the child had said? But the child no longer saw the world as she had.

It was all because of the phoenix, she was sure. Everything had changed at that point. The visions had stopped, and the emperor had accepted her. The world was confused, and she didn't know where she fit.

She pulled herself into Remi's lap and put her head to his shoulder. He sighed, and she could feel the relief flow from him as he closed his arms around her. And then Yang was there, whispering and calming, and she felt the barrier move. It didn't disappear, but it let the two men into it. She tucked them in and held them safe within her net. Then Yang sat heavily on the floor.

Curiosity filled the little world she had locked them in. He smiled as he took her hand and rested it on his knee to feel her pulse. Worry mixed with the curiosity and her own confusion.

'Breathe,' Yang whispered, and she did.

He nodded once. She pulled the barrier back and then tried to release it. It held tight for a moment longer and then was gone. She knew she could call it back if needed.

'I can sense everything around me, but amplified, as though the owner of the emotions is pushing them onto me.'

Yang nodded, and a small smile lit his face.

'Am I sick?'

He shook his head.

'Will it pass?' Remi asked.

'Not quickly.'

'Yang,' Lis cried, reaching for him. 'What is wrong with me?'

'You are with child,' he said. 'An extremely strong magical child. That explains the barrier, I hope, and why you feel as you do.'

'Confused,' she murmured. She had only just become a wife. Was she ready to be a mother as well?

Her father clambered to his feet and staggered. 'General,' Lis called. 'Would you see my father to the boat? I don't think he should stay here any longer.'

'Don't worry, Lis,' her father slurred as the general reached for him. 'I will protect you.'

She nodded and then curled back into Remi's arms.

22

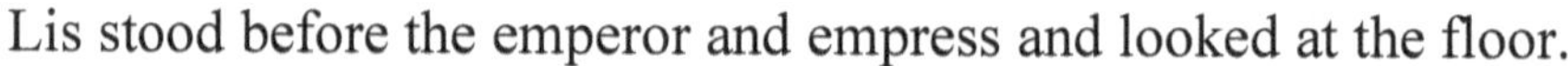

Lis stood before the emperor and empress and looked at the floor.

'It wasn't an attack,' Remi said, again.

'You were supposed to be helping the people, finding out what they want, bringing this Empire back together. Instead you land on Fourth and attack the people. They will side with the magics whether they want to or not, just to remove us.'

The general sighed.

'It is my fault,' Lis said.

'She isn't well,' Yang said, and she felt the frustration flow from Remi. Mixed with the anger of the emperor and the disappointment of the empress, it was overwhelming. Lis wanted only to sit down.

Advisor Gan was surprisingly quiet, and Lis wondered whose side he would take. She watched him for a moment, then bowed low before the emperor again. 'Forgive me, Your Eminence,' she said, 'but I need to rest.'

'Do you feel unwell?' Remi asked, leaning over her.

'I don't feel myself,' she admitted, her head pounding. 'I'll go back to the laundry.' She climbed to her feet, feeling more unsteady.

'I think we could find something more suitable,' the empress said, stepping forward.

Lis took a step back. She didn't know what she might do in her current state, and she didn't want to risk the empress. 'It is suitable.' She bowed again and then headed out of the room.

Remi jogged after her.

'You need to talk with your father,' she said. She turned her hand, and the pins that had held her hair so tight against her head appeared in her hand. She handed them to Remi and ran her fingers through her hair. 'I just need to be away from people.'

'Away?' he asked, pulling her to a stop.

'I feel everything,' she said. 'It confuses my senses, and I'm worried what I might do with it.'

'And your father?'

'I'm not ready to see him yet.' She shivered at the idea of the turmoil of emotions he would radiate.

He nodded slowly and kissed her forehead. 'I'll find someone to take you back.'

'I can find the way.'

'Not on your own. There may be magics waiting for an opportunity…'

'Just let them try,' she said. 'I have been taking down those I care for; imagine what I could do to those who threaten me.'

A guard appeared from the doorway and bowed low. 'I can ensure she makes it back to the laundry safely.'

Lis tried not to sigh as Remi nodded. He watched as she walked out into the morning sunshine, the guard a few steps behind. She could feel Remi's concern follow her, and she wondered how long this was going to last. If something did happen, such as an attack from the magics, she wasn't going to be able to defend anyone; she would be too overwhelmed by the emotions of those around her. If she could find a way to channel them back again, that would be useful.

The silence of the island was comforting, and she felt far more like herself when she made it back to the laundry. Although she could feel her father's sadness, it was lessened, and she imagined he must be sleeping in one of the small rooms. The guard bowed and then returned the way they had come.

The sheets had finally been taken down, and she could smell hot broth. Yang sat cross-legged in the dirt over a small fire with a sturdy pot. He projected a calmness that she hadn't felt in some time as she walked across to join him.

'That smells nice,' she said, sitting on the edge of the step that led to the covered walkway.

'I thought it might help you sleep or rest, and it had some effect on your father.'

'He hasn't really allowed himself the time to grieve,' she said softly. It was not so long ago that he had lost her mother, and then Ting along with her child. 'The child came early,' Lis said.

Yang nodded as he stirred the soup. 'How do you feel?' he asked.

'I hurt,' she murmured, 'but I'm too overwhelmed with everyone else to focus on myself, and I'm not sure that I should. I fear what might happen.'

'Your barrier?'

'Or worse. What if I attack those around me?'

'I'm sure you will be fine,' he said.

'You don't know that,' she said, more harshly than he intended.

'Your body is adjusting. It is all very new at this stage, and once you have had the chance to settle into your condition, things may be different.'

'Maybe. What do we know of other magics with children? Surely, they had them, or we wouldn't have the magics we have now. But did they all lose control?'

'Maybe it is the child.'

'Can you tell if the child is a boy?'

'Does it matter?' Yang asked.

Lis stared at him. 'Of course, it matters. The eldest child of the

Rei-Een Empire is always a boy.'

'Is it? We know what they do when they don't feel the child is what they want. Look at Wei-Song—do you think she would have been allowed to live if she were the eldest, magic or not?'

'Do you think they kept the magic secret before now if it was born into the royal line?'

Yang shrugged and refocused on the pot before him.

'Remi said there was no magic in the royal line. But he has it. This child may have it.'

'I certainly felt something.'

'Yang,' Lis said softly. 'What if it was me you felt? Can you tell if it is a boy?'

He looked up at her seriously. 'It is too early to tell such things.'

'Then how can you be sure the magic is so strong?'

He put down the spoon. 'I can.'

'But you couldn't get close enough before. Look again, please, and see what this child is.'

He put his hand on her arm and closed his eyes. She watched his brow furrow.

'Tell me,' she whispered.

'I'm not sure,' he said slowly. 'I can't sense the magic at all.'

'So, it was mine.'

'You sound relieved,' he said, moving back to his pot.

'Actually, I think it would be nice to work magic together, see what the child can do. My parents lived in fear of capture, and although they let me play with my skills, they never encouraged me to test them or see just what I could do. They never taught me what I could be. I had to learn on my own, in the midst of battle. I don't want that for my child.'

'I'm sorry,' her father said, leaning against the doorframe of his room. 'We couldn't encourage you. If the hunters sensed you, they may have traced you and killed you at any stage. I spent half my life watching for them.'

'They couldn't sense me,' she said.

'We didn't know that. We didn't know what you were.'

'I was happy,' she said softly.

'But it wasn't enough,' he said, taking a shaky step forward and sitting heavily. 'And now you are more lost than before.'

'Now I am more a danger to the Empire than its chance to save it.'

'You saved the prince,' he said.

'I nearly killed him,' she returned. She was so sure that she had, and she didn't know what she could do to make it better.

Yang held out a bowl of broth, which she took without hesitation to sip at. It was hot and good, and it helped calm the turmoil that burned within her. They sat in silence for some time. Lis could feel their uncertainty, but she tried not to focus on it. She wondered how Remi's discussions were going with his parents. It had been his mother's idea for them to marry early, and Lis wondered if she regretted it already. The empress had been such a stern, cold woman when Lis had first entered the hidden palace. She hadn't wanted Lis at all, yet it had been her choice.

It was the loss of her son and the confusion that followed that Lis thought was the reason behind it. And as much as she had cared for U'Shi, she had accepted Lis for who she was without question. Lis wondered if they would still be as accepting if they ended up in a war again, and because she was too overwhelmed by fear to know what she was doing.

She stood slowly and headed into the big room. She nestled down within the blankets and closed her eyes. Another war was coming. She could feel it, but there was nothing she could do to stop it, for she feared she was the catalyst.

She was sorry they hadn't been able to visit Fifth. It was the one place she had known, and she wanted to revisit the temples and families that she knew. She wondered if Peng and his family would have spoken to her, or if he would have openly blamed her for her sister's death.

Lis had only wanted to keep her safe, and safe from Peng. He had smiled and laughed when she played her magic tricks, opening flowers and creating little paths amongst the stems. Would that have changed if they had married? Would he have looked at her differently if he had seen what she could really do?

Her head pounded, and she tried to think about her child and the joy the news would bring. She wondered if Remi had told his parents. There were enough who knew the truth, such as those who had been inside her father's house when Yang had discovered the reason behind her odd behaviour. Was the child trying to protect itself, or was it her body knowing the danger they were in?

She imagined Remi's arms tight around her, holding her close as he did so often. Despite what they had done to each other in the past, and the fear he held for her safety, it was only love and acceptance she felt from him. There had always been something comfortable between them—from that first time when she had been lost, sunburned on a cot in a prison cell, and he had held her as though it was the only thing to do; to when she had wanted to die, allowing the rot to take her body, and he had pressed himself against her in the night, willing her to live.

She smiled at the idea, running her hand across her stomach. She had been so sure she would never be able to have a child of her own. And now she had one turning her world upside down. She could only hope this little heir of the Empire would have an empire left to rule over.

She blew out a soft breath. She could feel the sun shining through the doorway of the large room, despite her closed eyes. She just needed rest, and she would be able to better control her emotions.

Just as she started to drift, she thought she felt something else, a stab of anger and curiosity, and then nothing.

Lis dreamed of Remi. He was leaning over her, his hair loose about his face, his smile relaxed, his shoulders bare, fire dancing behind his eyes. He burned, the flames dancing over his skin. She waited for the phoenix to show itself, but it didn't. He burned hotter, and then the world around them burned. He cried out for her, but there was nothing she could do. His skin bubbled and split, and he screamed.

Lis sat up quickly, her throat dry as though she had screamed with him, his slow death still too vivid in her mind. It was dark, and she wondered how long she had slept. The ground was hard beneath her, and she ran her hand over the rough wood. When the sound of water sloshed against it, she wished for the gift of fire. Above her, slim slits of light marked out the boards above her. Footsteps moved back and forth as the wood creaked, but there were no voices. She reached out, but she couldn't sense how many were on the boat with her, and she couldn't feel any emotions either.

She put her hand to her head. It ached as though she had been hit, but there were no bumps or cuts that she could find. She wondered how long until she learnt who had taken her and what they wanted.

23

Remi tried to maintain his calm and keep the fire at bay. The conversation with his parents had gone around in circles. The emperor was clearly worried for what might happen next, and although Remi reassured him, he had the same fear.

'What do you propose we do next?' he asked the emperor.

'You have formed some allies, allowed the people to see who you are and what you are prepared to do for your Empire. I think it worthwhile that you attempt to continue your tour. Start with Fifth and try a different route to Fourth. Other islands were willing to greet you. I wonder why they were so keen to attack.'

'It may be that they feared what he was,' Advisor Gan said quietly.

The emperor drew in a breath, but Remi stepped forward. 'He is right,' he said, 'and the princess was not herself.'

'Ensure she knows how to behave and head back out tomorrow,' the emperor said.

'She knows full well how to behave,' the empress said before Remi could leap to her defence. 'There must have been something particular for her to act that way.'

Remi glanced at the advisor. He wasn't ready to announce the child to his parents yet. He wasn't quite sure what it meant, nor what it could mean for Lis going forward, and he would rather she had the time to come to terms with it before his mother started fussing. He was fairly certain she wouldn't let Lis leave the island again if they knew the truth.

'What of the phoenix?' his father asked. 'How did they react to that?'

'We didn't get the chance to use it.'

Advisor Gan gave him a sideways glance. Remi waited, but the man said nothing. Was he on their side, or was he saving up the knowledge to use against them at a later date?

'General Long?' the emperor asked. 'How is my old friend?'

'Not what he was,' Remi admitted. 'I think with some time, he will be himself again.'

The emperor nodded.

The small group bowed and left the throne room. As soon as they hit the sunshine, Remi noticed two of Lis's guards walking by the bottom of the steps. He hadn't sent anyone with her, since she was always so sure she could look after herself, but a guard had walked with her back to the laundry.

'Is someone watching over her?' he called after them, and they looked back at him with some confusion. Remi took the stairs two at a time to reach them.

'The princess is with you,' one of them said, looking around Remi and up the steps.

'We left her with you,' the other one said.

'She can be somewhat persuasive,' Remi admitted. 'She headed back to the laundry, but a guard followed.'

They glanced at each other before bowing as one, then followed him towards the laundry. He looked about the silent streets, wondering if the city would ever be what it had been before. Not that it had been as active as he'd heard it had been before the war. Fear had driven them away, fear of being caught or suspected of magic, and fear of the magics themselves. Remi had done nothing of late to help that, only to make it worse.

It was then that he realised the advisor had not joined them. The soldiers ahead of him broke into a run, and he rounded the corner to find Yang sprawled in the dirt, a pot of something he had been cooking knocked over and spilled out across the ground beside him. A bloody gash marred the side of his head. General Long was similarly positioned, as though he had stepped forward and then been knocked from behind. His face in the dirt, a mat of brown crust hardening in his hair.

Remi felt instantly sick, and he wasn't sure how he made his limbs move to stand in the doorway of the large chamber they had been sleeping in. Movement had stopped in the yard behind him.

'Go for the general and Hui Te-Sze,' he said, then pushed the door open.

The room was dim, even in the sunshine, and he formed a large flame in his hand. He needed to see, but he was so scared of what he might find.

The room appeared to be just as it had been, the sleeping mat spread out on the floor, the cover thrown back as though she had just stood up. The table was bare and untouched. Other than the fire marks along the walls and platform from his own loss of control, there was nothing to indicate there had been a fight. He wondered for a moment if she had willingly left with whoever had come. But he returned to the doorway and watched as a guard carefully helped Yang to sit up. She would not have willingly done anything for someone who had hurt Yang.

'Lis,' Yang murmured, and then he was fighting against the soldier trying to help him. 'Where is she?' he scrambled to his feet, but he leaned heavily on the soldier, and he stumbled as he tried to walk.

Remi stepped forward, took the man by the shoulders and lowered him back to the ground. 'Go for a healer,' he directed the soldier.

'I am a healer,' Yang said. 'Where is she?'

Remi shook his head. 'Gone.'

'No, she was sleeping.'

Remi kept a hold of him to stop him from trying to get up again. 'What happened?'

'I don't know. We had broth, I checked her over, we talked a little, she went to rest. Then I was being helped out of the dirt... I should have been more careful.'

'This isn't your fault.'

'She is scared,' he said, leaning in closer to Remi. 'She doesn't know what this child might do to her, and she is worried.'

Remi shook his head. 'She hasn't been herself. If the child has magic...'

'I don't know that it does,' Yang said, putting his hand to his head and flinching before looking at his hand and the blood there.

'You said it was powerful.'

'That might have been Lis protecting it. I couldn't sense any magic in the child today.'

Remi nodded and looked across at General Long. It appeared that he too had been taken unawares. He stood up quickly, releasing his hold on Yang, and he nearly fell back in the dirt. 'Come with me,' Remi said to a group of soldiers standing by the doorway.

'Where are you going?'

'I know where they were hiding,' he said.

'You can't take them on yourself. Wait for the general. Wait for the hunter,' Yang called after him.

'It might be too late,' he said, running from the compound as the soldiers followed behind. There were other soldiers around the Palace Isle, and he might meet up with more of them. He ran with everything he had. They couldn't be too far ahead of him—she had only left him within the hour, he thought. His father had talked in circles for so long. Remi still wasn't sure if the man trusted him or blamed him, but either way he was expecting Remi to fix the problems of the Empire.

They ran down the long street towards the gate he had once melted shut and pushed through it with no effort. The soldiers piled into the courtyard behind him. They waited, but there was no sign of life within the space, as though no one had used it in hundreds of years. He wondered how that could be. He stepped forward slowly. There wasn't even the mark from where Lis had created her cage of flowers to get his attention on the wall. He looked up but saw nothing.

He raced through the black gate, his heart pounding. It looked just as it had that first night, the dust and cobwebs heavy. There was no one in the dormitory where he had spent long recovering from his fight with Lis. The water in the pond looked just as black, and the cobwebs around the gazebo nearly stopped him entering.

He pushed open the door to the room with the faces, but there was nothing there. He pushed open the next and the next, and again they looked as they had when he had first found them. He stepped inside the room, and the image of Lis smiled down on him. He was sure it looked different, as though angled differently from when he had first found it.

What had happened to his world? It wasn't anything like he had thought it was. Although he had loved her from the moment he had seen her, there was a time when he would have killed Lis. Fearing what she was and what she might do to him. What she had done to him. And now they were more closely linked than ever before, but he had no idea where she was.

'Could the child be Hidden?'

'Sire?' a soldier asked at the door.

'Is that why Yang could sense magic and then not?'

'Healer Yang is Hidden; he can sense them.'

Remi nodded acknowledgment. Nothing in his world made any sense at all, and it wouldn't until he found Lis.

'They aren't on the island,' Remi said.

'The magics?'

He nodded. 'Get on the wall and find out if any boats have recently left. Now!' he cried, and the man bolted. He walked back along a gravel path he could barely make out amongst the weeds and past the black gate. The silver characters sparkled in the sunlight. Remi stopped and ran his hands over them.

'The phoenix returns' they said, and as he brushed his hand over them, they shifted beneath his fingers. 'Save them.'

'Gather every man you can,' he called to the nearest soldier, 'and get to the dock. As soon as we know where they were headed, we will be close behind.'

24

Lis squinted into the light as she was led onto the deck of the boat. There was nothing around them but water, and despite her recent trouble with her barrier, she couldn't seem to muster any magic at all. She blew out a soft breath and felt a tingle in her fingertips. But it was gone as soon as it had formed.

'That won't work,' a voice behind her said. A familiar voice, although the hatred laced in it was something new.

'Wu Peng,' she said softly without turning. 'I see that you abandoned my father as well as your wife.'

'My wife died,' he spat, grabbing her roughly by the arm and spinning her around, 'and it is your fault. Filling her with magic and the like.'

'I think you filled her with magic,' she said. 'You married her; you created the child growing inside her. It was the child who took her away. It had nothing to do with magic.'

He spat in her face. The action was so unexpected, she wasn't prepared for it. She wanted to step back, but he still held her tight. She wiped her face with her sleeve. She had a sudden urge to throw up, unsure how she managed to hold it in.

'I am a lot stronger than I was when I opened blossoms for you,' Lis said.

'Not now,' another man said, and she turned to him as he

reached for her. She was trapped by Peng's strong hold. It wasn't allowing her any chance to move away from these people. The man tapped something on her chest, and she looked down to find a bag hanging around her neck. A small cloud of spices hit her nostrils, and she sneezed.

At least she couldn't sense their emotions, but she wondered just what they wanted from her. Looking at Peng, it was clear he wanted revenge.

'You have fallen a long way,' he said.

She blinked back the stinging tears caused by the cloud of spices and longed for a breeze. 'I am the crown princess of the Empire of Rei-Een,' Lis said.

'I thought she was the hidden princess,' one of the others said, and Peng hushed him.

'You are nothing but a concubine. The prince and the royal family know you are not worth the title of princess. He has taken advantage of you, and you have let him. Pretending to push out the magics when you were fighting them together.'

'Taken advantage?'

One of the men sniggered, and she turned on him.

'We heard the stories of his visiting your bed. That is what princes do with concubines.'

'He never took advantage,' Lis said. 'He just watched over me.'

'He watched something,' one of the others said, and the rest joined in the laughter.

Lis sighed. She had no idea the Empire spoke of their relationship, but then he had never done as he should when she had been hidden, and that was his own doing. She had never asked anything of him. But she was grateful all the same that they had been given the chance to get to know each other. If she hadn't, she might not have realised how much she cared for him and had needed to return to him, and the Empire might have been lost.

'Whatever you may think, we are wed now.'

'I don't think so,' said the man who had laughed.

'I was presented to the people. We have been touring.' She hoped she didn't sound as desperate as she thought she did.

'It is a ploy. I wonder that the emperor would have allowed a son of his to live with magic, but then it may be that the emperor has no choice.'

'The emperor may be dead,' another said.

'It would be easy enough for you to see for yourself,' she said.

'The Palace Isle is crawling with magics; it isn't somewhere anyone in the empire wishes to visit.'

It had been abandoned since the fighting, and Lis realised that no one was returning. The ministers had more or less been saying the same thing as these men.

'We want the world to be as it was,' she said.

'It can't be,' Peng snapped.

'Where are we going?' she asked, looking out across the water. A ship this big would be seen, and they didn't seem to worry that she was visible to anyone else, although there were no other boats around. She wondered how long it would be until Remi realised she had been taken. The ocean was a large expanse; the Empire was just a small part of the world in the middle of it. They could be anywhere, and it could take weeks or more for Remi to discover where she was.

She pulled at the bag around her neck, but it had been stitched into her clothes. And the more she tugged at it, the more the spicy dust filled her nose. She gave up and let it go. She tried to will her clothes to change, but they wouldn't. She spun slowly on the spot, and again nothing happened.

Several of the men around her started to laugh. She tried to push out with her barrier, but there was nothing—no protection, no magic. She balled her hands into fists to stop them reaching for her stomach. The last thing she needed was for these men to guess that she was with child.

She looked over the railing at the churning choppy water. Perhaps the water could wash the spices from her senses. But as she leant forward, a strong hand closed around her arm again.

'I need you,' Peng said, his voice dark and cruel. 'You are the best bargaining chip I have.'

'Are you working with the magics?' Lis asked.

'I am negotiating,' he said with a grin, his hand tightening its grip. 'We will leave them alone if they leave us alone.'

'They won't,' Lis said.

He pulled her closer, and she tried to lean away from him, his breath hot on her face. 'I am in control now. I have the power to render them helpless.'

'Where did the spices come from?' she asked.

'You can't win,' he snapped, pushing her away. She gripped at the railing to prevent herself from falling.

An island glistened in the distance. There was something familiar about it as they drew closer. It was a small island, like the one she had grown up on, only there were no flowers and no dock, and she wondered if anyone had visited it before.

Remi stared as Advisor Gan clambered up the gangway to the ship. He shook his head and kept moving. Yang and General Long had stayed behind, and as much as he had wanted to bring Wei-Song with him, he'd insisted that she stay with Yang.

'You don't know where you are looking,' she had said.

And he didn't. A boat had been seen, but it had headed straight out to sea. It could have then sailed in any direction, or it might have kept going. All Remi felt was a steady rhythm of panic. For both Lis and the child. She had been so strong, so determined to keep them safe that she had pushed everyone else away without even realising she had done so.

How then, in the name of all the gods, had they managed to take her without incident? Other than the injuries to Yang and the general—but he was sure that had just been to keep them quiet.

The magics had disappeared completely, and he could only assume it was the only way they could get what they wanted: removing Lis from the equation. He felt sick at the idea of it, and he leaned heavily on the rail.

'If they wanted to leave her as a message to you, we would have found her body,' the general said. As Remi turned on him, he held his hands up in defence. 'I am saying she is alive and that they need her that way. My only hope is that they don't realise she is with child.'

'What if she pushes against them as she did with us?'

'Then they would never have got her out of the laundry. Maybe they drugged her, or knocked her out. Either way, our main concern is to get her back.'

Remi watched the water wash past the boat, but no matter which way they looked or how fast they travelled, they couldn't find any sign of the magics or Lis. There were moments when he thought he saw something in the water. He wondered if they might not have brought her far out to sea to kill her and keep him busy looking while they took control.

He looked back towards the Empire. Was he putting the world in more danger by chasing after Lis?

'What of the Crescent Isles?' the hunter asked.

'They aren't going to take her to anywhere we might have found them before.'

'Where could that be?'

Remi shrugged.

'What if the magics are not the ones who took her?' Advisor Gan asked.

He looked at the little man closely for a minute.

'The ministers are not that stupid,' Gan murmured, looking out across the water. 'Although they aren't as bright as the Empire thinks they are.'

'Who would have her then?' Remi asked.

'Those against magic,' Gan offered.

'Peng,' Remi muttered.

'He would know how strong she was,' the general offered. 'He knew her before. Why would he take her and how?'

'Could he have coerced her into going with him?' Advisor Gan asked.

Remi shook his head. There was nothing between them now, and she was angry that he hadn't accepted her sister and her child as he should have. Although Remi was sure the man was angrier at the death of them than Lis could understand.

A light misty rain started to fall, and their vision across the sea diminished.

'There is nothing out here,' Gan called above the wind.

'Turn west,' Remi directed.

'What is to the west?' Gan asked.

'The Sacred Isle,' Remi said. Someone in the Empire must have answers.

There were far more priestesses on the shores of the Sacred Isles than Remi had thought existed in the whole of the Empire, and he wondered if every priestess had returned.

Amongst the white, he saw no pilgrims. As the boat touched against the dock, every face turned towards them.

He took a deep breath and instructed the men to push out the plank. Then he walked down into the white. No one came forward to greet him or announce themselves as the high priestess, and he turned back to the boat. Advisor Gan gave him a not-so-subtle wave into the crowd.

'Priestess,' he nodded to the nearest one, and she stepped back. He worked his way through the crowd towards the nearest temple, nodding acknowledgement to each priestess he passed. They all stepped back out of the way, forming an open walkway through to the temple.

Once inside, it was empty and silent. He moved directly to

Goddess Aga and knelt before her. She had chosen him to be a member of this family, after all, and in a way the heir to the throne. He had briefly thought himself worthy, but in losing Lis he was no longer sure. Another test, another barrier.

He tried not to sigh as he stood. He noticed an older priestess standing beside him, her head bowed. 'Are you the high priestess?' he asked.

'We do not currently have one,' she said, her voice soft yet firm, and there was something familiar in it.

'Do I know you?'

She shook her head. 'I knew your father,' she said. She knelt before Remi, and he stared at her. 'I saw your brother's death,' she said. 'Long before your father was man enough to father him. I warned him of what the magic would do.'

'You caused him to turn on the magics.'

She shook her head. 'I only warned him of what they might become. I fear at the first sign of trouble, he took it upon himself to end it before it could start.'

'By killing every one of them to save Ta-Sho.'

She nodded once.

'But it didn't. In a way, it caused his death.'

'I am sorry,' she said. 'You were always meant to be Emperor. I didn't see that then. I was only a child, and I didn't understand what sharing the vision would do.'

'And now?' he asked. 'What do you see now?'

She shook her head and turned to the goddess.

'You fear I will misinterpret your vision.'

'There are no more visions. There have been none since you and the princess created the way out of this.'

'The phoenix? We didn't create it; it was there. Lis said she saw it when we stood against each other. But somehow it works together with us.'

'I cannot answer your questions. I don't know the answers, I haven't seen them, and there is no one now who sees what is to come.'

'Why was a high priestess not selected?'

She shook her head. 'I fear it is a sign of what is to come. The gods have granted us so much, and now they choose not to.' She reached for the stone of the goddess before her but stopped short. 'Not all questions can be answered, and it may be in some distant time that we return to what we were.'

He bowed his head in acknowledgement of what she had said. As she turned to leave, he reached out suddenly and grabbed her robes. She turned slowly and smiled at him as though he were a boy.

'I don't know where she is. Yet there may be a way for you to find her. Come,' she said, leading him through a back room and out into a narrow street.

He followed her through the labyrinth of laneways, not seeing anyone else along the way, and then they moved through a gate into a small green courtyard. He immediately thought of Lis when he saw the thick green grass and tall bright flowers that grew against the walls. He could imagine her standing here, her eyes closed, feet bare, arms outstretched and enjoying the sun.

'Has she been here?' he asked.

The priestess shook her head. 'Come,' she said again, leading him through the garden, and he stopped at a black gate. It was bright and smooth as though recently lacquered, and he ran his fingers over the surface. The same characters appeared that he had seen at the hidden princess compound. 'Save them.'

He sighed. 'Where are they?' he whispered to the wood.

The characters changed, and he stepped back. 'Only you will know,' they read.

'Find her,' the priestess whispered. 'You must find her for the world to be as it should.'

25

Lis walked across the dead, dry grass of the island and wondered just what they were going to make her do. The wind blew around her, and as much as she hoped it would blow the spices away, it only seemed to make them worse. They clung to her or were somehow magicked to remain with her.

'How did you do this?' she demanded.

No one answered her, other than someone jabbing her in the back to get her walking faster. She still wore the heavy navy outfit that marked her as a royal, and she wondered why no one had taken that into account when they'd called her a liar for being married.

She could remember the horror on Remi's face when she had mentioned other options for him. That was a time when she had thought they would never end as he'd originally hoped they would. She had been so sure she would die then, that there was no future for her at all let alone with Remi. Now she was so relieved that they had not only survived but made that promise to each other. She only hoped she could protect the child in the same way.

The island was long and flat, and she wondered if anyone else knew it was out here. She remembered the maps from when she had first entered the hidden princess palace, the small dots out from the main islands of the Empire. Her family had lived on one such apparently insignificant dot on that map, and it was only now that she thought of the others. Were there other families living in isolation from the Empire? And could it be for reasons similar to her own family's isolation?

The wind continued to blow, and Lis longed for shelter. There was something ahead of them, and it took several more steps before she recognised it as the ruin of a building. The wood had rotted away, and there was very little evidence left to show what the building had been or who might have lived in it.

Another jab to the centre of her back kept her moving, and she lifted her skirt so that she wouldn't trip in the soft sand. They were already too far from the water, and Lis wished she had been quicker to jump in when she had the chance, but Peng had maintained a tight hold on her. She could feel the bruises forming where his fingers had pressed too hard into her skin. She glanced at him now, walking a little behind her. Despite no one being around, he had his hand on his sword.

She wondered if he would consider killing her. What had she seen in him for all those years? She had nearly married him, and if she hadn't been selected by the prince, she would have. Again, Remi had saved her, and she hadn't realised just how much until that moment.

Ahead of them was a sand dune. She slipped as she was directed over it, and one of the men had her back on her feet and moving before she had a chance to even reach the ground. With a fist full of sand, she might have a chance to get away. But she wasn't given an opportunity to grab any.

As they slid down the other side of the sand dune, she was surprised by the lack of wind. Cut deeper into the island was a small compound. High fences kept the sand back, and several buildings filled the space. The man with her pounded on the fence, and a gate opened. He pushed her through and then followed. The man held the gate open and pointed to one of the buildings, and then she was led to it.

The compound contained several buildings, but the one she was being pushed towards was small and sat up off the ground on round logs. The man's sharp fingers in her back directed her up the steps and through the squeaking door.

Before she could ask him anything, the door was shut behind her, and she felt like she was back in the hull of the boat. She was thankfully out of the wind, but her ears still buzzed from the journey across the sand. The gaps between the boards allowed the cool air in and only a little light. There were no windows, and although she hadn't heard a bolt, she was sure she wouldn't be able to get out very easily. She crawled forward across the boards, cringing at the sound of her skirt snagging in something, and then her hand caught on something sharp. She carefully felt across her palm and found a long splinter poking through. She pulled it out with a squeal. If only it had been something she could use.

A blanket was balled up in the corner, old and dusty and damp. She could smell the mildew and realised just how small this building was. She pulled it around her shoulders. It wasn't ideal, but it could keep her a little warmer when the temperature dropped during the night.

Lis woke to the sound of arguing. She strained to hear what was being said, but she couldn't tell. Nor could she tell who was doing the arguing. She tried to remain still as the sound drew closer.

'You can't be serious?' one voice said.

'I am. We know what they want, and we can help them get it.'

'They'll kill us.'

'Not if we help them.'

'They don't need our help. They can take on the Empire on their own. There is nothing to stop them now.'

'What about the prince?'

'He was on their side. He fought with them.'

'He is not fighting with them now; he is out searching the Empire trying to work out where his princess went.'

'You said he didn't care about her. That she was just a woman he bedded.'

'She is more than that. She was always more than that.'

Peng, she realised. What did he think he could get? The other man was right—the magics wouldn't give them anything. If they thought they could negotiate, they would all end up dead. Lis included.

'Why did you marry her sister when it was the magic you wanted?' the other man asked.

But the crack and thud that followed suggested he didn't get the chance to answer. Was it power he wanted, and was he hiding amongst these men to get it?

A sickening chill ran over Lis, and she only hoped he didn't think he could use her in his plan. Yet he had some idea of using her, and that was why they had taken her in the first place. She wondered then if he had been on Fourth the day she had lost control. He hadn't seen the phoenix, or what she and Remi could be together. She wondered if they could be that again.

The door banged open and the lantern was bright. Although she couldn't see his face, she knew it was Peng.

'You heard that then?' he said, his voice heavy with hate.

She shook her head. Had he always been this man? she wondered. Had he always been something other than what he pretended to be? He pushed the door shut, and Lis heard the bolt then. If only she had known it was there in the first place, she might have been better able to protect herself.

He sat the lantern down, and the room glowed oddly. Despite the light, it still looked grey. She tried to shuffle back against the wall, but she was nearly already there. And given the size of the room, there was nowhere for her to go to get around him. She rubbed at her arm where it was already tender from the firm hold he'd had on her earlier.

When he squatted down before her, she no longer recognised him. This man might have used Peng's name, but he didn't even look like him.

'You are going to give me what I need to rule the Empire,' he hissed.

She shook her head and he leaned forward, just enough to be able to run a finger down her face. She slapped his hand away. 'You were always more beautiful than your sister,' he whispered, and her skin crawled. 'She was only too happy to take me as her husband, but I had to imagine it was you lying beside me of a night,'

Lis gulped down her rising fear. She tugged at the bag around her neck. The only way to remove it would have been to remove her clothing, for it was sewn too well in. She was suddenly glad she hadn't thought of that previously. But if she had managed to remove it, she might have been better able to escape.

Peng reached forward then and took the pouch in his hand. If he pulled it free, would she regain her powers immediately, or would she have to wait until the dust cleared her nose? The longer he held it, the more spices filled her senses.

'You sent me back,' she whispered, trying to look around him. There was no way out of the building unless he was prepared to let her out.

'You had to go back. You had to win him over.'

Lis shook her head, and then he had her by the throat as he leaned over her. She could feel the weight of him across her, and she worried for the child. There was something else, but her senses were off and she wasn't sure of anything.

He pulled at the blanket, throwing it back towards the door. The musty smell filled the small space as he still pinned her down.

'I can't give you what you want,' she said.

'You will,' he said, pushing her head against the wall. She felt the echo it made, and she thought she could hear someone outside the walls.

'I can't,' she wheezed, finding it harder to breathe as his hand pressed tighter against her throat.

'You gave it to him,' he whispered hoarsely, too close to her face. In the shadow of the lamp, she couldn't tell what he might do. He pressed his lips too firmly to hers, and she struggled, trying to push against him. His hands fumbled in her clothes, ties were pulled, the cold air wrapped around her, and his rough hands ran across her skin. She wanted to vomit.

'I won't give you my magic,' she screamed in his ear. As he sat back, there was a bang on the door, and then another before it gave way, pushing the lamp over. The damp blanket started to smoke and Lis kicked out at him, but he punched out at her face before someone else jumped on him.

26

Chonglin wondered whether this was a good idea. Answering a summons from those who most likely wanted you dead was a good way to end up that way, and he wasn't sure how the magics had been found in the first place for the message to be delivered.

He might be able to get some answers in coming here, he thought as he made his way across the sand. This also seemed like the strangest place to meet. An island in the middle of the Empire, with no cover. If the prince was out looking for them, he would find them without much effort at all. Although Chonglin wondered if the stories he had heard about the prince were true. That he and his princess had married, and then she had disappeared.

The man ahead of him led him over a sand dune and then stopped. A small settlement was nestled out of the wind and sight of anyone passing. There were several small buildings on the edge of the camp, one of which had a man tied to the leg of it, although he seemed to be directing his anger to whoever was inside.

He scowled at Chonglin as he passed. They moved between several other buildings, all built higher off the ground but still out of sight. He wondered if smoke might be a problem, but he hadn't seen any yet.

The man led him into a cottage-sized building, which was airy when he entered. There was no fire, but blankets and furs covered the floor, and he sat where directed. It might have been a mistake coming here alone, but he could burn the place to the ground before any of them could raise a sword.

The man who had escorted him leant forward and blew something from his hand. Chonglin sneezed as the spices filled his senses. 'What is this?' he asked, calling the fire to his palm, only nothing happened.

He tried again.

'A precaution,' the other man said. 'We just want the chance to talk.'

'You want the chance to end us,' Chonglin stammered, unsure how he could take these two on if it came to a fight.

'Please, sit down,' the man said, waving the other man from the room. 'We needed to meet on neutral ground, and this was the only way to make that happen. It will wear off.'

Chonglin nodded acknowledgment and sat back. He had little option now. 'Who are you exactly, and what do you want?'

'I am Li Sho-Ma. I am just a man, a merchant from Fourth. We want the Rei-Een Empire to end. We don't want a return to what was.' He held up his hand again as Chonglin leant forward. 'You can have half of the current empire if you leave us in peace with the other.'

'Do you think it that easy?' Chonglin asked, trying and failing not to laugh at the man.

'It could be.'

Chonglin had only answered the summons to try and get some answers, and so far these people were making less sense than he'd expected. 'What happened to the high priestess?' he asked.

The man cocked his head but said nothing.

'Did you kill her?'

'Why would we kill a priestess?' Li Sho-Ma asked too calmly. 'They all returned to the Sacred Isle, and they can stay there as far as we are concerned.'

Chonglin nodded once. 'And the crown prince and his hidden

princess—they are stronger than you think. Do you really think we can take the Empire from them?'

'We have that in hand,' he said.

Chonglin shook his head. 'She can't be underestimated.'

The man grinned and stood up. 'Let me show you something,' he said, opening the door. Chonglin climbed to his feet and followed. They moved back towards the hut with the man tied to the leg of it, who continued to yell.

He opened the door and then motioned another man forward with a lantern. Chonglin could hear movement inside the small space. As the lantern was passed up and the room lit up, he locked eyes with a bruised and dishevelled princess. He tried again to raise the fire to his hand.

'She is harmless,' the man said.

'They want the magic,' she cried, her throat raw, and he noted one eye was swollen shut. Her clothes were in tatters around her. 'They want to take the magic for themselves,' she rasped.

'Give it to me,' the man beneath them cried out.

'They want the power,' she whispered hoarsely. Whatever was left of her voice was nearly gone. 'Run.'

He backed down the steps and bumped into the man waiting there.

'We want,' Li Sho-Ma said, appearing in the doorway, 'a truce. Continued fighting will only destroy what is left of the Empire. And it is dying already. You know this. You've seen it. The Palace Isle is not what it was, and now there is no one there but soldiers and royals and healers.'

Chonglin looked back at the broken princess. A lone tear ran down her face, and he knew what it had taken for her to try and warn him. 'What happened to her?' he asked.

'We found a way to subdue the magic,' Li Sho-Ma said. 'The spice dust. We have it sewn into her clothing.'

'What is left of it,' Chonglin muttered.

'One of us lost the way,' Li Sho-Ma said, his voice harsh, and he turned to the man tied to the pole. 'He wanted to end this, but really he only wanted her and her power. He will not be a problem.'

Chonglin stared at the man trying to pull himself free, the ropes cutting into his arms, his hate spilling out, and he wondered what else they had done to the woman trapped in the room. 'Kill her and we have a deal,' Chonglin said.

The man tied beneath the house started to laugh, an odd cackle that wouldn't stop.

'We need her to keep the prince from the Palace Isle,' Li Sho-Ma said. 'She stays as she is.'

'She is much stronger than you realise.'

'Not with the dust she isn't. She can't pull any magic, not even a little flower, with that filling her senses.'

Chonglin nodded.

'We mean to show that we are dedicated to this truce.' He waved the other man forward, and he held out a bucket of water. 'This will clear you of the dust.'

Chonglin braced himself as the man threw the water over his face. He blinked back the salty water and then he felt clearer. A small fire sparked in his hand.

'It will take a little time,' Li Sho-Ma said. 'What else could we do to prove our loyalty to the cause?'

Chonglin looked at the mad man who struggled even more.

'We will prove to you that it is not the magic we seek—far from it, only peace.'

'Peace,' Chonglin said, holding out his hand. All he needed was to get off this island and back to his own people so they could decide what to do next. But as they shut the door on the broken princess, he wondered which of them would win the Palace Isle. 'She doesn't need to be alive for the prince to search for her; she only needs to be hard to find.'

The leader of the small group laughed and slapped Chonglin on the shoulder. 'You see,' he said, 'we are working together already.'

Chonglin bowed and followed the other man towards the fence.

'We are working for the same thing,' Li Sho-Ma called after him.

He turned back for the fence and hoped he would find those on his boat just as he had left them. He didn't think that peace or understanding with this man would be what he claimed.

27

Remi stood at the front of the boat and sucked in a deep breath. The hunter beside him did the same.

They had been sitting in the same small area just off the Sacred Isle for a day and a night. They were two of the best hunters in the Empire. Any hint of magic, anywhere within the empire, and they would be able to detect it. But there had been nothing.

Remi tilted his head to the side. 'There,' he whispered.

The hunter nodded once. It was barely anything, a hint of magic rather than any real use of it. He held out his hand in the direction he was sure there might be something. The sails were raised, and the boat sailed forward into the nothing of the ocean. Remi remained where he was well into the night, but he sensed nothing further. He wondered if the magics were deliberately keeping their magic to themselves to prevent being discovered.

As he stood in the dark, he wondered at the people they had met during their tour. How many of them had magic or some other skill they were keeping to themselves for fear of what the Empire might do? What would he have done? Before Lis, before his own magic had flared. Would he have hunted these people down? It seemed more important now to pull them together. To build the Empire back to what it had been. His father appeared to have lost the strength he'd had before, but that didn't mean they would not see the end of this fight together.

The boat knocked against something, and they tipped to the side, Remi lost his footing and hit his shoulder on the railing. There was a general cry from amongst the men.

'Drop anchor,' Remi called. They might be close, or they might be far away. They might even have been sailing in circles. The moonless night wasn't helping them, although the captain assured him the stars were enough. 'Not if we run aground,' Remi muttered. It wouldn't be too long before they would be looking at the rising sun.

He rubbed at his eyes and then his shoulder.

'Get some rest,' Hui Te-Sze said.

Remi nodded, but he didn't move. He didn't want to sleep through a possible sign of where she was.

As the morning light shone across the water, Remi realised they had come up close to some small rocky islands barely big enough to stand on, and it was only luck they hadn't taken out the side of the hull. Ahead of them was a long, flat island of sand. 'Let us see if we can make it to that island,' he said, pointing ahead.

'We might need a moment on dry land to gather our thoughts,' the hunter offered.

'Or we keep looking,' Remi said.

They sailed around the island looking for somewhere to get close enough to shore, and Remi stared across the flat, dry land at a sand dune in the middle. It didn't matter from which angle they approached the island, it was always rising away from them.

'Lower the boat,' he called, standing at the railing as he studied the sand. 'You can wait here,' he called back to the captain.

He was one of the first in the boat and then the first out of it, helping drag it through the shallows and onto the sand.

'What can you see?' Te-Sze asked.

Remi shook his head. 'It doesn't feel right,' he said.

The soldiers were still trying to get out of the boat as he splashed through the water and onto the dry island. It was wider than it looked. He took off running, feeling as though the flat world wasn't changing around them, and then all of a sudden they were standing at the edge of the sand dune.

Despite his instincts to pull his fire to the surface, Remi took his sword and headed up the sand. He stopped at the top, looking down at the little village hidden from the world. There were several grey, weathered, wooden buildings dotted around the area, in no particular order and of various sizes. Someone hung from a rope in the middle of the space, and he almost fell trying to run down the sand dune before he hit the fence. He felt along it, banging, and then a gate swung open.

From this angle, he could only tell it was a man. He threaded his way between the buildings. Then he stopped and looked up, wondering for a moment how they had managed to hoist him so high. And why Remi hadn't seen him from the water.

The hunter stopped beside him.

'Wu Peng,' Remi said. 'But why?'

The hunter shrugged.

'Check every building,' Remi called to the men, and they started carefully checking each building.

Remi pushed open the door of the largest one, but other than furs and blankets there was nothing. No hint of who these people were or what they were doing out here.

'I didn't know anyone lived on these islands,' he admitted to Hui Te-Sze.

'I am starting to wonder if I understand anything of the Empire and its people,' the hunter admitted.

Remi stopped to look at the rope marks burnt into the leg of a small building. He looked back at the hanging man and wondered if he had been held captive. He took the first step and as it creaked, he heard something move inside. When he took another, there was a distinctive shuffle. He pulled his sword and quickly took the remaining steps, then pushed the door open.

His heart broke. Lis sat in the corner, her arms up. 'No Remi,' she cried, but he stepped forward. 'Stop,' she cried, her throat raw. 'It isn't safe.'

He stopped and looked around. She kept her hands out in front of her, but she shook. Her clothes were tattered, and anger flared across his skin.

'What is that smell?' the hunter asked, coming in behind him.

'Spice dust,' she whispered. 'It stops the magic.'

A strange noise filled the cabin, and he realised she was crying. He stepped forward.

'No,' she said, and it caused her obvious pain.

'Ok,' he said, squatting down where he was, his hands out. 'I'm not coming any closer. Where is it?'

She carefully put her hand to her chest and then pulled the material away to expose a mesh bag. 'As soon as you move it, the dust gets everywhere, it burns my eyes and I can't smell or sense anything. I can't put my shield up.'

He nodded slowly, looking over her battered body.

'They will find you,' she said. 'Go.'

'There is no one here,' he said. 'There are all gone.'

She cocked her head to the side. 'Are you sure?'

He nodded.

'I need to get to the water.' She took a shaky step up and leaned against the wall. He noticed her skirts were ripped then, and he wondered just what they had done to her. She swayed and then leaned back against the wall.

He stepped forward, but she waved him away again. 'You don't want this,' she said.

'I'll help,' the hunter said, directing Remi out the door.

'I don't know what this will do to you either,' she whispered.

'Well, if we run into trouble, it is best that the two of you are working to full capacity.'

Lis nodded and leaned into him. Remi backed down the stairs and gave them a wide birth. She looked for a moment at the sand dune as though it would be too hard, then turned back to Remi with a smile. She must have seen Peng behind him, hanging by the neck, but the only movement was the smile slipping from her face before she allowed the hunter to lead her out of the village and across to the water.

Remi followed as close as he dared, but as the wind picked up, he stood further back.

He watched her walk directly into the waves with the hunter, who tried to hold on to her tight despite not wanting to look at her as the material floated away around her. She ducked beneath the waves. Then, sitting in the shallows, she started to remove her clothes. The hunter turned his back. She dipped under the water again and then stood, running her hands through her hair. Remi could see the bruises from this distance, and he only hoped the child had survived.

By the time she reached the sand, he expected her to have created something to wear, but he raced forward, pulling his coat off and wrapping her in it as he had done when she had been attacked in the baths. She leaned into him heavily, and he had her up and in his arms. The soldiers had started to move over the sand dune, and the hunter seemed to be fishing around in the water.

Then he pulled at something and stood with the bag held high.

'Is that a good idea?' Remi asked him.

'I think we should have the healers look at it. See exactly what makes it up and if you need to inhale it. We will keep it locked in a box, or wet.'

Remi nodded once.

'Do you want us to cut him down?' one of the soldiers asked, catching them up.

'No,' Lis murmured, her eyes closed and her head on his shoulder. 'Leave him there.'

'Your Highness.' The man bowed, and they surrounded the group, escorting them back to the boat.

Yang paced back and forth across the laundry space. It was surprisingly long and, despite the distance one way before he turned and headed back in the other, it was quite calming. Although not for Wei-Song, as she screamed at him to stop. He raised a finger to his lips but did as he was bid.

General Long was resting, or at least Yang hoped he was. After they had stopped his supply of rice wine, the man had started to come to terms with what had happened. Despite what Yang had heard about how strong he was, the man had gone to pieces. He had spent the first couple of days crying, but Yang doubted he had given himself time to do that, to grieve properly, despite the fact he had tried to drown himself in rice wine.

Yang had tried to calm him as much as he could, but it was important he face what had occurred. Not that Yang was too keen to face what might have happened to Lis. He put his hand to his head and tried not to wince. The Imperial Healer had looked him over and treated the wound, but there was a bruise across nearly half his face.

Then another bruised and battered face appeared around the edge of the building, and Yang ran towards her. She held up a hand, and he stopped. He bowed low, but he itched to throw his arms around her and ensure she was safe. She walked past him and into the large room they had shared, then closed the door after her.

He looked at the prince, who ran a hand across his face.

'What happened?'

The prince shook his head.

'Is it that bad?'

'I don't know,' he snapped, then pulled himself together. Yang was tempted to take a step back as he saw the angry fire behind the prince's eyes, but he kept his ground. 'She won't say. She won't say anything.'

'I've sent it with two soldiers,' the hunter said, coming into the compound.

'What?' Yang asked.

'They used a spice or herb to keep her magic from working. We have sent it to the healers to learn what it is, but I don't think anyone with magic should get close to it until we know more.'

'Has her magic returned?' Wei-Song asked, standing by the door.

Remi shook his head. 'She was covered in it. It might take days to leave her system.'

'She couldn't lift the barrier?'

Remi shook his head again.

'Hence the bruises,' the hunter whispered.

'The child?'

Remi turned his back then and walked away.

Yang wasn't sure what he could do, but Wei-Song nodded towards the closed door. He took a deep breath and stepped up onto the walkway. She gave him a small smile. He knocked once and then entered.

She sat against the far wall, in a corner out of the light. But she didn't move as he crept closer. He had seen her scared before, but this was something more, like an angry fear, and he almost felt hit in the face with the intensity of it.

'Do you want to talk?'

She shook her head.

'Can I look you over? There seems to be some significant bruises. I'd like to make sure there is nothing more serious.'

She nodded once and used the wall to climb to her feet.

'Come and sit in the light,' he said, reaching out for her. He could feel the hesitation before she took his hand.

'I don't want you to feel the loss of magic if I still have it in my system.'

'Does it work like that?'

'I don't know. I washed it off, and it seemed to help. I felt lighter, like I could sense the world around me again, but I can't use it.'

He nodded. 'Don't push. Let's make sure you are physically well first.'

He looked her over slowly. There were some scratches on her hands, and some serious bruising on her arms as though someone had held her down. The finger marks were still clear. Her face was dark, as though someone had punched her, and one eye was swollen, although she appeared to be able to see from it.

He sighed. 'What did the magics think they would gain from this? It seems somewhat risky—they might have removed their own magic.'

'Not magics,' she whispered.

'Do you know who they were?'

She shook her head.

Lis didn't think she really wanted to know if something else had happened while she had been locked away in that building. She could still taste the spice that had been tied around her neck. The whole idea of it made her sick, not just the taste, but that she could do nothing to protect herself. She shivered again at the thought of Peng and his hands on her body. In some ways, it was a relief to know he was gone. She was sad in a way, but more relieved.

'What can you feel?' she asked Yang, scared more of the answer than the worried look on his face.

'I can feel something, I'm still not sure about the magic, but all is fine.'

She sighed with the relief and then burst into tears.

She leaned on Yang, and he tentatively patted her back, which just made her cry all the more.

She hadn't said anything to Remi on the journey home because she wasn't sure what she could say, what she could do to make any of this better. She hadn't been as safe as she'd thought, and Yang and her father had been hurt.

She pulled back then and looked at him closely. She raised a gentle hand to his face, but she didn't touch him. 'Does it hurt?'

He shook his head, but she could tell he lied.

'How is my father?'

'Suffering more from his loss than the bang to the head.'

Lis nodded slowly. She too had felt her sister's loss, but after spending time with Peng she knew in some ways that Ting was in a better place, and she hated herself for thinking such a thing.

'Is it my fault she died?' she asked.

'No. It sounds as though the child wasn't fully formed, and there was a lot of bleeding. Nothing could have been done for her. No matter where she was.'

Lis nodded once. The girl at the school must have known that, and it was why she had sent her away. Lis didn't think she would have blamed them if her sister had died in their care, but grief is a strange thing.

'I think you should sleep,' Yang said softly, looking around for the bedding.

'I'm not sure I'm ready to face the darkness alone,' Lis admitted. 'I would like to sit in the sun, but I'm not sure I want to be seen.'

'Did you tell him what happened?'

Lis shook her head again. 'I don't want him to be disappointed in me.'

'He would never be disappointed. The moment you are in trouble, he forgets everything else and races to rescue you. You are his everything. Both of you.'

'I don't know that I can live up to that.'

'You chose to be here.'

'I did, and I wouldn't be anywhere else. But what if he is better off with someone else? What if he had chosen someone else?

Someone without magic.'

'Then he wouldn't be happy. Now rest.'

'Would you fetch my guard?'

He nodded and climbed to his feet, leaving the door open. She heard him call to some soldiers, who then appeared before her and bowed.

'Would you mind waiting inside the door?' she asked.

They bowed again and stood to attention.

She allowed Yang to help her into the bed. Although her body ached, it was a relief to lie still and warm. Lis closed her eyes and, knowing that they were safe, she tentatively rested her hand on her stomach. But she couldn't feel anything there, nor could she sense any life yet.

28

Remi stood in the throne room; his hands clenched before him with a nervousness he wasn't sure how to deal with.

'Where was she?' his mother asked.

'On a remote island. We thought nothing was there and…'

'Who took her?' the emperor interrupted. 'Magics? Are they so determined to destroy us?'

'She hasn't said, and it wasn't clear. They used something to hinder her magic, so I'm inclined to believe…'

'Hinder her magic?' the emperor interrupted again.

Remi took a deep breath and nodded once. He worried that with all the tension, he would burst into flames at the slightest provocation, and she wasn't here to stop it. She nearly wasn't here at all, he thought as he clenched his fist tighter.

'There was a death?'

'Wu Peng, her sister's husband. We found him hanging in the middle of the settlement.'

'Why?'

'I don't know,' Remi said through clenched teeth. 'It is isn't clear if he was taken too or if he was somehow involved.'

'Why would he be involved?'

'His wife died…'

'Poor Lis,' the empress said. 'Does she not know what

happened?'

'I think she does. She may not know how to tell me.'

'Does she think you will not support her?' his father asked.

'She might think I will burn them all to the gods.'

His mother chewed her lip. She had seen him lose his temper, and she had reason to fear him. Thankfully, Yang had the skill of no other, and there wasn't even a mark where he had cut her that day. He wondered for the first time whether she had shared his outburst with the emperor.

'The healers are looking over the substance they used. I don't want to replicate it,' Remi said quickly, beating his father to another interruption. 'I want to understand it, and it may be that we can form an antidote.'

'If we could take out the magics,' his father mused.

'You might also take out our best defence.'

'How long until it wears off?'

'I don't know. Lis still seems to be suffering the effects. She rinsed it from her body, but inhaling it seems to do the damage.'

'Do you think she will heal?' his mother asked.

He hoped so. It had taken her so long after he had tried to kill her, and she had been so broken. He only hoped she was more determined to survive now for the child's sake. He opened his mouth to tell his mother the news, but he decided against it. Something may have happened while Lis was locked away that changed things, and he needed to be sure she was safe. That they were both safe.

'Go,' his father said. 'As soon as you have word, return. We need to move on whatever is happening in the Empire as soon as we can.'

'Or there will be no Empire left.'

The emperor nodded once, and Remi turned and left the room.

He hurried across the Palace Isle to Lis. She had needed some space. Although he had sat with her while she had curled up and cried on the journey back from the island, she had almost shut down the moment the boat reached the docks and the soldiers started unloading. He only hoped she had not pushed them away this time.

He rounded the corner into the laundry to find Yang and Wei-Song in quiet conversation. The hunter and the general were sitting near General Long, who sat staring out at the world. Remi could sense the soldiers around the space, but he couldn't see Lis. Although she was possibly resting, he had to see her.

He pushed the door open a crack and came eye to eye with a soldier. The relief was overwhelming, and the man put his finger to his lips. Remi nodded and slipped into the room. Another soldier stood a little further into the room. Both watched the sleeping princess. Remi felt as though he could breathe for the first time that day.

He knelt down beside her and brushed her hair from her face. She murmured something in her sleep. She didn't appear frightened, but he couldn't understand what she said.

He brushed his lips over her forehead and sat back. What would he do if he lost her now? All of this was a risk. They may have to face the magics again, and she had nearly died the last time, although they would be fighting together. He wondered if the phoenix would ever be of use.

He jumped when her soft hand touched the side of his face. Lost in thought, he hadn't noticed her wake.

'We are ok,' she whispered.

He kissed her forehead again, and when he made to kiss her lips, she moved out from beneath him and sat up. She reached for his hands, but before he could say anything she looked to the guards and nodded her head. They bowed low and filed from the room, quietly closing the door behind them.

'Wu Peng was behind this,' she said softly.

'Peng?'

She nodded.

'Because of your sister?'

'I thought so, but he wanted my magic. When we were at the island, he was determined that I could give it to him like I had given you yours.'

'Well, not exactly…' he murmured. 'How was he going to take it?'

She shook her head.

'Did he…?'

'It wasn't what the others wanted. They want a truce with the magics. They see the end of the Empire coming, and they think they can share it. Their spice dust is a way to stop the magics taking control of the whole Empire.'

'They hung him because he wanted what they were fighting against?'

'I think so, but I think it was something the magic said. He wanted me dead.' She swallowed loudly. 'But they wouldn't let him. Peng had become a liability, and I think they were willing to give him up.'

'Who was the magic?'

'I know he was there in the square that day. A fire bearer. He was near you. But I don't know his name. They didn't use names. I didn't know any of the others either.'

'They weren't from Fifth?'

'I think they were at Fourth.'

Remi let out a long sigh. 'We are trying to bring the two sides together, and they are trying to work on a truce without us.'

'They want to rule instead of the emperor. They will split the Empire down the middle.'

'Who gets the Palace Isle?'

'I don't know.'

'It may not be as easy as they think. They may imagine different halves, different solutions, and it will be another war. Only this time they have something to fight the magics with that will level the playing field.'

'The emperor wants to use the dust,' she said.

'He has considered it, but it would do more harm than good.'

'Because of the impact it would have on us?'

'And on the Hidden. We need to find some middle ground. And at the moment, this island is it, as there is no one else here.'

'Could we offer it as refuge, for either side? Both sides?'

'And what will we do if one side tries to take advantage of that?'

Lis sighed. 'We need a vision, an idea of how we can do this. There has been nothing but empty promises and vague ideas.'

'The visions have stopped.'

She waited silently.

'Not just the child Wei-Song knew—all of the visions. In our search for you, we visited the Sacred Isle.'

She clutched his hand.

'I met a priestess who once knew my father. She was the one who told him the magic would kill his son. She told me that when we came together, something shifted.'

'When the phoenix showed itself?'

He nodded. 'All visions ceased. There has not been one since that time. No one is able to tell us what is to come or what we might need to do to make it happen.'

Lis closed her eyes, and a large tear rolled down her cheek. 'Thank the gods,' she whispered.

'I thought you said we needed a vision,' he said.

'But without them, we aren't trying to live up to anything—we aren't trying to be something the people want. We can be what we think we need to be. What we can be.'

29

Remi and Lis stood before the emperor and empress, trying to stay focused on why they were there. The ministers stood to the side, their neat rows giving the indication of attentiveness and obedience, and yet their quiet murmuring showed that they were anything but obedient.

'You can't seriously bring a whole group of magics onto the island,' the emperor said.

'We need to work together,' Remi said.

The ministers glared at him as though he should be locked away somewhere, and the emperor sighed.

'We are strong enough without their help,' another said.

'Are we?' the emperor asked. 'We couldn't stand against them last time. Perhaps it is better to find a truce.'

'They will demand land and resources,' a third minister said, 'which we cannot give.'

Remi wondered just how much land they already had. So much of the Empire was empty, sitting vacant since the magic war when they had killed so many. 'If it comes to war again, the Empire will not survive,' he said.

The ministers grumbled amongst themselves.

'He is right,' General Long said, bowing again before the emperor. 'I can only add my advice. The Empire is not what it was.

The Palace Isle is a shadow of the great city it was. Even before the fight when I escorted my child here to be...' He stopped and looked at Lis before he cleared his throat. 'I may have lived on my island for a long time,' he said more clearly, 'but I soon realised that the world was not what it was when I left the Palace Isle.'

The emperor nodded wearily.

'The Empire of Rei-Een was once a strong and thriving nation. Let us help restore it to what it was.'

'Could we consider trading again with other nations?' Lis asked.

'What would we trade?' one of the ministers snapped. 'We barely have grain for the people we have, and you want to give it away.'

The emperor stood from his throne, and the room hushed. 'Truly, minister?' he asked, and Remi felt the threat in the quiet question.

The man nodded, then seemed to remember himself and shook his head.

'You are the minister in charge of such things. When were you to tell me you had failed in your duty?'

The man stammered and looked amongst his friends, but the other ministers looked away.

'The Empire is falling,' the emperor said with a sadness Remi felt wash across the room. 'Our world is coming to an end. It appears to have been happening for some time. Maybe the magic war was the beginning of the end.' He sat heavily in his throne.

'But we can restore it,' Lis offered. 'Working together, we can make it strong again.'

The emperor stared at her unseeing.

Advisor Gan stepped forward and bowed low. 'I think the crown princess is correct,' he said softly, and Remi wondered if the man truly believed what he said. He had changed his mind too often for Remi's liking.

'I suggest a council, Your Eminence.'

The emperor turned slowly to look at the man, and Remi wondered whether he would survive this. If the Empire ended as they feared, would his father die with it?

'Who would you suggest to bring together for this council?'

'The prince and princess as the voice of the Empire,' Gan said clearly, bowing. 'Representatives of the army, perhaps a minister or two,' he said, looking back over the men standing beside him with apparent disappointment. 'The elders of the Hidden, representatives of the common people, be it those willing to settle with the magics or others,' he added, 'and of course, the magics.'

The murmuring increased in the room. Some clearly approved his suggestion; others didn't, and Remi wondered if that was more about it encroaching on their power rather than it being a bad idea.

'And how do you propose to bring these people together without them killing each other, or us?' the emperor asked.

The little advisor looked uncomfortable for just a moment, but then he glanced at Remi and took a deep breath. 'We invite them,' he said. 'We send notices around the Empire to be posted in halls and gathering places, markets and the like.'

'And if no one comes?' the emperor asked.

'Then we think of something else.'

Remi nodded once to the man, and he stepped back. It was a good idea, but it could also end as badly as his father feared. And Remi wasn't sure he wanted to be stepping between magics and those without to keep the peace. He glanced at Lis, who may have been thinking the same thing, for she looked quite serious.

He leaned towards her, but she gave a little shake of her head. 'Could we offer some form of protection?' she asked.

'You want to get between them?' Remi asked quickly.

'No, but I think we need to reassure those with magic that this is not an attempt to capture them, and to reassure those without that they are not entering a fight.'

The emperor nodded once. 'Send out your notices,' he said to the advisor, who grinned broadly. 'You have until the sun rises the day after tomorrow to have them here, or the world may end before you get a chance.'

His smile faltered, but the advisor bowed low and raced from the room. The emperor waved his hand at the room and sat down slowly. The empress stepped up to him as the room emptied, and Remi took Lis's hand and moved forward.

'I don't want to talk about it any further,' he said before Remi could speak. 'Has your magic returned?' he asked Lis.

She shook her head. Remi wasn't sure if it was the amount of time she had breathed in the dust or that she carried a child that had caused it to have such an effect.

'Take her to the healers,' the emperor said. 'I know you trust your own, but another may be better able to help you.'

They bowed low to the emperor and, with a glance towards the empress, they left.

'A visit to the healers may alert my parents to your condition,' he murmured.

'I am sure they will learn of it soon enough. I thought my father would have said something. There are too many who know our secrets.'

'But there are many who will keep them,' a soldier behind them whispered.

Remi turned to nod at the man.

They headed towards the healers' compound, which Remi thought was the only part of the Palace Isle not to change. People had come and gone, but the healers always remained. They walked in silence, but Lis still allowed him to hold her hand, and he wondered what else might change as the Empire was rebuilt. If it could be.

As they entered the healers' compound, the Imperial Healer raced forward with his hands out. 'Stop!' he cried.

They both stopped dead.

'I fear that any one of these herbs might trigger something,' he said.

'I have walked through here before with no effect,' Remi said, although he remembered wondering what impact the herbs might have on magic.

'But our little princess has been compromised.'

'Do you have any idea what they did to me?' she asked.

'It is a combination, but I'm not sure which spices have affected you so badly. The water helped you?'

'It washed the dust from my skin, but I fear I inhaled too much of it.'

'Come,' he said thoughtfully. 'I would have you examined away from here.'

She nodded once, and he walked past them out into the street. He paused for a moment, then led them through the streets until they reached a rivulet passing though the grounds of the island. Ahead of them, Remi could see the bridge Lis had thought was so beautiful the day she had become the hidden princess, and where his mother so often found her way.

'Why here?' Remi asked.

'If this doesn't work, we can throw her in the water.'

Lis's eyes widened as the old man smiled. 'A precaution.'

Lis nodded once, and he produced a small package from his pocket. She looked at it warily. Remi wondered if the man was going to test the dust on her directly.

He moved between the two of them.

'This will make you cough,' he said, leaning around Remi and blowing the spice into Lis's face.

Remi turned, worried that this would only do more damage. She looked at him and crinkled her nose, but nothing happened.

'Maybe we need to try some more,' the healer murmured, and then Lis sneezed. She shook her head and, as Remi closed his fist to prevent himself from thumping the old man, she started to cough.

It was like a little tickle, a delicate thing, but it didn't stop. It got worse and worse until Remi thought she would drop from it. She doubled over and then a hacking cough started, as though her body was rejecting not only the dust but her own lungs.

Remi didn't know what to do. As he reached for her, she held out a hand for him to keep his distance. And then it stopped. She took several deep breaths and glared at the healer. Then she disappeared, and the old man squealed for joy. Then he squealed in fright, and Lis reappeared with her arms around him.

'Thank you,' she said. 'Thank you.'

'I don't think I ever want to see that again,' Remi whispered.

'I don't want to experience it. Is it an antidote to the spices they used?'

He shook his head. 'It was because you had breathed it in. I feared it still stuck in your lungs and might have remained there for a very long time. This helps with coughing, mostly for infections we can't shift from the lung.'

'It worked,' she said.

'Come,' the old man said, taking her by the arm and leading her to the bridge. He sat her on the first step and sat beside her as though they were old friends. 'I would like to check that you are well.'

She nodded, but she looked up at Remi. Their world would be different again once this news escaped. He leaned in and put his head to her chest. Then he looked into her eyes.

'Magic me something?' he whispered.

She took a deep breath and then held out her hand, and a cake appeared on it. He looked at it suspiciously.

'Lotus seed paste?' he asked.

She nodded, and he snatched the cake up and pushed the whole thing into his mouth. He nodded slowly with his eyes closed, and Lis giggled, a sound it seemed Remi hadn't heard in a long time.

'Now,' the healer said through a mouthful, 'about this child.'

They both glanced at each other. 'You haven't even felt her pulse,' Remi said.

The old man waved him away. 'I can see it on your face. Yang assures me you are well, and if you can both withstand the power of the spices you have been subjected to, I have no concerns.' He looked up at Remi. 'Women have been having babies without my interference for a very long time,' he said with a smile. 'You will have to do far more than a woman of your position would be expected or allowed to do in your condition. You do what you must before the empress learns of this.'

Remi bowed before the man. Lis kissed his cheek, then presented him with another cake.

'Run along,' he said. 'Stay away from the healers,' he added in a serious tone.

They both nodded and, taking her hand, Remi ran back through the streets towards the laundry.

30

Lis stood beside Remi at the docks and watched the boats arrive. The docks were almost as busy as they had been when she had come to the Palace Isle for the Choosing. When the news had first reached them at the laundry that boats were arriving, Lis was apprehensive. She had thought this a good idea, yet the men who had taken her were foremost in her mind.

The number of people surprised her, and she was almost tempted to stand behind Remi as the number of boats increased. Yet as soon as Master Yangshing stepped onto the dock, the world made more sense.

Not all of those getting off the boats were from the Hidden school, and Lis wondered if there were more islands on the outer rim of the Empire hiding magics and their allies. She shook her head, and Remi gave her hand a gentle squeeze.

Wei-Song pushed past her and out onto the docks, throwing herself into the arms of the older man. He smiled as he ran his hand over her hair, and Lis knew this man was more of a father to Wei-Song than the emperor ever could have been. The emperor and empress were waiting back at the throne room. Lis was sure they would be standing at the top of the steps when the others came through to meet them.

Master Yangshing stepped forward and bowed low to Remi,

then to Lis. She smiled, and he reached out to touch her face, but then stopped.

'He should be taking better care of you,' he whispered, leaning in closer.

'He is always there to rescue me,' Lis said in return. 'Who else have you brought with you?' she asked.

'Not all magics. Some who have supported us over the years, and I have given my word they will not face persecution for that action.'

'I can second that,' Remi said. 'Welcome,' he said, indicating the large open gates behind him. 'We don't have some of the comforts we did before, but the island is yours.'

Many bowed low as they passed him, and Lis noticed that some carried barrels of food. They hadn't had much help of late, so Yang had been doing most of the cooking for their small group. She wasn't sure about the soldiers, and she felt bad for not checking on them. Although she was sure they looked after themselves when they travelled.

Advisor Gan appeared beside her, grinning continuously at the people arriving by boat. The moment the emperor had dismissed him, he had set the scribes to work creating the posters and sending them out to the main islands of the Empire. Lis only hoped that all of those who should be involved were able to.

Some of the faces arriving looked familiar from their journey around the islands not so long ago, but they had little to say as they passed Remi and Lis on the docks. They bowed and kept moving. The soldiers acted as runners, showing people to accommodation.

They had asked people to come together in the main square, but some had been standing there most of the morning, and there were still boats arriving. Lis searched the crowd for anyone familiar. Despite the number of Hidden on the island, they stood out amongst the rest. Lis was surprised that no one was hiding.

Others moved around the edges of the group. Looking at who was there, trying to find people. Lis only hoped this didn't develop into a fight before they could talk to them. She had hoped the emperor would stand before them, to show that he wanted the Empire united. His brief stint on the steps of the throne room had been just that.

As one boat arrived, Remi stiffened beside her, and a man stood at the top of the gangplank as the soldiers tied up the boat. The man looked directly at them and gave Lis a smile before he stepped from the boat. As he headed towards them, Lis took Remi's hand.

'He is the magic,' she whispered.

'Chonglin,' Remi greeted the man before he could say anything, and he bowed low.

'I see you found your princess,' Chonglin said.

Remi bowed his head. Lis could feel the tension in his body and what it took not to attack this man.

'We are here to listen to what is to be said,' Chonglin said. 'Not to cause trouble, I assure you.'

'I'm not sure I believe you,' Remi said, his voice low, and Lis felt the heat rise around him.

'You are welcome,' she said. 'Please...' She held her hand out, and Remi glared at the man.

'I was led to believe all are welcome,' he said.

'You are,' Lis said quickly.

'Did you try to kill my wife?' Remi asked, leaning forward.

'Didn't you?' Chonglin asked.

Lis slipped between them and took the magic's hand. 'You are most welcome,' she said again, then nodded to a solider by the gate to escort him inside.

'This was your idea,' she hissed at Remi. Then smiled as another man bowed when he passed them. 'No matter what we think of them, we must be accommodating, or this won't work.'

Remi nodded and huffed, and the heat died away.

By the afternoon, Lis was ready for the shade and a rest. She had insisted on standing by the gate to welcome everyone, and she was sure it would help them see they were all welcome in the same way. She sighed and stretched when one last boat arrived. There hadn't been a boat in a little while, but they were thinning out, and she guessed all those who would come were already here.

The man who marched towards her caused her heart to jump, and without a thought she had her hand up and her shield in place.

He stopped and glared at her before he looked at Remi. He had his arm across her and was trying to reassure her it was well, but her mind raced.

'Search that man,' she said to the guard.

'Are we not welcome?' he asked, the voice grating on her fears. Her shield pushed out further.

'He may be carrying spices that are dangerous,' Lis said, and the guard stepped forward again.

'We have come in peace,' the man said, holding up his hands. Others joined him on the dock, many of them familiar to Lis. They really hadn't thought she would survive. 'I am sorry for Wu Peng,' he said, bowing low again.

'I'm not,' she murmured. The guard nodded, and she looked away.

'You are welcome,' Remi said. 'But you will be watched.'

The man smiled and headed through the gate. Some of the others following him didn't bow to Lis or Remi, and she wondered what they really wanted here.

'This might have been a bad idea,' she whispered, taking Remi's arm and following them through the gates.

'We'll soon find out,' he said.

'Where is the emperor?' someone in the crowd called out.

Lis was surprised by the number of people in the crowd. Watching them unload one boat at a time, they hadn't seemed so many, but now she was somewhat overwhelmed.

'He won't be coming,' someone else called. 'Why would he? They are rounding us up to take us out.'

Lis wondered why he had come if he believed that to be true.

'That is not why we asked you to come,' Remi said, his voice carrying across the square as he walked through the people and up the steps of the temple.

Lis followed close behind and noticed Chonglin in the crowd, smiling. She was reminded of the last time Remi had been on these steps addressing people.

'The Empire is dying,' he said, and a whisper moved through the crowd. 'We must work together to save it.'

'It is magic that is killing it,' someone cried out, and Remi took a breath.

'We hope that by bringing the Empire back to what it was before the magic war, we can find a way to succeed.'

'Your father started the magic war. There was no need to turn on his own people like that. He turned on more than the magics.'

Lis wanted to agree, but they had to stop the Empire being overthrown. Siding against the emperor wasn't going to help.

'And you have magic,' someone else said. 'How can we trust you don't want it for yourself?'

'We know what you did that day,' an old woman said.

'Please,' Master Yangshing said, putting his hand in the air. 'Let us listen to what they have to say. They may have fought each other, but they stand united before us now.'

'Master Yangshing?' a voice asked in the crowd. 'I thought you were killed in the war.'

'I'm tougher than I look,' he said with a bow, and some laughter followed. 'I understand that we all come from different places, and that we have experienced different lives following the magic war. But we are all Rei-Een citizens, and I'm sure we want our world to continue.'

There was some general agreement in the crowd, along with some shouts about not trusting magic.

'What does the hidden princess say?' a voice cried out above the rest, and Lis focused on Chonglin. 'You fought against the magics with the soldiers and hunters. Why do you want to end this now?'

Lis cleared her throat. 'I fought to save the prince,' she said, and the crowd hushed around her. 'It was my fault that he had become what he was, that he struggled to control his skills. He had been led to believe that we couldn't live in harmony. I believe we can.'

'You tried to kill each other,' someone said.

'No, I was trying to stop him from hurting himself.'

'But you don't have the control to do that either, do you?' a familiar voice cried out, and Lis searched the crowd of faces for the man who had held her.

'You don't like what those with magic are,' Lis said, still trying to find his face, 'but you would have the magic if you could.'

He pushed forward then, and Lis focused on the anger before her. 'I want a world where there is no magic.' He turned back to the crowd. 'And I have the means to take it away.'

'I thought you wanted a truce, Li Sho-Ma,' someone else said, and from nowhere a gap formed around the two men as they pushed at each other.

'This isn't helping,' Lis pleaded.

She felt the hum of magic before it sparked, but the man called Li Sho-Ma threw a hard punch, and the other man was out cold before the magic formed. 'They still want control,' he snapped. Then he turned and stalked away.

Lis looked up at Remi.

'There are a lot of opinions as to what we should do,' he said, and although the murmuring continued, the crowd watched him instead of the man still winding through the crowd.

Remi waved a soldier over. 'Don't let that man back on his boat, and I want it searched. Any sign of the spice mix—call in the healers.'

The soldier nodded and disappeared.

'We want peace,' Remi said again. 'We want the Empire to be what it was. Please think of how we can make that happen, and we will meet again in the morning to discuss more ideas.' He looked across at Advisor Gan, and the little man stepped forward.

'If you have any questions in relation to your accommodation or needs for your stay here, please step forward and I will do my best. Otherwise, the island is yours to explore.'

'I suppose we did tell them the island was theirs,' Remi murmured.

Advisor Gan shook his head. 'Most of it, but we have soldiers stationed where people shouldn't go. The empress would see you,' he said without looking as several people moved forward to ask him questions.

Lis looked back at the crowd. Several people watched them go, including Chonglin, and she shivered. A little way from the group, Lis came upon her father talking with the general.

'I'll see what can be done,' the general said, nodding to one of the soldiers with him, who then bowed and raced off. 'That could have gone better,' he said, turning to Remi.

'It could have gone a lot worse,' Remi said.

'You didn't think about showing them your little trick?'

Lis shook her head. She wasn't sure that it would be enough, and she wasn't sure it would work. It hadn't when Remi had tried on Fourth, although she hadn't been focused on him at the time. She felt much better, and her barrier was working again, but she wasn't sure she could try. Remi was highly agitated, and if it didn't work, she might not be able to pull him back into control before someone was hurt.

'You shouldn't have mentioned that it was your fault,' Remi said.

'But it was. It is because I'm here that all of this has happened.'

The general opened his mouth, and Lis pointed at him. 'If you say destiny, I shall banish you and Yang to the far reaches of what is left of the Empire.'

'You would never do that to Yang,' the general said with a grin. 'But I agree with him. The gods have conspired to bring you together, whether you think they have or not.'

Lis shook her head.

'Can you heal it?' her father asked, his voice rough and broken. Lis wondered if he would ever be the man he had been before all of this.

'The damage we have done?' she asked.

He surprised her with a smile. 'The Empire. Can you really bring all of these people together?'

'I hope so,' she said.

Remi tapped her on the shoulder. 'Mother,' he said softly, indicating the woman standing on the steps of the throne room. Lis was reminded of the fear she had felt on that first day, how distant and untouchable the empress seemed to be. Only she knew a different side of her now, although Lis wasn't sure she knew the woman as well as she thought she did.

She kissed her father's cheek and took Remi's arm, and they went to meet her.

The empress led them straight into the throne room. Lis was surprised to find it empty. The empress stepped forward and sat on the throne. She smoothed over her skirt, and Lis and Remi both bowed before her.

'Now tell me what you haven't already.'

'I think we have told you everything,' Remi said quickly.

'Where is Wei-Song?' Lis asked.

'With Master Yangshing,' the empress said with a wave of her hand. Lis couldn't remember seeing her in the crowd, but she nodded once. 'What happened while you were away?' she asked.

'When we travelled?' Lis asked.

The empress nodded once.

'I lost control,' Lis said.

'There was more to it than that.' The empress maintained her firm features and stern voice. Lis wanted to sit at her feet and beg for forgiveness, but she wasn't sure why she felt she needed it.

'Mother,' Remi said softly. 'What is it you want to know?'

'Only what occurred. You were supposed to make things better. I threw away the last of the traditions for you, but you haven't made things better.'

'I'm not sure anything would have,' Remi said. 'The ministers are right. The Empire is collapsing, and if we don't act now there will be nothing left.'

The empress shook her head.

'The emperor has lived in fear,' Remi said, taking Lis by surprise. 'He feared what he had been told about the magics, and he decided to end them before they could end him. But it didn't work. It didn't save him, and Ta-Sho still died. All these years since the war, he still lived in fear. People died who didn't need to, and a group of our own people plotted against us. In trying to save it all, he has destroyed us.'

The empress stared at him open mouthed.

'He insisted you kill your own child. You knew it was wrong. It was why you saved her and sent her to those he would have killed.'

She pushed up from the throne, her face pale. 'I have done all I can for this Empire,' she hissed.

'And you have kept far more from it than I ever did.'

She stopped and stared at them, then sat down again. Lis reached out her senses, half expecting the emperor to be close by. There was only a servant waiting in the shadows.

'Did you break from what is right and bed this woman before she was your wife?' the empress asked, but the strength had gone from her voice.

Remi shook his head. Lis wondered how they had returned to such a place when they had seemed so much more only days before.

'What would I keep from you?' Lis asked. 'What do you think I haven't shared? That I lost control, that the fear of the men caused my own to flare, that there is a way for those without magic to take from those who have. That my father is broken. That your son and I have some connection neither of us can explain. That a man I once cared for tried to rip the magic from my body with his hands.'

Remi put an arm across her then and moved her around behind

him. Her heart beat too fast, and she was lost to the sound of it pounding in her ears.

'Being empress is a sacrifice,' she said. 'You are the crown princess now. Life is different; life is harder than it was before.'

'My life has always been hard,' Lis said, clinging to Remi's back. 'I was nearly lost,' she whispered.

'You don't matter,' the empress said, the harshness of her words jarring Lis. 'Your only purpose is to produce an heir. Not to try and save this Empire, not to guide your husband. A son is all you must do.' She waved a servant forward and he bowed, holding out a golden cup. 'Drink the tea.'

'No,' Lis said.

The empress stood slowly, and the anger rolling from her made Lis step back as the servant stepped forward.

'We shall try to bring back to this Empire what we can. You will drink the tea. And on the seventh day, when we are sure your womb is clean, you will bed your husband before those who should observe it.'

'No,' Lis said again, pushing out with her barrier and knocking not only the tea from the servant's hand but the man to the floor.

'We must be sure that any child you carry is of the line. That man may have done more than try to take your magic.'

Lis stared at the woman, and she felt the heat of Remi's fire simmering under his skin.

'He hit me,' she whispered, indicating her still-bruised face. 'He choked me,' she said, lifting her chin. 'He ripped my clothes, but he did not get near enough to father any child.'

Remi blew out a soft breath and stepped between them again. 'She was lucky in some way,' Remi said softly, and Lis leaned into his back. Her hands balled around the material. No matter what they said, the empress would feel she had lost something. 'They both are,' he whispered. 'The child was confirmed by the healer before she was taken. I know, we know, that there is no doubt to the lineage. There will be no tea,' he said, and the certainty in his voice made Lis shiver. 'There will be no observing of our private moments.'

The world was silent, and the servant picked up the cup and scampered away. Lis remained hidden, only able to see him scuttle away. She couldn't sense anything from the empress. She wasn't sure if that was due to her shock that her son would speak to her in such a way, or that he shielded them as he did.

When nothing more was said, Lis released her hold on Remi and he turned, pulling her into his arms and out into the sunshine before the empress could say anything further. She baulked at the top of the stairs. Remi, still with his arms tight around her shoulders, directed her along and through a doorway she hadn't realised was there. He pressed a finger to her lips, and she nodded.

The room was dark, and it took a moment to adjust. Remi waited before stepping further inside. There was no one there.

Then Lis heard a door open, and in the darkness she sensed someone else. They waited, her hand in Remi's, his finger still pressed against her lip. She took his hand and indicated he could move it.

'What has happened?' the emperor asked in a stern voice. 'I wanted to talk with them about the meeting. Why would you approach this without me?'

'I didn't ask about the meeting,' the empress said, her voice just as stern, and Lis felt a shiver cross her skin. 'I wanted to know what they were doing. You heard the stories as I did, of his sneaking in and out of her palace. Some aspects of our society must be maintained.'

'What does it matter if the girl was bedded beforehand? As long as it was only Remi doing the bedding.'

An angry silence followed. Lis glanced towards where Remi was, wondering what he thought of this.

'Do you think it doesn't happen?' he asked.

'She must be pure,' the empress stammered. 'U'Shi…'

'Was a silly girl, and I can understand why Ta-Sho found

interest in others. I understand some of the traditions—it reduced the fighting, stopped brothers killing each other—but we are men.'

Lis held her breath.

'Pardon?' the empress asked, her voice wobbling.

'Where have I confused you?' the emperor asked. He certainly wasn't the sullen man he had been earlier.

'Are you saying that my son…'

'Bedded the maid, I believe, or was she a guard? Maybe both. She had some involvement with Remi, but I don't think he wanted her in the same way.'

Lis could feel Remi's heart beating at the same fast pace as her own.

'Did you…' the empress stammered, and Lis imagined her sitting on the throne, learning her world was not what she thought.

'Of course,' he said. 'I didn't want the first time to be in front of a room full of officials watching my every move.'

'But…'

'An act,' he said. 'I was not as kind as I could have been. They like a bit of blood, my father had said, and then they would leave us alone and we could…'

The slap was loud in the following silence of the room.

Lis was reminded of the kindness and fun she and Remi had shared in that very room. It would have been very different with the officials watching. She wondered if there was more in the world she wasn't aware of. He had spent so many nights simply curled around her. But had he sought his pleasure elsewhere?

'I thought the girl not mine,' the emperor said, the levity gone from his voice. 'I knew what the tutor was, and as soon as I saw the magic in her, I knew she wasn't mine.'

'She was,' the empress whispered. 'She was every bit of you. Yet he would have taken us both,' she said, the sadness at a life lost evident in her voice. 'I could have left and raised her in peace without you.'

He laughed then, a bitter sound that caught Lis unawares. 'You wouldn't give up the power. You might not have killed her, but you abandoned her, passing her into an unknown world to ensure you maintained the hold you had over the one you knew.'

The empress cried out, and Lis wondered if he had hit her then. A small shutter opened to reveal the screen before them as the emperor and empress struggled on the other side. She had one arm raised as though to hit him, and he had hold of her forearm. He grabbed the back of her head and forced a kiss on her. Lis shivered and looked away, reminded of Peng.

Remi leaned against her, and she stifled a scream.

'Is someone there?' the advisor's voice whispered hoarsely. Lis bit down on her lip. The hatch was raised, and she heard a distant door close softly. She wanted the light. But she could still hear muffled conversation within the throne room.

The weight of Remi against her kept her pinned to the wall. She could smell his skin and hear his heartbeat. Then she felt his breath by her ear. 'When they are gone, we can move.' She nodded against him. 'I thought he didn't know about Ta-Sho,' he whispered.

Lis was desperate to ask what he might have kept from her, but she didn't.

31

Lis missed the sheets hanging in the laundry. The early morning sun slowly coloured the building, and the air around her felt pink. She wondered how the sheets would have reflected the light.

Remi walked around the edge of the building and stopped. She looked up and then back to the space that used to be sheets. There was a hesitation with him since hearing the emperor the day before. Lis wasn't sure she could look at him in the same way, either. Remi might not be the man she thought he was. But then, she didn't really know him. In this world, no one seemed to know anyone for who they really were.

Peng came to mind as she shuffled her toes in the dirt. He had been very clever at hiding who he was and what he wanted. Her time on their island home isolated from the world might have done her far more harm than her parents imagined. Remi sat beside her and laced his fingers in his lap. With his own feet firmly on the ground, she was reminded of how much taller than her he was, how much bigger, and she hoped they wouldn't be facing each other again across a battlefield.

'Any more boats?' she asked, watching the pattern her toes made in the dirt rather than looking at him.

'No. It appears everyone who is coming is here.'

She nodded once.

'Did you sleep well?' he asked, and she wondered how long he had been gone.

She shook her head, and they continued in silence.

'Will you bring them back together, or do we ask for spokespeople?' she eventually asked.

'That might be more useful. We can pull them into a safer environment, talk more rather than have them yell ideas.'

She nodded. She slipped off the step and took a couple steps forward. 'Where have you been?' she asked. Again, she couldn't look at him for fear he would lie to her.

'I have been with the healers.'

'I thought he said to stay away,' she said, thinking of the Imperial Healer.

'He was testing something with Yang.'

'I don't think it is safe for him to be there either.'

'He wanted to help.'

Lis nodded and walked across the courtyard to the little garden by the wall. When she turned back, Remi was gone.

She must have dozed in the morning sunshine, for she woke to Wei-Song shaking her. 'Are you well?' she asked, the concern not only clear on her face, but flowing off her in waves. Lis held out her hand, and Wei-Song pulled her to her feet.

'I didn't sleep well last night,' she said.

'The prince sent me to find you. They have nominated representatives and decided to meet in the throne room.'

Lis waited a moment.

'He needs you with him.'

'Oh,' she said. She looked across at the guard waiting for her by the gateway. He bowed once, and she followed him towards the throne room.

Lis joined the people entering the throne room. With the guard still a step behind her, she moved over to Remi. He indicated the cushion beside him, and she silently sat down.

The guard stepped behind her.

'Are you concerned?' Remi asked.

She shook her head and then followed his gaze to the man behind her. 'He is doing as he does,' she said, turning back. She noticed then that there were no other guards in the room, although she thought there should be, with such a gathering and the emperor, she guessed, looking at the empty throne.

'It is a sign of faith,' he murmured.

Lis waved the man out, and he left without question.

'You don't seem yourself today,' Remi said.

'Don't I?' she asked just as the emperor entered the room and everyone stood and bowed.

'I thank you for taking the time to consider the best way forward,' he said, glancing at Lis and Remi.

She nodded, but she wasn't quite sure how she could hold a conversation with this man again. She had learnt too much of him, and she wondered what else had been learnt from that little room. She looked at Remi then, and he smiled at her. She tried to indicate across the room.

'Gan,' he whispered.

She nodded and hoped he was certain he was alone this time.

'The survival of the Empire is utmost. I know there will be some complex matters to discuss, but if you have any clear ideas, now is the time to share them.'

'You are thinking about the people then,' Li Sho-Ma said, and Lis shivered. She hadn't noticed him when she entered the room. 'Are their needs forefront?'

'Your needs,' the emperor said. 'Is there something particular you consider in your question—food, livestock, vessels?'

'I am from Fourth,' he said, and Lis tried not to move around on the cushion. 'We used to have traders, before the war.'

'What did you trade for?' Lis asked.

'We created fine cloth, and we would trade it for a range of items.'

'Did you have trouble with magics?' someone across the room asked, and she wasn't sure who they were or who they represented.

'We had magics amongst us,' Li Sho-Ma said. Lis wondered if that was true. He had been determined to take their powers away. Although he was willing to share the Empire with them, or so he had claimed.

'Do you fear magic?' Lis asked.

He grinned at her as he shook his head. 'No need to fear what we can control,' he said.

A man across from Lis leapt to his feet, and a wind swirled dangerously around the room.

'There is no need for hostility,' Remi said, standing, his arms outstretched as though he were putting himself between them.

'He wants to end us, not work with us,' the man stammered, and the wind died down. 'I heard there were some who thought they had a way to control the magics.'

The man tipped his head.

Lis could feel the crackle of magic as it built, and then Remi was holding a sword of fire in his hand. She wondered how he had managed such a thing. Chonglin's eyes narrowed, and Lis knew he had connected the skill with something else. She moved slowly to stand beside him. She didn't think there was anything she could do to help if he lost control, and she wasn't confident they could bring the phoenix forward.

She glanced up at the emperor, who looked as though he had the upper hand. He smiled at her, but she turned back to Chonglin. The emperor was hoping for something she didn't think they would be able to give him.

'We don't have a representative of the priestesses,' Chonglin said, and the sword died in Remi's hand. 'The high priestess should be here.'

He stepped out and around his table. Lis wondered what he might do with his guess, although it confirmed for Lis that the priestess had been working with the magics and sharing her visions with them. She wondered how the world might have turned out if she hadn't died.

'There is no high priestess,' a priestess said in a clear voice from the doorway.

Murmuring started around the room.

The priestess stepped forward, ignoring the noise around her, and knelt before the emperor, touching her head to the floor. Lis was surprised, for she had never seen a priestess offer such reverence to an emperor before. 'You have grown into a fine man, Emperor Rei.'

He stood then, and the noise increased. Lis could see he was torn between helping her up and sitting on the floor with her, but he stopped before he did anything that would draw any more attention. He indicated that she rise.

'We are grateful the priestesses could spare you,' he said softly. 'Let me prepare a place for you.'

'There is no need,' she said softly, sitting on the step to the throne.

He looked lost for a moment and then sat back down.

'The high priestess,' she said, looking at Chonglin, 'was not working with the gods. They have deemed not to choose another high priestess. I don't know if they will change their minds.'

He bowed his head to her. Lis thought they had all been working together, that it was their way, but she supposed power did different things to different people. And all that knowledge would have been difficult to hold.

'Please continue,' she said.

The room broke into hushed conversations and the occasional shout.

'You have no right to control the magic,' someone called out.

'You must understand the danger. We have to protect ourselves.'

'But if we work together…'

'The magics will just try to take control. It is only a matter of time.'

Remi blew out a frustrated breath.

'People worked together before,' Lis offered. 'Why can it not be like that again?'

'They didn't allow us to be ourselves. Magic was tolerated if it was on their terms.'

'What would you like?' she asked. 'Schools? A chance to learn?'

The man nodded.

'A chance to grow stronger,' someone else said.

'It would be better to learn exactly what could be done, and to learn control. We could be a better, more useful part of the Empire rather than just growing crops and colouring cloth.'

Li Sho-Ma coloured at the man's comment, and Lis wondered how he had used those with magic for his own betterment in the past.

'You didn't stop trading because of the magics,' she said to him. 'Not in other lands, but because you could no longer use the ones here. If you use your dust, they will be even less able to help you.'

'You would have been too young for such a business before the war,' someone else said. 'What are you hiding?'

The man raised his hands in a show of defence. 'My father ran the business, but it would have been mine. It destroyed him, and I wouldn't want that to happen to anyone else.' He stood then and looked to the man sitting with him, who also stood. Lis recognised him for the one who had walked her across the sand and locked her in the shack.

'Who do you represent?' an older woman asked. She was the woman who had fixed Lis's clothing, and she sat beside Master Yangshing. Lis wondered then why Wei-Song hadn't joined them.

'Ourselves,' the man spat, and they turned and marched out.

The old woman looked at Yangshing and sighed. 'There may be too many differences,' she said.

Chonglin nodded, his eyes on Lis.

32

Lis walked towards the laundry, disappointed that the negotiations still weren't getting anywhere. Everyone wanted something different, and no one trusted anyone else. Remi had stayed behind to talk to his father and although Lis had chatted a little with some of those present, she wanted time alone.

She was just rounding a corner when she heard screams. Before the guard with her could think of stopping her, she was off and running. Some people were in the main square, but there were many staying at various palaces around the island, just as her family had when they had visited for the Choosing.

A man before her, clearly Hidden, reappeared, and the guard took a step back before he pulled his sword. Lis put her hand out to stop him, and the man dropped to his knees.

He coughed and Lis backed up, then put her sleeve over her mouth.

'Get to water,' she cried.

'What is it?' the guard asked as she ran from the square, her sleeve still blocking some of the air—and, she hoped, the dust. Wei-Song stumbled in front of her, and Lis scooped her up by the arm, pulling her along.

'Don't breathe it in,' she said as Wei-Song covered her face, but it was too late.

'Where are we going?' the guard asked.

Lis pointed towards the throne room, but the dust was likely across the island. She turned back, looking into the sky. It glittered in the sun. 'On the wall,' she said.

She pulled Wei-Song along and into the throne room, where she barred the door. 'Take as many non-magics as you can and get on the wall,' she said to the soldier. He bowed and ran back out.

Wei-Song coughed and dropped to her knees. Master Yangshing rushed forward, but Lis leapt between them. 'Don't touch her,' she said. 'Dust—it's everywhere. It might be on her clothes.'

'Water,' Remi called.

A servant stepped forward with a jug, and Remi splashed it in her face. She sighed, but then looked over her clothes. He stepped towards Lis, but she held her hands out. 'More water,' he said. 'And fetch the healer, the Imperial Healer,' he called after the man. 'Tell him it is time to test.'

'What are you thinking?' Lis asked.

'Where were you?'

'It is everywhere,' she said, looking at those with magic around her. Chonglin still stood to the side. 'They have gone high, I think. It covers the whole island like snow.'

'We could blow it away,' Chonglin said.

'Unless it takes your magic before you can,' Lis said.

He nodded once.

'Not everyone wants to share,' Yangshing said. He inched closer to Wei-Song, but Lis moved between them.

'You don't want this,' she said.

'How long does it take to wear off?' the emperor asked.

'It depends how much is inhaled,' Lis said.

'Days,' Remi said.

'This will put people on edge,' the emperor said. 'Who is behind this?'

'I think we know,' Lis said, but she looked at Chonglin rather than Remi. He nodded once.

'He is willing to share if he can have all the control.'

'The healers may be able to stop it,' Remi said.

'There isn't enough water,' Lis said as the servant reappeared. Remi took the jug and got her to tip her head back. He poured it slowly over her face, rinsing the dust from her skin.

She shook a little and smiled.

'You could have done that for me,' Wei-Song said. 'Instead of throwing it at me.'

'More effective,' Chonglin said, stepping closer. Lis raised her hands. 'I have bigger problems than you,' he muttered.

'What did she tell you?' Lis asked. 'What did she see that had you so determined you would win this?'

'She saw the end. She saw us win.'

'But she saw different versions. She knew to keep us apart or you couldn't win. You tried to turn us on each other. You knew you couldn't win against us.'

Chonglin shrugged.

Lis sighed.

'I'm sick of hiding,' the master murmured.

'I'm tired of pretending to be someone I'm not,' the old woman said.

Others started to chime in with their reasons for being there.

Lis looked at the master, his focus still on Wei-Song. 'We did make up part of this Empire once,' the master said. 'We had a purpose without bringing fear to others.'

'I would like it to be that way again,' Lis said.

'You have magic,' someone said. 'You want a place, but what does it mean for us?'

'We wouldn't take your place. I think there is a way for the magics to help the Empire, so that we can build a better, stronger world together.'

Another man shook his head. 'What happens when they want to

take over?'

'We don't,' Yangshing said. 'We want to live in peace like everyone else.'

'I think there is a long way to go. Just because the prince has magic doesn't mean that it is right for the Empire. We have done just fine since the war.'

'Have you?' someone else asked, and Lis wasn't sure if they had magic or not.

'Will you capture and punish these men?' another person asked. 'Do we know this won't happen again?'

'The healers are sharing something that will counter the effects of the dust,' Remi said. 'It may still take a few days to fully take effect, but it will render the other harmless.'

'Except we are already covered in it,' Lis said. 'Any movement could send it around this room.'

The empress appeared at the end of the room, silent and serious. Lis bowed in her direction, and others followed her lead. 'Is it only the two of you?'

'Yes,' Lis said.

'Come this way,' she said, leading them back towards the front door. 'We don't want it inside. Splash this room down,' she said to the servant. 'Make sure no particles have attached themselves to anyone else. I don't want it in the palace,' she said. 'It will be a risk to everyone, magic or not.'

Lis struggled to keep up with her broad stride. They hurried through the streets, Wei-Song taking her hand and looking around them. Lis was sure this put them at more risk. It was only when she noticed that she had sent the guards to the wall, and they were without protection, that they were standing outside the baths.

'What a great idea,' Lis said. 'We should open them...'

The empress turned a dark look in her direction. 'You are essential to the Empire. Both of you. Rinse this from your clothing and your skin, and change.'

She glided away gracefully but still managed to look angry,

leaving them alone in the small garden.

'She is not herself,' Wei-Song said, entering the baths and heading straight through to the royal section.

'She has recently realised that the world is not what she thought,' Lis whispered.

'If she knew you were with child, she might soften.'

'She knows,' Lis said, carefully removing her clothes.

'Did the healer dust get us?' Wei-Song asked.

Lis shrugged and stepped into the pool. She quickly ducked beneath the surface and ran her fingers through her hair. Wei-Song did the same. They sat for a moment on the steps, splashing in the water.

Lis tried to relax, hoping the water had rinsed the dust from her system before it could take hold. The sound of banging made her look towards the door, and again she regretted allowing the empress to pull them away without protection.

She was out of the water, dry and in fresh clothes before Wei-Song had even moved. There were dry clothes put aside, but Lis didn't need them. She was out the door and in the street before she thought it was a good idea.

Chaos reigned.

People, magic and not, ran in every direction. Swords clashed. People cried out. Lis pushed forward with her barrier, only it faltered, and she knew the dust had affected her enough that she wouldn't be able to use it.

As she ran back through the streets, she fell over a man, dead and bleeding across the flagstones. She picked herself up. Her hands stung from the graze across the stones. He held a short, sharp blade in one hand, and she took it from him. People everywhere were fighting, but she couldn't tell who was on what side, and it appeared that those fighting didn't know either.

Lis looked firstly for the empress, for it hadn't been so long ago that she had left them. She might have gotten caught up in the fight. But Lis couldn't see her.

She couldn't see anyone she recognised amongst the people, and they were fighting down every street. She had hoped they could bring people together in some way, but now that was looking very unlikely. If this continued, the entire Empire would be fighting each other and no one would survive. She only hoped they had discovered those who had released the dust.

She didn't feel quite like she had before, but her magic wasn't right. And given the limitations she had felt previously, she wasn't sure they could do very much even if she found Remi. He at least had been inside, and it could be that he was protected from the dust.

The square was filled with shouts and the sound of metal on metal.

Someone bumped her from behind and she fell to her knees, the blade skittering away across the stones. She wasn't exactly experienced at fighting with magic, outside of that one day, and she had no idea what to do without it.

'Your Highness,' a man said, reaching out a hand to pull her to her feet. 'Why are you out here?'

'I was at the baths,' she said, well aware that it didn't explain why she was where she was. For a moment, she wondered if the empress had deliberately put them in danger, but she didn't think the woman would do that to Wei-Song. She hoped Wei-Song had stayed at the baths and not wandered out into this. She looked round for a guard or someone she could trust to send for her. Then she stared at the man before her.

'Why are you fighting?' she asked.

'The people are trying to stop us being what we are. They have,' he said, running his hand across his nose. 'I can't breathe.'

Lis nodded. She remembered that feeling all too well. 'It is just a few who are trying to do this,' she said. 'We can't treat them all the same. We need to find some middle ground.'

'They don't want middle ground,' he murmured, then swung around as a man charged towards them, his sword out before him.

He went down with a groan, and Lis bent over him. The other man looked her in the eye and then fell to his knees.

'There needs to be another way,' Lis murmured, but as she looked around, she didn't think she could get that message to everyone.

'This shows they want control,' the man who had run at them said. 'The magics want to take over.'

'It wasn't a magic who started this,' Lis said. 'It was a group from Fourth, trying to stop those with magic from using it.'

'How can they stop magics?'

Lis shook her head, scanning the madness around her for a familiar face.

'That is why they aren't using it,' the man said.

Lis nodded absently.

He grabbed her arm then, and she looked up at the desperation in his face. 'We are never going to stop,' he said.

Lis tried to pull from his hold.

'This madness will go on until there is no Empire left,' he murmured, letting her go as another man approached with a sword.

She saw someone from the school through the crowd, a young man who had travelled with Master Yangshing. She raced away from the others and then spun as a blade caught her arm. There were too many around her to know who had nicked her or whether it was deliberate. When she turned back, the man she'd been looking for was gone. She needed someone to go for Wei-Song.

'We need to get you out of here,' the magic said.

Lis nodded, putting her hand to her arm. It stung. She wished she had something to protect herself with properly, so she could find someone to stop this. The two men who had been fighting each other only moments before did their best to get her safely out of the fighting.

But as they moved along streets and between buildings, Lis soon realised the fighting covered the whole island. They were never going to bring the Empire together. There was too much hate between those with magic and those without, and the war wasn't the end of that. There had been too much fear in the years since.

There were some who already worked together, such as those who had protected the Hidden and allowed them to live amongst them. Lis thought of the old woman from Third, whose neighbours must have known what she was.

'Everyone has some magic,' she muttered to herself, and one of the men with her stopped. She turned and looked back at him.

'What did you say?'

'I saw something that indicated everyone has some magic, that there is a little in everyone who lives here, and if they took the time they might be able to learn how to use it.'

He shook his head. 'No,' he said.

Lis put her hands up slowly. 'Maybe I was wrong,' she whispered.

'Lis!' Remi called behind her, and she turned to see him racing towards her. She held up her hand, and he slowed down.

'I'm ok,' she said, looking back at the man before her. 'Wei-Song is at the baths.'

'You left her?' he asked. She was surprised by the accusation she could hear in his voice.

'I went to investigate the noise and got caught up. I couldn't find anyone.'

'You have found two men here,' he said slowly.

'They have helped me.'

He noticed her arm then, reaching for it. 'What happened?'

She shook her head. 'We have to stop this. No one will win.'

The two men glanced at each other and then bowed to Lis. 'Let us go for your maid,' one said.

The other nodded. 'We will bring her back to you safely.'

They headed off together.

'Can we trust them?' Remi asked.

'They were trying to kill each other not so long ago. But with the dust, no one seems to know who is magic and who isn't.

People have kept to themselves for too long. They don't know who they can trust because they feared being found out and killed, or suggested to be helping magics and killed. There has been too much fear.'

He nodded slowly. 'I have been part of that.'

'You were only doing what you were raised to believe.'

'I was doing what I thought would benefit me. Let's get you out of this.' He took her hand and led her up the steps of the throne room.

33

'What were you thinking?' Remi asked Lis quietly as he sat her down.

'This isn't my fault,' she whispered.

He took her hands then and tried to pull her attention from the people in the room. 'The baths were a good idea.'

She appeared to be searching the room for someone, and he glanced over his shoulder. Most of those who had come to the throne room to meet were still there, yet Chonglin had disappeared. 'Does he know the dangers?' Remi asked.

'You said the healers released something.'

'They have been trying to find a way to counter the dust. Possibly with more dust. That was what Yang has been helping with. Did it help?'

She shrugged.

'Lis,' he said, sitting beside her. 'Did it help?'

She sighed and looked into his face before she leaned against him. 'After I was in the water, I had enough magic to dry and dress. But my barrier wouldn't hold.'

'Why did you go out?"

'I needed to.'

'And the guard?'

'I can't remember if they followed us or not. Maybe your

mother took them.'

'She isn't herself,' he murmured, looking around the room and wondering where she was. 'Do you think she still sacrificed Wei-Song in a way, leaving her with people she thought the war would kill?'

'In some way, it would have been your father who killed her if that had occurred. I don't know,' Lis said, trying to cover a yawn. 'Nothing appears to be what we thought.'

'You could rest against me,' he offered. He didn't want her heading back out into the world, although he knew they should be out there trying to stop whatever had started this fight. They had aimed to bring the two sides together, and they were already killing each other in the street.

Wei-Song stepped into the room. The two men who had been with Lis bowed low and then appeared unsure whether they should leave or stay. One of them saw Lis and bowed low again as Wei-Song ran to Master Yangshing. Lis was on her feet and across the room before Remi could hold her back.

Wei-Song threw her arms around Lis and held her close.

'Thank you,' Remi said to the two men. 'Has it settled down?'

'Your Highness,' one of them said as he bowed. 'It appears to be worsening. There is a fear that no one knows who the enemy is. Every man fights for himself and his family, only sure of those he arrived with.'

'Is there any magic?'

'A little,' the other said, looking at his own hands. 'It is unpredictable and…'

'It will return,' Remi tried to reassure him. 'It takes time, and it depends on the dust.'

'There is more dust and spice in the air. It is difficult to breathe,' the man said. 'It is difficult to know if we can ever be what we were.'

Remi looked across the room at Lis, still standing with Wei-Song and talking in hushed tones. Wei-Song wore a reassuring smile, and he was sure Lis was apologising for leaving her behind. But it might have been the safest place for her, despite being alone. The madness was in the open.

'She put herself between us with a little blade,' the man said, and Remi turned to find him watching Lis as well. 'I heard what she did in the square that day. The world thought you both dead.'

'I think we thought the same for a time.' Remi turned back to look at Lis. 'Where did she get a blade?'

The man shrugged. 'From a dead man, perhaps.'

'Where were the soldiers?' Remi murmured.

'I haven't seen many soldiers out there,' the other man admitted. 'Some, trying to stop the fighting, but not in the numbers I expected.'

Where had they gone? Could it be Chonglin? But the island had been covered in soldiers not so long ago, as though every soldier in the Empire had been on this one island, and other than the healers they had been the only ones here.

'Where is Yang?' Remi asked, and both Lis and Wei-Song turned to him.

'You said he was helping the healers,' Lis said as they walked towards him.

Remi looked at the doorway. He needed to know if the dust the healers had developed was a way to end this, if it really was working. Lis wasn't as badly affected by the dust as she had been previously, but she wasn't working to capacity even though she had only been exposed to it for a short amount of time.

'I want you to stay here,' he said to Lis.

She glared at him, but she nodded once. He headed out into the square and paused in the doorway. Despite his wanting to keep Lis safe, he was sure it would only take her a couple minutes before she was following him out.

But it was the master from the school who appeared in the doorway.

'I may be able to do something,' he said.

Remi nodded, and they headed towards the healers. People ran past them, but no one seemed to pay them any real attention. 'I don't think the healer's dust is working,' the master said, looking over those around them.

A tickle started in the back of Remi's throat. He thought he must have breathed in the dust, but then the healers had spread theirs just as easily. He looked up at the wall, distracted by the idea of the dust, and noticed many of the soldiers around the top of the wall. They may have gone up to help spread the dust, but they weren't coming back. It might be that they didn't want to get caught in the fighting. It might also be that they weren't able to get back down.

A man with a sword nearly caught Remi off guard as he lunged at him. Remi lifted his own sword in defence, and the master was pushed against him. 'Do you have a sword?' Remi asked as the man before him suddenly dropped his and moved away. 'That was strange.'

'I have some skill with the mind, but my own feels quite foggy.' The master took the sword Remi offered. 'I am a teacher. I never expected a time when I would need one of these.'

Remi nodded. Half of the men on this island weren't trained for fighting, and he hoped some of the soldiers had remained near the healers to ensure they were safe. The sounds of swords and fighting were all around them, and Remi wondered if the Palace Isle would ever be what it was before. They were trying to restore an Empire, and they couldn't even keep the peace on an island they had invited the only current inhabitants to.

Chonglin was ahead of him in the crowd, moving through the people, and he appeared to have some skill with a sword as well as fire. Remi watched it splutter in Chonglin's hand, and then he held out his own.

Someone nudged him from behind. He tried to ignore the people around him as he focused on the flame struggling in his own palm. He took in a deep breath, but the flame didn't grow any further, and then it died.

'Something is wrong,' he said. 'Why isn't the healer dust working?'

'Perhaps it hasn't quite covered the whole island yet,' the master murmured, and Remi turned then to look at him properly. He held the sword out in front of him, but he leaned forward, and there was a slick red line across his side. Remi just caught him before he fell.

He crouched over the master in the increasing noise of the square and wondered if he could make it to the healers. He lifted the older man up, his arm around his waist. He took a moment to orientate himself completely and then, as the sword dropped from the master's hand, he ran.

The fighting wasn't as intense as he'd thought. Or perhaps it was more so, as the fighting seemed limited to swords and blades. There didn't appear to be any magic working at all on the island, and Remi thought the dust must have worked. Could they have spread it across other islands of the Empire? Might this actually be the end? Although he had seen fighting like this before, the world had never quite looked the same for Remi since he had faced Lis in the square.

He wasn't quite sure how he had made it as far as the healers' compound, but it was not what he had hoped to find. There wasn't a soul present. He pushed his way into the Imperial Healer's office. The whole place smelt of herbs and spices, just as it had before, and he wondered if the coughing medicine might be of any use.

His mother sitting in a corner of the room was a surprise, as was the look of fear on her face.

'Why are you here?' he asked.

'I wanted his advice on a matter,' she said formally, standing and brushing at her skirt.

'Mother?'

She waved off his words and focused on the master. Remi lowered him down to the floor. 'I hoped for some help,' he said.

'There is none left,' his mother said matter-of-factly.

The man groaned and then clutched at Remi's hand with surprising force. 'You will take care of her?' he asked, his voice a shadow of what it was.

'We'll find help,' Remi said, looking around.

'Promise me,' the master croaked.

Remi nodded slowly.

'You are so alike,' the master murmured, and then his eyes closed and his body relaxed.

The empress closed the distance between them quickly. Kneeling down over the master, she shook him wildly, but Remi knew he was already gone.

'Why didn't he ask me?' She looked even more lost than she had when Remi had found her in the corner.

'You abandoned her once already,' Remi said, standing and looking down on her.

'That was not my choice,' she stammered. 'You know that. If I could have kept her…'

'There is always a choice, Mother.'

She cleared her throat and stood slowly. 'Where are the healers?'

'I don't know. I thought they were working on a way to stop this. Have you seen anyone?'

'Not here,' she said.

'Where is Yang?'

She shook her head. 'Will you take me back?'

'No,' he said, heading for the door. But he paused. He wasn't sure where he was going, or who he was looking for. If Yang was in the middle of all this, it might already be too late, he thought, looking back at Master Yangshing.

34

Lis couldn't wait any longer. Not that she had waited very long. She understood why Remi had asked her to wait behind, but there was too much happening. If she could help, then she should. She tested her barrier, nodded to Wei-Song and headed out the door.

'He has taken the master with him,' Wei-Song said, catching Lis on the steps. 'Where are the soldiers?'

'I think they went to help distribute the healer's dust.'

'Do you think we have enough magic strength to be out here?'

Lis longed for the little sword then, unsure if she should have the confidence in her magic that she did. It didn't take long for her nose to twitch, and Wei-Song rubbed at her throat.

'We are looking for Yang, aren't we?' Wei-Song asked.

Lis nodded. He had been working with the Imperial Healer, and he would know what they could do. Only the last time the two of them had come out alone, it hadn't gone very well. Even the men who had found her and helped her back had now disappeared. There was no one near the throne room, yet she could hear fighting. The shouting and screams, metal on metal.

'I can't feel any magic,' she said softly, taking a step towards the fight.

'Maybe your senses are still dulled,' Wei-Song offered. When Lis turned back to her, she shrugged. 'I can't sense any either,' she admitted. 'I'm not sure I want to head into this fight. We aren't what we were, and you are not safe from them just because you are the crown princess. What if they have pulled the prince in again? What if they can turn him as the priestess did?'

'He isn't so easily swayed,' Lis said. 'Not now.' She pushed out with her barrier, and it failed. 'I thought the Imperial Healer had found a way to fix this. That their dust countered the other.'

'I don't know how it works, but the prince thought it safe.'

Lis shook her head. 'I don't think it is as safe as he thinks. My barrier is gone,' she added softly, taking a step closer to Wei-Song. 'Try something.'

Wei-Song held out her hand, and her forehead crinkled in concentration. She lowered her hand and shook her head.

'Do we continue to find Yang? Or do we go back inside and wait?'

'Yang,' Wei-Song said determinedly.

They headed down the steps and towards the main square. They would still need to go that way if they were to reach the healers' compound. She wasn't sure if he would be there or not, but it was the best place to start since they hadn't heard anything other than that he was helping them. The square before them was a different matter.

It was much like Lis remembered the square on the day she had fought Remi. Only there was no magic in the air. Men, magic and not alike, faced each other with swords.

The sound was overwhelming. She wondered why they hadn't heard it inside the throne room. The noise distracted all her other senses. And without her magic, she was feeling increasingly vulnerable. Then she saw Remi across the square.

He held his sword out and moved through the crowd as though he too was looking for someone. He had headed out to find Yang, and Lis wondered why he wasn't at the healers'. Or was there no one there? Several people moved out of his way. She wondered if he was still the great hunter, rather than a prince with magic—if the people would still fear him as they had.

Another man took him on without hesitation, and Remi tried to push rather than fight him. Given his size and the small man trying to jab at him with a sword, she was pleased he was trying to stop more death.

'Where is the master?' Wei-Song asked beside her, but Lis could only shake her head. So far, they hadn't really been noticed, but it wouldn't be long.

One of the men who had helped her stood up on the steps of the temple, raising himself up above the crowd. He was calling into the people, but Lis couldn't hear his words with the noise of the fighting. The other man joined him, but the fighting continued.

Lis looked back into the people, but she had lost sight of Remi. She only hoped he hadn't been hurt. She took off towards where he had been, Wei-Song just behind her and calling out for her to stop. She could just feel the flicker of magic and recognised it as Remi's, and then it was gone. She turned on the spot, trying to make him out amongst the people, and a sword came crashing down towards her. She put her arm up. The sword bounced from the barrier and out of the hands of the man using it. And then her barrier disappeared.

She had really hoped the healer's dust would be working by now. But there was no consistency to her magic. The man before her glared, and she recognised Chonglin. She held out her hand, but he swatted it away before he stumbled and dropped to his knees at her feet. Wei-Song was between them, and another man stood behind him, a bloody sword in his hand.

'The magic must stop,' he said, stepping forward.

'It has,' Lis said, and he paused. 'The dust in the air has stopped our use of magic.'

He looked out across the square then. Lis felt a pulse of Remi's magic, but she couldn't see the flames.

'Then we have won,' he said. The look on his face made Lis step back, and she pulled Wei-Song with her. For a moment, she wished Mu-Phi and her sword were there, but Mu-Phi might have sided with this man. Lis tried to pull her barrier around the two of them, but it wouldn't work.

Then another man was there, fighting the man who had killed Chonglin. Lis wondered if this would truly continue until nothing and no one was left. She tugged at Wei-Song, pulling her away from the men and through more fighting towards where she hoped Remi was.

Amidst the crowd and fighting, she had lost sight of him. If his magic was also failing, she wasn't sure what he might be able to do. Although, she tried to reassure herself, he had once only fought against magics with a sword.

Then she caught sight of him across the square, knocked to his knees. Blood covered one side of his face, and she hoped it belonged to someone else. A man stood over him with a sword.

'No,' Wei-Song cried beside her. Lis wondered where her own voice had gone. The world appeared in slow motion as the sword was drawn back and Remi lowered his head. Yet Lis's heart beat so fast, she thought it would burst through her chest.

And then one of the men who had saved her was pushing the large man out of the way, and the other man was pulling Remi back and helping him to his feet. Lis found her ability to move then and raced forward, unseeing of those around her except Remi. Then she was standing before him, wanting desperately to throw her arms around him, yet too scared to touch him in case he wasn't real.

She turned to one of the men first and took his hand. 'Thank you,' she said.

'You should not be here,' he said.

'I thought the magic would return,' she said, turning to the other man and bowing before him. 'And I'm looking for my friend, a healer, Yang.'

'No one should be in this, Your Highness,' the first man said again.

'They shouldn't,' she admitted. 'And if this continues, there will be no Empire left.'

Remi wrapped his arms around her. She could feel the fast beating of his heart, and he squeezed her tighter.

'Did you find Yang?' she asked.

'No,' he said. 'There are no healers at the compound. I…' He stopped then and let her go. He looked over her head and then smiled. 'I am surprised every day that he has managed to survive.'

35

Remi watched as Yang put his hand on another magic. He coughed, and then a wind blew around them. Pushing the dust up into the sky, it sparkled in the sunlight. If Remi hadn't known just how dangerous it was, he might have been impressed.

Yang wore something over his face, and despite the dust in the air, Remi moved closer. A fireball sailed into the sky, but as it neared the spinning cloud of dust, the movement shifted it. It dissipated, again falling to the ground. The magic standing beneath it, whom Yang had helped shift the dust from, looked about in a panic. Remi could see the dust settle back on his clothing even as he tried to run.

The fighting and noise were still too loud, and although Yang was covered in dust, he continued to lay his hands on people. It was only when he stumbled and Lis stepped in to take his weight that Remi realised she had followed him across the square.

Any more exposure to the dust and she might never get her magic back to what it was. She had returned to normal when the Imperial Healer had helped her to cough up the dust. Was that what Yang was trying to do? As he reached them, the wind bearer sighed. He wasn't a man that Remi knew, not someone who had fought with the magics in the square that day, and he wondered where the man had been hiding. Although he too was wearing a dark cloth tied around his face, like Yang.

'Are you Hidden?' Remi asked him.

He shook his head. 'You should not be here.'

'None of us should be,' Remi said.

'I couldn't leave Yang,' Lis said, coughing a little, as though something scratched her throat.

'No one should be out here until we can remove this dust.' Yang said.

'How will you do that?' Remi asked. 'You are just spreading it around.'

'And using all the power you have to do it. What if someone is hurt and needs your skills?' Lis asked.

'Every magic on this island is hurting, and so is everyone else. Look around you,' Yang said, his voice husky behind the mask. His anger was apparent, even though he spoke to Lis. 'There is nothing but turmoil. I am trying to stop this, but we may just be standing in the middle of the end of the Empire of Rei-Een.'

'Why are you trying to use wind and fire?' Remi asked. 'You are spreading it. Use the antidote the healers developed.'

Yang looked down then. 'It doesn't work. It works once, but when a magic comes in contact with the dust again, the healing dust no longer stops it taking hold.'

'Lis walked back through it from the baths,' Remi said.

'My barrier isn't working at all,' Lis said. 'Only some of my skills returned, and now they seem to have disappeared as well.'

'We have to destroy the dust,' Yang said. 'It is the only way. I can help expel it from the body. Then if we can move it away and burn it while we find a way to prevent it getting back into the body…' He put his hand to the mask across his face. 'The water in this helps slow it down. But the movement of the flames pushes the dust about, and I fear we can't remove it at all. They may have the entire Empire covered in the stuff by now, and we will never be able to work magic again.'

Lis looked at Remi and then around the square. The fighting

continued around them as though they were islands in a stormy sea.

'What of the phoenix?' Remi asked, stepping in closer to Yang in case anyone heard the word over the noise.

'We can't form it like this,' Lis said. 'I have nothing, and now you won't even be able to lift a flame.'

Remi smiled and held out his hand, but she was right. Nothing happened, and he didn't realise he would miss the fire as much as he did. But as he let his hand drop, she stepped up to him and took his hands in hers. The smile on her face lit up the darkening world around her.

'The fire still burns,' she whispered.

He shook his head.

'I can see it in your eyes,' she said, and then Yang was close behind her, looking into his eyes as well.

'There may be a way,' he murmured.

'What are you thinking?' Remi asked, and for the first time he was nervous of the lean healer. There was a spark of a different kind behind his eyes, and Remi wondered what he might do to help end this.

He called the wind bearer closer. 'I am going to expel the dust,' Yang said. 'The wind will blow it away from you.' He looked at Remi and nodded. 'Long enough that you can burn.'

'Burn what?'

'All of you, let it go—let it take control. That will stop the dust from settling on you again. Then while you burn, I will do the same for Lis and she can step into your flames and...' He held his arms out.

'And what?' Remi asked.

'You let the phoenix fly.'

'How is that going to help everyone else?'

'I think he might be right,' Lis said softly.

Remi cleared his throat and then looked around the square. If they didn't do something, there would be nothing left. Too many had died already. He nodded once.

Lis took a step back. The wind bearer nodded, and Yang placed his hand on Remi's back. He wanted to cough as a strange sensation filled his chest and a bitter taste filled his mouth. And as the dust sparkled in the sunlight before his face, a wind blew it away from him.

He watched for a moment as it moved over the people around them, and then he allowed the fire to take hold. It moved quickly across his skin, the heat comforting. He let it burn, allowing it full control.

Yang moved behind Lis, and Remi assumed he held his hand to the middle of her back as he had done with him. Again, the dust sparkled in the sun as it was lifted away from her by the wind, and she was stepping into his flames.

She wrapped her arms around his waist and leaned into him. They stood for what seemed like an age, the fire raging around them. And as others in the square moved away from them, he thought he could die happy here, if that was their fate, together.

As he allowed the thought to take hold, he felt the shift in the flames, and Lis glanced up at him. Then he was sure they lifted off the ground. The great wings of the beast surrounding them beat slowly as they lifted higher.

Everyone in the square dropped to their knees, and he assumed it was at the sight of the phoenix as so many others had done before. But then they appeared to be doubled over coughing. Remi wondered how Yang could reach so many, but he too was on his knees.

The dust swirled up and around the square, glistening in the sun like a silver cloud. As the wings continued to beat and the phoenix they created carried them higher into the sky, the cloud moved with them. He looked down on the world, appearing like a map beneath them. The Palace Isle and the boats dotted the deep blue sea around them. Long wisps of silver cloud moved towards them from the other islands, as though pulled to them.

'I dreamt this,' Lis whispered, 'only the world was burning.'

As she said it, the cloud rushed at them, and she clung to him a little tighter. As the silver cloud reached the phoenix, it burst into flames. The fire fuelled their own, and it continued to grow as the dust flowed into the flames.

They stayed where they were for a moment, and then Lis carefully moved one arm up and around his neck, then the other. As she kissed him, the fire flared and the beast around them grew larger. Remi could make out the feathers of flames across the broad wings, and he could almost see the face. It was an odd sensation, as though they were the beast, inside the beast and beside the beast all in the one instant.

And then Lis was releasing her hold on him. For a moment he thought they might fall from the sky, until he felt the firm ground already beneath his feet. Around them, the world was silent.

36

Lis allowed Yang to check her pulse, but as they sat together on the edge of the covered walkway, her arm across his lap, his focus was on Wei-Song sitting in the small garden by the wall.

She had said very little since the phoenix had cleared the dust and the world had changed. The fighting had stopped as though they had all realised they had been fighting the same thing, magic or not, and a different conversation had started. Several leaders had been asked to meet again as the council they had tried to form, and they were to meet with the emperor.

Pulling from Yang's loose hold on her, Lis headed across to sit with Wei-Song in the sun. They sat in silence for a time, Wei-Song not even acknowledging that Lis was there, and then she took Lis by the hand.

'I can't seem to get warm,' she murmured. 'All this sunshine, and the heat is pulled from my body like I can do to a room.'

Lis pulled her into her arms, and as Wei-Song's head rested on her shoulder, she started to cry. Yang stood up, but Lis gave him a subtle shake of her head, and he sat back down again. There was little they could do for her, other than support her and give her the time she needed to heal.

'Remi would like you to be on the council,' Lis whispered.

'I can't,' Wei-Song said, pulling back.

Lis smiled. 'Who better to represent the school?

'It is not the same,' she murmured.

'Excuse me, little hidden princess, but I think you are the perfect person. Master Yangshing taught you as he did for a reason. He raised you to use your magic to help the Empire.'

Wei-Song nodded and wiped her nose with the back of her hand.

'I know you miss him. When my mother died, I thought I would be consumed by the pain, but it gets easier.'

'He was more than my teacher,' Wei-Song whispered.

'I know,' Lis said. 'He was your family, as we are. Let us help you carry some of the pain.'

'Please let us help,' Remi said, and Lis looked up with surprise, unaware that he was there. As Wei-Song nodded, he pulled her to her feet and wrapped his arms around her. 'It is so good to have you here, little sister.'

Wei-Song smiled and wiped again at her face as Remi let her go.

'I never thought you would truly accept me,' she said.

He bowed before her and then gave her a bright smile. 'It is time we stand before the emperor.' He held out his hand to help Lis to her feet, and she looped her arm through his.

Yang stood slowly from the step. Although Lis wanted to run forward and support him, she remained where she was as Wei-Song stepped in. He smiled sadly down on her head as she guided him forward.

The ministers stood in their neat ordered lines in silence. Advisor Gan stepped forward and bowed low to them as they took their place before the emperor. Others had gathered in the room as well, including the men who had helped Lis return from the baths and then tried in vain to stop the fighting in the square.

Lis smiled at them, and they bowed to her before turning their attention back to the emperor. He, as he stood from the throne, appeared to be the man he had been before—firm, strong and confident. Although Lis couldn't think of him in the same way. Too many had turned out to be not what she had thought.

The empress stood silently to the side of the throne. She appeared as she had when Lis had first seen her at the Choosing, and Lis wondered at the times they had laughed over the little table in her palace. Had the empress had a chance to be who she really was in those private moments, or was it another act to get from Lis what she needed?

'We have representatives of the Empire for the council,' the emperor said. 'Is there anyone you would like to nominate who has not already been named?'

Remi pulled away from Lis, Wei-Song's hand tight in his. They bowed together before the emperor. 'I would nominate my sister, Yangshing Wei-Song,' Remi said, and Lis noted the small smile Wei-Song gave him before she put her hand to her chest and bowed again to the emperor. 'To represent the Order of Huans, the Hidden.'

The empress opened her mouth and then closed it, then looked at Lis with the disappointment Lis had hoped she would never see again.

'I am honoured to have you,' the emperor said, a little less enthusiastically than his previous words.

There was a long way to go, but together, Lis was sure they could create an Empire stronger than the one they had shared before the magic war.

Epilogue

Lis watched as the children ran free around the courtyard. Flames, wind, and small clouds of lightning all tumbled around the space. She watched her son, Te-Sho, run at the front of a group, striking the ground with lightning and then watching as the ground opened and closed before him.

His twin sister, Ying, sat in the grass and looked up at the wall. Although she often ran around with the others, she hadn't shown any signs of magic. She gave Lis a small sad smile as she sat beside her and wrapped her in her arms.

'It isn't fair, Mama,' Ying said, but there wasn't a whine to her voice. 'I can't do what they can.'

'Maybe you are made of different stuff,' Lis said softly. 'What would you really like?' she asked. 'If you could wish anything forward?'

Ying held her hand out over the grass, but nothing happened and she let her hand fall.

'Why don't we try together?' Lis offered.

Lis held the child by the wrist and allowed her to guide what they did. She could feel the wanting in her, trying to push through the skin. 'Let it come,' she whispered.

A blade of grass pushed a little taller than the others, and then it shot up and caressed Ying's hand. Leaves sprouted along its length, which quickly turned to thorns, and a plump bud developed on the end. Lis waited, her breath held, and a bright yellow flower burst forth, its long, slender petals pulsing back and forth.

Te-Sho ran over. 'Well done, Mama,' he said.

The flower grew taller and thicker until it was the height of the boy, and then the petals pulled together to form a face that snapped at him. He laughed and ran off. The flower turned to Ying, kissed her cheek and then withdrew to the size it had been before.

Lis could feel the disappointment ebb from the child. She wrapped her arms tight around her shoulders, pulling her closer.

'You should be happy with that,' Lis said. 'I have never seen a flower behave in such a way.' The flower turned to look at her, and she was sure it smiled.

'But you did it, Mama.'

Lis shook her head.

'Did you do this?' Remi asked, walking towards them.

Lis gave Ying a nudge. 'Make it grow,' she whispered. She let her go, and then Ying raised her fingers to the sky. The plant grew quickly, reaching Remi's height easily. He looked a little nervous as the flower folded its petals inward. Lis wondered if it would snap at him and what he might do in return. But it arranged the petals differently, and she was sure it grinned at him.

He scooped the child up and swung her around. When he set her down, she raced off to join the other children. The eldest of the group, Ku-Aing, smiled towards Lis as she took Ying's hand. Not really a child anymore, Ku-Aing was a young woman. She had very little magic skill, but she was content and had happily joined Lis and Remi and their children, easily becoming part of the family.

Lis had not hesitated when the girl had asked to be given the name Lis had considered so long ago. Now that the visions had returned, she still smiled and answered to her name, but as yet, Ku-Aing wasn't willing to tell them what she saw.

Lis was grateful that she didn't know what was to come, and that the visions rarely gave the girl nightmares.

ACKNOWLEDGMENTS

Special thanks to the team at Deranged Doctor Designs (DDD) for facilitating absolutely brilliant cover design work and all the marketing extras. Thank you for your support and beautiful covers.

TWG members: Melissa, Matthew J Morrison, John Hargreaves, Sue Larsen, Nicholas Jansen and Chantelle Griffith for listening and support in all things writing related. Special thanks to Yasmin and Belinda for taking the time to read and comment on my stories.

Allison E Wright for wonderful editing work. She smooths out my words and saves me from a lack of commas.

My parents, Francine and Ken Smith. Amazing, supportive people who I don't thank often enough. Thanks for keeping me grounded and being the best grandparents ever.

As always, Temwa for being my biggest supporter.

ABOUT THE AUTHOR

Georgina Makalani survives life as a servant of the public by hiding in her office at lunch time with dragons, witches, a laptop and a little bit of magic.

For more about Georgina and her books visit her website: www.theflowofink.com